continued . . .

Praise for
Ride for the Roses

"*Ride for the Roses* is a delectable plunge into Regency times. A wonderful read with warm, complex characters, a page-turning plot and a delightful ending."   —Pat Potter

"A wonderful not-to-be-put-down read."   —*Rendezvous*

"This is a delightful Regency tale of mistakes and match-making following a traditional plotline that is enhanced by a cast of endearing characters. *Ride for the Roses* is a debut that heralds a new talent."   —*Romantic Times*

"A pleasant Regency romance that includes a number of charming characters. . . . Christina Kingston shows she is a talent worth reading, for her audience will find much entertainment value in her debut novel."   —Harriet Klausner

"Pick this book up—it's exciting to see such a strong debut romance! If you enjoy a well-written historical with a smart heroine and an engaging hero with a good sense of humor, this is one ride you'll be glad you took."
—*All About Romance*

"A most enjoyable Regency historical. This is an impressive debut and I look forward to many more fine books from Christina Kingston."   —*The Romance Reader*

Ride the
Winter Wind

Christina Kingston

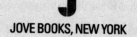
JOVE BOOKS, NEW YORK

RIDE THE WINTER WIND

A Jove Book / published by arrangement with
the author

PRINTING HISTORY
Jove edition / April 2002

Copyright © 2002 by Christina Strong.
Cover art by Judy York.

All rights reserved.
This book, or parts thereof, may not be reproduced in any form
without permission.
For information address: The Berkley Publishing Group,
a division of Penguin Putnam Inc.,
375 Hudson Street, New York, New York 10014.

Visit our website at
www.penguinputnam.com

ISBN: 0-515-13279-9

A JOVE BOOK®
Jove Books are published by The Berkley Publishing Group,
a division of Penguin Putnam Inc.,
375 Hudson Street, New York, New York 10014.
JOVE and the "J" design
are trademarks belonging to Penguin Putnam Inc.

PRINTED IN THE UNITED STATES OF AMERICA

10 9 8 7 6 5 4 3 2 1

Prologue

They were coming again, the three of them. The big one held that blasted bludgeon at the ready, tapping its weight against the palm of his hand as if the blows gave him a sense of deep satisfaction.

They'd ask him questions again, of course—questions to which there were no answers, for they wanted none. Nor would he give them any if there'd been answers to give. The interrogation was only a flimsy excuse to see if they could make him cringe or cry out.

They wanted him to beg for mercy.

Michael would die first.

Seeking to distance his mind from the pain he knew was coming, he cast about for a train of thought to occupy him while he survived this. Oddly, the thought that came was that he found it interesting that courage rose higher when a man was free to retaliate against his enemies. Just now, hanging half-starved in chains was certainly playing the devil with his own resolve.

Then the thought went flying as the big brute swung the bludgeon straight at Michael's face, all his strength behind it. Rough iron manacles bit deeply into his wrists as Michael twisted in his chains and took the full force of the blow on his left shoulder. The darkness of the cave in which they stood exploded with the brilliance of a thousand stars as pain flashed through him like lightning. He heard an agonized cry, and knew from the triumphant laughter of his captors that it was his own. Then the darkness swallowed him.

In the luxurious guest bedchamber at the manor known as Cliffside, Michael Mathers awoke bolt upright, sweat-soaked. Shuddering. Gasping for air. The echo of his cry still reverberated through the room.

The door to the adjoining dressing room flew open, and a disheveled man ran to the bed. "It's all right, sir. Just that bad dream again, I'll wager."

Michael ran a shaking hand through his dark hair. "Aye, Gris. That same damned dream." He listened to the whispers in the hall outside the door. "I'm fine," he told his host's former batman. "Go back to bed."

Gris stood silent for an instant, then ventured, "There's nothing I can do?"

Michael clenched his teeth to hold back the obvious reply. There was nothing anyone could do. "Just go back to bed, Gris."

"Aye, Major. I'll go."

When he was gone, Michael dropped his head into his one good hand and muttered, "Yes. And that is what I myself must do. I must go. I've disturbed the sleep of my friends for the last time."

He looked toward the door, through which he could hear Bly tell Kate, "He's all right, Kate."

And heard her softer voice protest, "No. No, he's not all right."

There was a pause, then Bly said, "Come away. Michael doesn't want us right now."

And as they went back to their own bed, Michael thought he heard a muffled sob from Kate.

It was more than he could bear. He had no heart for this. Causing his friends such grief was worse than any torture he'd endured in the caves. His resolve to leave strengthened. He straightened and said aloud, "In London no one will hear me if I cry out in my sleep, nor care if they do." He drew a final shuddering breath, and firmly promised himself, "The matter is settled. Come hell or high water, I leave tomorrow."

Naked as the day he was born, he rose and stalked across the room to the dressing room door. "Gris," he ordered through it, "tomorrow I want you to pack my things and send them on to the house in London. I ride as soon as I have said my good-byes."

From his place just on the other side of the door, the older man shook his head in defeat so profound that it showed in his voice. "Yes, sir."

Michael turned away and strode back to his tumbled bed. At least his friends would find peace in his absence.

Chapter One

Guy Michael Mathers, Fifth Viscount Kantwell, had made his decision. Now it was time to act.

Standing beside him, his big gray gelding tossed its head and moved restively on the sun-dappled stones of the Cliffside courtyard. Michael calmed him by smoothing his hand affectionately down the horse's satiny neck. Gladiator responded with a soft nicker and nudged his master's shoulder.

Chalfont Blysdale, Michael's best friend and former colonel, laughed. "It looks as if Gladiator is ready to go."

Blysdale's bride took a step forward and said, "Must you go, Michael?" Lady Katherine looked across the lush, green, rolling hills in the direction of the capital. "The weather toward London looks threatening. Surely you can postpone your departure until it clears."

Lord Blysdale slipped a possessive arm around her. "Kate's right you know, Michael. That solid bank of clouds looks like snow. You'd do well to wait awhile." His eyes held a speculative expression as he regarded his friend. The expression had nothing to do with concern for the weather.

"Wait awhile!" Michael Mathers threw back his handsome dark head and laughed. "My God, Bly. I've camped on you all summer and autumn."

Blysdale smiled, but the watchfulness in his eyes didn't diminish. "Not so. You spent what was left of the spring and half the summer at Taskford with Harry and Regina."

Michael laughed again. "While you and Kate were away on your wedding trip." He turned eyes as blue as Blysdale's to Lady Katherine, and his smile softened. "And I strongly suspect that I was the cause of your cutting your trip short, Kate. I deeply regret that."

"Nonsense, Michael." Kate put her hand on his arm and smiled up at him. "Cliffside was nagging us. We couldn't be certain the new bailiff would remember all our instructions, and there is always so much to do. We had to return."

"Aha," Blysdale teased her. "Now I see how the wind blows. I'm to have my good friend Mathers to keep me company in my wife's neglect." Turning to his old comrade-in-arms, he said, "Nice of you to join me. Sometimes I get lonely in that place where I am second to Cliffside, that I occupy in my beautiful bride's esteem."

In a flash, Kate turned in his embrace and slapped him on the chest. "Stop that! You know very well . . ." She cut her sentence off, seeing the mischief in his eyes. Fighting down laughter, she scowled at him in pretended disapproval, then turned back to Michael and demanded, "Surely you aren't going to go and leave me alone with this dreadful man, Michael. Winter is coming, and just think how dreary that will be."

Michael and Blysdale exchanged a glance. Michael was more pleased than he'd ever hoped to be to see the happiness in his friend's face. His lips twitched with the effort to hide from his hostess the message that had passed between them. "I feel certain," he said in a voice that trembled with suppressed laughter, "that Bly has plans for your entertainment through the next few months."

"Yes." Blysdale's deep voice was even deeper as he nuzzled his wife's hair. "And even beyond them."

Kate didn't fail to catch the implication. "You are both beasts," she told them, her voice full of loving laughter, "but, in spite of that, I wish you would stay, Michael."

A cloud scudded over them from the Channel then. Blocking the sun. Chilling them momentarily.

The gray gelding shook his mane and struck sparks from the paving stones with an iron-shod hoof.

Their laughter died. It was time for Michael to leave.

Kate moved out of her husband's embrace and hugged her departing guest fiercely. He held her tightly for an instant in the steel circle of his right arm, then returned her to her husband's embrace with a husky "Good-bye, Kate."

Blysdale held her with her face against his shoulder. His own face was grim. "Good-bye?" It was clearly a question.

Michael turned away to Blysdale's manservant, Griswold, without answering him. "And thank you for all you've done, Gris. You're a champion." He shook the man's hand with vigor and smiled a tight, crooked smile.

Gris was as grim as his employer. "When you come again, I shall know more of what we can do for your arm, your lordship."

Michael gripped Griswold's shoulder hard, and his eyes said it all. He wouldn't be coming back.

Eyes narrowed as he looked up at the sky, he told them, "You might be right about the weather. It's past time that I got about my business."

Griswold stepped forward to hold his horse as Michael reached for the pommel of the saddle to haul himself up into it.

Bly kept Kate turned away as he watched with bleak

eyes the clumsy effort of this man who'd once have been able to vault onto his mount with ease.

Michael turned his horse, threw a "Good-bye" back at the little group standing in the sunny courtyard and cantered away.

Kate and Griswold both called out, "Farewell!"

But Blysdale stood silent.

Fifteen minutes later, his ancient campaign cloak billowing around him in the rising wind, Michael topped the last hill from which he could look back and see the estate he'd just left. He reined his horse to a halt and sat looking back toward the Channel—back toward Cliffside Manor. God, he was going to miss them there! He was going to miss them all. Then his attention passed over the manor, resplendent in the sun against the sparkling waters of the Channel, and went to the rock-strewn hill beyond it. Memories rushed in on him as he focused his gaze on that distant, innocent-appearing hill—horrible memories of the cave under it that had been his prison for months and of the atrocities that had taken place there.

Just to look at that hill sent emotions he could barely control surging through him. He shuddered. Even though he was free of the chains that had bound him to the cave's dank wall—free and out in the glorious sunlight again—it still haunted him. Maimed by the treatment he'd received while a prisoner there, his left arm was useless. That loss made him feel like no more than half a man, but he was alive. Reluctantly and resentfully perhaps, but alive. Smythe—David—his dear friend, was not so lucky.

That cave had been David's prison, too, and David was gone. David would never see the sun again, never breathe this fresh clean air, nor ever again see the lush, emerald carpet that was England's soil spilling down to the sea.

And the blame for David's untimely death lay heavily on Michael's heart. If only he hadn't . . .

Michael shook his head to throw off his guilty thoughts—to rid himself, at least for now, of the pain of them. Shifting his regard from the rocky hill to Cliffside Manor, he thought instead of all they had tried to do for him, and told himself that recalling those memories was better than hopelessly lamenting the death of a comrade.

In the early spring, when he'd been rescued by all that were left of the "Lucky Seven," Michael had been in pretty bad shape. No one had remarked on it, of course, but they'd taken him on as their project.

Harry and Regina had nursed him back to health, coddling him all spring and well into the summer at Taskford Manor, putting weight back on him, and walking him like a pampered dog to help him regain his stamina. Then he'd returned to stay with Blysdale and his bride at Cliffside when they returned early from their honeymoon.

Consulting over him like a gaggle of London physicians, the bunch of them had met behind his back and decided that Bly's man Griswold was Michael's best chance of recovering the use of his arm. There'd been no deterring them.

How diligently they'd all labored to help him regain the use of his left arm. Griswold had applied himself to searching out any and every remedy that even vaguely suggested it might be of benefit for the paralysis Michael suffered from. Kate had looked after him as if he were an invalid child, and Bly had watched over him like an eagle.

Twice every day Griswold had soaked and massaged his arm all through the autumn—until Michael could bear their concern and valiantly hidden frustration no longer. Finally, he had called a halt to it all, pretending to accept his infirmity with good grace. Though deathly disappointed that all efforts had failed, he prided himself that he'd carried the deception off well. That he'd convinced them all.

All except Blysdale, of course. Bly knew that Michael's

seeming acceptance was a ruse. Sitting there on his horse in the blustering wind, Michael smiled ruefully. No one ever deceived Bly, blast him. Those piercing eyes of his could see into a man's very soul. But at least he'd gone along with Michael's game, seeming to the others to believe Michael as he'd pretended that it didn't matter—pretended that despite the fact that he'd have to wear a useless arm strapped to his side for the rest of his life, he was the same carefree, charming, ladies' man he'd always been.

Now that the dreams were coming more frequently, though, Michael couldn't keep up the pretense any longer and he'd told them he must leave, using the excuse that he'd left the bailiffs on his estates without supervision for far too long. After what Kate had had happen at Cliffside in her absence, they'd accepted the necessity for his departure. How could they not? Hadn't Kate and Bly used the same excuse to explain their early return from their wedding trip?

Only that solemn expression in Blysdale's penetrating eyes at their parting had told Michael that his friend was deeply concerned about his state of mind. Bly looked past a man's mask into his heart, and Bly knew what having to have his food cut up for him and needing—not just accepting, as most gentlemen habitually did, but actually needing—help to get dressed was doing to Michael.

By far the worst of it all was that he'd seen Bly watching him sympathetically more than once while he'd been clumsily mounting a horse. Even here, miles from his ever-observant friend, his face flamed at the memory and a muscle jumped in his jaw. That was one of the things he was running from. One of the things he couldn't stand. To have a man he'd ridden beside into the hell of cannon fire silently grieve as he was forced to watch him lumber into the saddle was one more thing—the final thing—Michael couldn't endure. Dammit, he'd been a cavalry officer, by all that was Holy!

And what was he now? Despair ravaged his handsome face here where there was no one to see as Michael asked himself again, aloud, "What the blazing hell am I now?"

No matter. Whatever happened in the future, he knew that he had nothing to fear from Bly's almost supernatural powers of observation. His old commanding officer could be depended on to keep a still tongue in his head.

Michael sent a final salute in the direction of the friends he was leaving and spun Gladiator away. It was past time for him to stop feeling sorry for himself and to face what was left of his life.

Turning away from Cliffside and the sunlit Channel behind it, he gave his full attention to the weather into which he was riding. Just as Blysdale had predicted to support his wife's plea that Michael stay, the weather in that direction wasn't good. Not good at all. In stark contrast to the sunlit coast behind him, the rolling hills ahead were blanketed with moving shadows. Long, low clouds heavy with moisture hung against the sky ahead like sodden banners.

Michael scowled at them. Here it wasn't even Christmas yet, but obviously, it was going to snow. Since he'd left the milder climate of the coast, the sky had become leaden, and the temperature had dropped markedly. The distant clouds he'd observed from Cliffside Manor were no longer distant. Now they brooded oppressively over the landscape just ahead, pressing down in a solid, heavy bank of gray.

Michael eyed it with an odd mixture of alarm and elation. The alarm was for the safety of his favorite mount, Gladiator. The elation came from the realization that he might have been given this impending snowstorm as an opportunity to escape his tiresome problem. After all, who could blame him if, caught in a blizzard, he simply fell asleep in deep snow?

He was a man with a useless arm strapped to his side. Why should he be expected to survive?

The storm would break over him any minute now. Its proximity filled him with a strange impatience, and he put Gladiator into a gallop and rode hard to meet the ominous white wall ahead.

Within half a mile, the snow was falling fast and furiously. Thicker and thicker the flakes fell as he rode deeper into the storm. The road was quickly blanketed. Only the trees growing on the ditch banks that edged it marked the way well enough for him to go on. He slowed Gladiator to a walk, however, afraid that the drifting snow might conceal some hazard to his greathearted charger.

The storm grew fiercer. Blinded by the raging world of white that surrounded him, Michael rode on. He kept his head bent low, letting the brim of his hat keep the snow from driving into his eyes. As his mount had dropped its head for the same purpose, he sat exposed to the howling wind without so much as his horse's neck to shield him.

He didn't care. He was no stranger to discomfort, and he supposed that freezing was as good a way as any to part company with a life that had become . . . unpalatable.

Gladiator deserved better, though. Never would Michael forget the debt he owed the horse under him, nor in any way deny the strength of the bond that had been forged between them in the crucible of battle. All through the long years of the Peninsular War, the big gray gelding had served him tirelessly and faithfully, sharing Michael's every hardship and danger. Twice Gladiator had brought him safely to camp when Michael had been so badly wounded that he could hardly stay in the saddle. Often, when the fog had been so thick no human could have found the way back, Gladiator had returned him unerringly to his men's position after he'd ridden out to reconnoiter.

Most impressive of all was the fact that, even though the big gelding had himself been wounded three times, Gladiator had survived that battlefield hell to be shipped home to England when many another officer's charger had not.

After all that, Michael would be damned if he was going to let the great beast perish in a simple snowstorm. After all, he owed Gladiator his life. Now, at long last, he had the opportunity to repay the debt by getting the gallant animal out of harm's way. To see his horse to safety, he'd simply have to put up with life for a little longer.

Pity. He really was quite weary of it.

As Gladiator plunged on through the deepening snow, the wind tore the gelding's breath away in tattered white plumes. Then it sent chilling tentacles to search out and steal the warmth from under his rider's cloak as well.

Michael's breath formed ice on the collar of his worn campaign cloak where he'd pulled it up to shield the lower part of his face, and the fingers of his good hand, cold and growing numb in his glove, felt as if they would shatter if he had to clench his fist. It didn't matter. He could hardly clutch the cloak closed and hold the reins with a single useful hand.

Cold and stiff as he was getting, falling from the saddle into the nearest drift would be an easy thing to do, but for his horse's sake, former Major Guy Michael Mathers, Fifth Viscount Kantwell, rode on.

Chapter Two

"I can't believe this!" In the morning room of Collington Park, Lady Alissa Alana Collington stormed back and forth across the luxurious Persian carpet. "This can't be happening!" After a moment, she threw herself down on a chair and glared out the window at the acres of beautifully designed and carefully tended formal garden that ran down to the estate's huge ornamental lake. She was seeing neither as she fought for control of her fury. In her hand she held a copy of her grandfather's will, the cause of her anger.

Looking across the room, to the chair in front of the fire, where her grandfather's widow, the Dowager Countess Lady Ellen, sat, Alissa said, "I never suspected that he'd do this, Grandmother. Never!" She rose and went to the fireplace to be near her.

"Surely Uncle Gerald knows that Grandfather didn't ever mean for the provisions of his will to be carried out. He couldn't have." She took a deep breath. "And you'd certainly have thought that my uncle would have said something in the four years since Grandfather died to warn us of his intentions!"

Giving an unladylike "Ha!" Alissa stamped her foot and continued, "Why am I dissembling? I know better than to expect fair play from Uncle Gerald, the blackguard. He planned to do this all along! He's deliberately waited till the last minute. And he has sent this copy of Grandfather's onerous will as a goading reminder that he can do it! He *can* steal my inheritance."

Alissa shook the copy of the will in one hand and held out the note that had accompanied it with the other. "And this note! Look what he's written. Just look! *You have only one more week, Alissa.* And it's not even signed!" She crumpled it into a ball, and flung it into the fireplace. "The effrontery of it! Uncle Gerald knows very well that Grandfather didn't really intend that clause to be carried out!"

Lady Ellen pursed her lips for a moment, then said soothingly, "Indeed, I'm certain your uncle does know very well that your grandfather loved you too much ever to have brought you to this unpleasant pass, my dear. It's always been my belief that your grandfather merely intended to urge you to marry before you became a spinster like your great-aunt Isabelle." She shuddered delicately. "Isabelle was the bane of our existence, believe me, dear, and your grandfather was convinced that it was because she had never married."

"Hmm, yes. I know Great-aunt Isabelle very well." There was a world of understanding in Alissa's wry comment.

"I'm afraid we all know Isabelle better than we would like to. I only hope she stays away until we have the present difficulty resolved."

"Gracious Lord, yes. Now is *not* the time to have Aunt Izzy turn up! And she just might, too, with Christmas almost here." Alissa fell to pacing again.

Soft-voiced, her grandmother said, "Regarding your

grandfather's will, Alissa. You must realize that your
grandfather didn't really know your uncle Gerald very
well. All his love and attention were lavished on your father. Richard was his heir, after all. As a result, your grandfather never saw what Gerald was becoming. Maybe he
didn't want to." She bowed her head briefly and added,
"Possibly he didn't care." Then Lady Ellen frowned, as an
old resentment stirred. "I know he'd never listen to me
about Gerald. And certainly he had no idea that our second
son would become so bitter and greedy as to want to enforce the conditions of that exceedingly ill-conceived
will!" Lady Ellen was warming to her subject. "I know for
a certainty that he never believed that *you* would ever actually *reach* twenty-five without having been snatched up
by one of the many eager suitors that always buzz around
you."

Alissa laughed, and the laugh had a bitter edge. "If only
I could find a way to be certain that it was me they were
attempting to snatch, and not Grandfather's fortune. Then
I might permit myself the luxury of falling in love with one
of them."

Lady Ellen looked at her granddaughter. Alissa was so
beautiful that it was no wonder half the bachelors in England had pursued her. With her perfect features and huge
gray eyes, she was a prize to be coveted even without her
grandfather's fortune. With it, Alissa was irresistible.

But to wish for love? That was something few couples
achieved in marriages in the *ton*. "Love has very little to do
with marriage, my dear. Not in high society, anyway." She
sighed. "Love seems to be reserved for milkmaids and
scullery girls, alas."

"I know that, Grandmother." Alissa smiled and admitted ruefully, "But I'm stubborn, and I've always wanted to
marry for love."

"So you have frequently told me." Lady Ellen's tone
was dry, then it warmed and she said, "And it has been my

fondest hope that you could do it, my dear. Always. For that was once my own most cherished dream."

She sighed again, then straightened and said briskly, "But your grandfather, after seeing that love did eventually come to the two of us in spite of the fact that ours was an arranged marriage, didn't care whether you married for love or not, so long as you did marry. He couldn't stand the thought of your perchance turning out as did your great-aunt Isabelle." Her mood changed, and she said briskly, "And to be fair, we have to remember, Alissa, the will was written right after one of Izzy's chaotic visits here. And believe me, nothing short of a raging hurricane would be worse than a visit from my twin!" She paused to shake her head. "Even so, as time passed, I think your grandfather began to see that the will he'd had written—which he half meant as a nasty poke at your great-aunt, after all—was not such a good idea. In fact, I feel he'd have written a new will to negate that one if he hadn't broken his neck on that blasted horse!"

After a moment of silence to honor her husband's passing, she said, "If only your dear little cousin Robin had been your father's son instead of your late aunt Blanche's. Then *he'd* have inherited and we wouldn't be plagued by your uncle Gerald!"

"Oh, yes, that *would* have been wonderful." Suddenly saddened by the fact that Robin had become another of her responsibilities when he'd been orphaned, and worried that she might lose the power to be able to meet that, as well as all her other obligations, Alissa turned away, pacing again.

Isabelle and all else aside, her grandfather's will and her uncle's insistence on seeing its terms carried out to the letter were a mammoth threat to Robin's and their continued well-being. That damnable will would, in one week, give her uncle, the current Lord Withers, everything that rightfully belonged to Alissa. That fact, she knew, was obviously the strong inducement behind his eagerness to "do his duty."

Her uncle Gerald, who'd already received her grandfather's title and everything that was entailed to it, was a fabulously wealthy man. Unfortunately, he was proving to be a very greedy one, as well.

Alissa stopped her pacing when she arrived back in front of her grandmother's chair. Her eyes were narrowed and her lips were firmly set. "I'm not going to let Uncle Gerald have Collington Park, you know."

"Oh?" Lady Ellen smiled at her granddaughter's determination. "And just what are you going to do to stop him? I fear your suitors seem to have thinned out rather dramatically, of late."

"That's true." Alissa cocked her head, considering. "It's really too bad that Sir Hadley had that awful accident going home from dinner here. I hear he's walking again, but has to use a cane." She threw her grandmother an impish look. "Unfortunately, Hadley hasn't attempted to contact me lately."

"The Coxwains never were a particularly *intrepid* family, my dear. Courage was simply not their forte. Why should Hadley be any different?" She smiled slightly, remembering. "Your grandfather always said 'the apple never falls far from the tree.'"

Alissa shot her grandmother a pained look and walked over to the window. Outside, wan winter sunlight flooded the rose garden. "I think I may be getting to be considered something of a jinx in the matrimonial market, considering the fact that both Maunton and Peckingham died in odd accidents in the middle of courting me." She turned back to face her grandmother. "Though I didn't want to wed either of them, it's still a terrible shame. They were too young to die." She let a long moment pass, then said with forced brightness, "All this tragedy has put rather a damper on my marriage prospects, I'm afraid."

"Indeed, I'd have to agree." Lady Ellen's voice held none of the mischief of her granddaughter's. "We've not been under the usual siege of suitors for a while now."

Alissa tossed her head. "Oh, who wants to wed cowards, anyway."

"*A* coward, my dear. Only one," Lady Ellen corrected firmly. "We ladies are allowed but a single husband at a time here in England."

Alissa laughed. "Very well. So we will just say that Fate has spared me the temptation of accepting one of the men who might have come if they were guaranteed absolute safety in doing so." Her smile faded. "Now, though, with time running out, I just might be tempted to accept him should Sir Hadley hobble over."

Suddenly, as if a chill wind had blown over her, all the merriment left Alissa's face, and her huge gray eyes were solemn. "I've only one week left, Grandmother. I don't want to be reduced to putting you and Robin in some ghastly hovel while I slave away as a governess somewhere to support us."

Lady Ellen, who knew no wife in her right mind would hire her beautiful granddaughter for a governess unless all the children were girls and their father as blind as little Robin, rose from her chair and went to embrace Alissa. "You'll think of something, dear. I know you'll think of something. You always do."

"Of course I shall," Alissa said with a confidence she was far from feeling. She smiled brightly at her grandmother and changed the subject. "Now you must go have a rest. I shall see you at luncheon."

Lady Ellen gave Alissa a peck on the cheek, rose with her assistance, and left the room.

Alissa watched her go and saw that her grandmother's limp was back. Winter always brought the ache in her hip that caused it. She made a mental note to ask Kemp to see to it that the rooms Lady Ellen frequented were kept warmer than usual. The butler probably wouldn't even need to be asked to see to it. Kemp had been here at Collington Park before Alissa had been born, and knew better than she what pleased her grandmother—and what that aging lady needed.

She closed her eyes and pressed her fingers against them. She must hold on to her inheritance. Everything and everyone depended on her. The servants, the Park. She mustn't let it pass into her uncle Gerald's hands. She knew he wouldn't take care of the people who worked in the manor and on the estate the way that she did.

Oh, he'd take good care of the *possessions*, all right, but she knew he cared nothing for the living treasures of Collington Park. That task was clearly hers, and she had better have a brilliant idea to save it all immediately.

Less than an hour later, Alissa had finished her letter to her dear friend, Sir Thomas Lane, and given it to Kemp. "See that our most trustworthy man rides with this to London. It is to be put directly into the hand of Sir Thomas Lane." She hesitated only a moment, then added, "Have two armed grooms accompany him, and put all three on our fastest horses. They are to leave immediately."

Kemp bowed and left with the sealed letter in his hand. If he was astonished by his mistress's grim order, he hid it well.

Alissa didn't care if her butler was shocked. She'd had enough of her uncle! And suddenly, now that she'd been alone awhile to think, she wondered if the accidents that had befallen her last three suitors had been accidents at all! Could it have been that her uncle thought she was getting too near her birthday for him to risk her accepting one of their offers of marriage?

Absurd as she felt her suspicions to be, she couldn't seem to shake them, and finally stopped trying. Being on her guard wasn't going to kill her—and there was a slim chance that *not* being on her guard just might.

Well, she intended to be vigilant, and in her letter she had certainly done her best to warn Thomas to be careful. Now she could only pray that he'd arrive safely.

If he came at all.

Later, long hours away in London, Sir Thomas Lane was staring into the fire in his study, brandy at his elbow, the miniature portrait of his lost beloved in his hand. When his butler appeared, he looked up inquiringly.

"There is a messenger from Collington Park, sir. He says the matter is most urgent."

"Show him in." Thomas rose, straightened his cravat, and waited, leaning against the mantel. He hoped nothing had happened to Lady Ellen. She was getting up there in age—nearing seventy-five, if he recalled correctly—and he knew that in spite of her indomitable spirit, her body was getting frail. As he waited, he prayed that Lady Ellen was not the subject of this urgent message. Alissa had lost her parents while still a child, and her grandfather just four years ago. She didn't need to bury her beloved Lady Ellen and be left alone to raise a blind child. Especially with that bastard she had for an uncle.

The butler reappeared with a mud-spattered man of slight stature, deep lines of weariness in his face. Without speaking, the man handed Sir Thomas the letter he carried.

"Thank you." Thomas ordered his butler, "Take care of this man and his horse."

"Men and horses," the butler murmured.

Sir Thomas absorbed the fact that Alissa had sent more than one servant to deliver a single letter. That was interesting. Did she think that there was danger to one man alone? He nodded to his butler to tell him he'd heard, and waved the two men out of the study.

When they'd gone, Thomas opened Alissa's letter and read,

Dear Thomas,

I am certain that this will be the most peculiar missive you will ever receive, but I am in desperate need of your help. I do not know how to ask this of you, but I must. My grandfather's capricious will states that I must be married by the time I am twenty-five or Collington Park and everything I possess will be forfeited to my uncle Gerald, Lord Withers.

Neither Grandmother nor I ever thought that such a provision would be enforced, as the whole family thought of it as rather a joke. A slap at Great-aunt Isabelle, if you will. You'll remember that she and Grandfather positively loathed each other, and that he was always saying that she would not have been so difficult if she had married as she should have. He also used to say that he was going to see to it that I was not left to suffer her fate, but of course none of us paid any attention to that, more's the pity.

To make a long story short, Uncle Gerald has decided to enforce the terms of Grandfather's will, and I dread to think what provisions he will make for Grandmother, Robin, and me once we are destitute.

At this, Thomas cursed, then read the rest with a muscle jumping in his jaw.

I know that the wound of losing your dear wife and your newborn son cannot have healed. Indeed, it may never do so. I must ask you, however, to come to my aid, Thomas. I have no one else to turn to for help. Please, I beg you, for the sake of Lady Ellen and dear little Robin, to come and marry me before the week is out.

I am, as I said, desperate, and I know you will not fail me. I ask for no more than a marriage in name only.

*Please keep in the forefront of your mind, dear
Thomas, that accidents have befallen my last three
suitors—two of those accidents fatal—and do not—I
repeat, do not—chance coming alone. Bring Hardiston or some other of your comrades from your army
days. And be careful!!!*

It was signed simply, *"Alissa."*

Sir Thomas bellowed for his man. When he rushed into
the study, Sir Thomas ordered, "Pack my saddlebags for an
overnight trip. I must go to Collington Park. Right now I'm
going to look for Hardiston. I'll want to leave when I get
back from my club. I'll return shortly."

Sensing the urgency in Alissa's summons, he headed
for St. James Street to find Hardiston and get him to accompany him to Collington Park. Hardiston was not at the
club, however, which meant that he was probably not in
town. A quick inquiry gave Sir Thomas the information
that Hardiston had been called to the bedside of an ailing
aunt.

Lane was familiar with the situation. Hardy's aunt was
not only very dear to him, but she was also rich and had
made him her sole heir. A call to her bedside was something Hardy would never ignore—even without the
thought of inheritance.

Lane looked around the club. He could see no one else
present with whom he cared to share the arduous miles to
Collington Park, Alissa's concern for his safety or not.

"When will Hardiston return?" he asked of his infor-
mant.

"He'll be in tonight late, or tomorrow at the crack of
dawn. You can bet on it." The gentleman chuckled. "His
aunt calls him to her deathbed on a regular basis, you
know, and he never stays more than one night." The man
chuckled. "The old girl has remarkable powers of recov-
ery."

"Good." Now he would wait for Hardy to return and get on his way with him in tow early tomorrow. "We can start for Collington Park the instant he returns."

"Did I hear you mention Collington Park, Lane?"

Sir Thomas spun around to face the owner of the unctuous voice. He made no attempt to keep his face from showing the dislike he felt for this man. "Yes, Lord Withers." Contempt blazed from his eyes and filled his words as he told him, "I'm on my way there to marry your niece."

Lord Withers's eyes widened in an instant of shock, then narrowed with cunning. Both expressions were gone in a flash, instantly replaced by one of affability. "Ah. My felicitations. My niece is a beautiful girl. And, of course, a very, very wealthy one." Letting the implied insult that Lane was a fortune hunter hang in the air, Withers turned his head and made a show of looking out the window, bending down and craning to see the sky above the building across the street. "Best get going, then, Lane. Waiting for Hardiston might not be a good idea. The roads around Collington Park are treacherous in bad weather, and there's a storm on the way. Moments count, you know." He peered innocently at Lane and drawled, "Unless, of course, you are *afraid* to go alone."

Sir Thomas Lane was still seething about Withers as he rode through the night toward Collington Park. "Damn the man, and damn this foul weather!" His horse flicked an ear back toward him, then, when no more was said by his rider, turned it forward and gave his full attention to the road.

Sir Thomas patted the big chestnut gelding on the neck. It had been a weary ride, and he was anxious to see the end of it. He was doubly anxious to see Alissa and to place her under his protection. She'd been his late wife's dearest friend, and he was going to do everything in his power to keep her safe from the machinations of her despicable uncle.

Dawn was breaking, and the bitter cold seemed to recede only a bit with the rising of the sun. From the top of the hill he was cresting, Lane could see the road that led to the long Collington Park drive. Just before the drive began, there was a bridge spanning a rushing, rock-strewn river. Ice rimed the rocks, glittering in the dawn's early light, and told him the bridge might be treacherous with it as well.

The road to the bridge itself was patchy with ice wherever there was moisture on the descending slope, and both rider and mount were watching it carefully as they picked their way down it. With his hat pulled low and his head bent against the biting dawn wind, Sir Thomas didn't see the four men who rode out of a small grove of trees at the foot of the bridge.

Chapter Three

Alissa was alone in the study when her uncle Gerald arrived at Collington Park. She looked up to see him standing in the doorway, an agitated Kemp behind him. Her eyes narrowed. Her voice heavy with loathing, she uttered a single word. "You!"

"Yes, me, my dear."

"Aren't you a week early, Uncle?"

"I didn't come to bid you 'Happy Birthday.' Alissa."

"Then why are you here?"

"You are hardly being cordial, Niece."

"I'm so glad you noticed. I had no intention of being."

Her uncle stared at her for a long moment before telling her, "Alas, I am the bearer of sad tidings."

Alissa controlled the apprehension that flooded her. "Oh?" She managed to keep her voice cold and casual. "And they are?"

"I was at my club last evening, and chanced to meet Sir Thomas Lane there."

Alissa clenched her fists and waited. Was he going to tell her that Thomas had decided not to come? Whatever his news was, he was clearly enjoying drawing it out, making her wait. She refused to prompt him. Her nails bit into the palms of her hands with the effort it took her to remain silent.

Finally Withers said, "Lane informed me he was on his way here to marry you."

Relief flooded Alissa. Thomas was coming to save them! When her uncle just stood and watched her, she burst out, "You didn't really think I'd let you take Collington Park from me and treat those I love Heaven alone knows how, did you?"

"Ah, my dear, was that your plan? Were you going to wed Sir Thomas just to foil me?"

Deep in Alissa a knot of fear formed and grew, prompted by the look of sly triumph in her uncle's eyes—and the fact that he had used the past tense. He'd said, "*Were* you going to. . . ." The hair on the nape of her neck rose, and she watched her uncle without blinking, without breathing, her expression steely.

He watched her a long moment before he said, "Because if you were thinking of *marrying* Sir Thomas Lane, then it is with the utmost regret that I impart my news to you, dear Niece." His false affability dropped from him and he told her with a snarl, "Your friend has met with an accident. A fatal accident."

Alissa swayed and put a hand to her throat. Oh, dear God! She'd killed Thomas!

Her uncle was all concern again. "I'm so sorry, my dear. His horse slipped on the bridge at the foot of the drive—you know how icy it gets—and threw him down onto the rocks in our river. You know, too, how swiftly it runs. His body was swept away before I and my men could recover it."

Alissa struggled to find her voice through the horror

overwhelming her. When she did, she managed to gasp, "Get out!"

Lord Withers bowed sardonically. "As you wish, dear Niece. Until next week, then." He turned on his heel and walked jauntily across the room. Pausing in the doorway, he said, "Oh, by the way. I took the liberty of putting Lane's horse in your stable. It's lame from the fall. I suppose I'll have it shot when the stable becomes mine next week. But for now . . ." He let the rest of the sentence trail away as he walked out the door.

Alissa stood where she was for another minute, her mind filled with horror. Then she sat down at the desk in stiff little sections—like a jointed wooden doll. Putting her face in her hands, she mourned the death of her dear friend.

After a long time, when sorrow had been served, her tears of mourning turned to tears of outrage. Alissa lifted her head and dashed them away. Stony faced, she sat still as a statue. Then she rose and yanked the bellpull as if she intended to pull it out of the wall.

Never in her life had she been so angry. She was shaking with fury. Thomas Lane was dead, murdered by her uncle, and it was her fault! All her fault! There was nothing she could do to bring Thomas back, but as God was in his Heaven, she could avenge him!

She knew as certainly as she knew the sun would rise tomorrow that her uncle had caused Thomas's death. All she had to do now was go to London to Bow Street and place the matter in the hands of the Runners. If anyone could bring Thomas's murderers to justice, Alissa felt it was the newly formed Bow Street Runners.

There was a sound of hasty footsteps, and Kemp hurried into the room. "You rang, Lady Alissa?"

She knew he was alarmed by the way she had yanked and yanked the bellpull. It was not like her—but then, she wasn't feeling at all like herself. Frustration and guilt were vying to overwhelm her, and she had no intention of letting either of them slow her quest for justice. "Have the traveling coach brought round, please, Kemp. Order the maids to pack enough clothes for a week in London for Lady Ellen, Robin, and myself."

"Yes, my lady." Kemp bowed himself out.

A few minutes later her grandmother came into the room, frowning. "What is this that Kemp tells me about a trip to London? The weather is turning, Alissa. This is hardly an opportune time for travel."

"I know, and I'm sorry for it, Grandmother, but we must get to London."

Peering into her granddaughter's face, Lady Ellen asked, "What is it? What has happened, my dear?"

Alissa started, "It's Uncle Gerald. He was just here and he . . ."

Kemp charged into the room.

Startled by the expression on his face, Alissa demanded of him as her grandmother had just done with her, "What is it, Kemp? What's happened?"

"It's the traveling coach, Lady Alissa! It's been tampered with. The back axle has been sawn through. It will be quite impossible for you to use it to reach London."

Alissa paled. Her grandmother sank slowly down onto a chair. There was no doubt in either of their minds why the coach had deliberately been wrecked. No doubt, either, as to who was responsible. Clearly Gerald didn't want them to be able to leave Collington Park.

Grim determination filled Alissa. "Evidently my uncle wants to keep us here. Never mind. I'll ride. Have my mare saddled." She thought better of that and changed her mind. "No, saddle Jupiter. He has more bottom. Stamina will be important if the weather turns." She started to leave the room. "Send Button to me. I'll need her to help me with my riding habit."

"No!" Her grandmother struggled up from her chair. "I have a far better idea. Send someone down to the Dower

House to see if any of the carriages left in the stables there will do. They'll be very old, but perhaps they'll still be serviceable."

Alissa smiled. "What a splendid idea."

Lady Ellen grinned at her. "I had to think quickly. I wasn't about to be left behind."

Alissa came back to her grandmother. "You mean that you weren't going to let me go alone."

"That, too, my dear. That, too."

Kemp hurried out to dispatch a footman to order the head groom and coachman down to the Dower House at the other end of Collington Park to look for a vehicle to take his ladies to London.

He sent pistols with them.

When he'd finished seeing to that he came back and stood waiting to be acknowledged.

"Yes, Kemp?" Alissa gave him her full attention.

"I was wondering if you want a baggage coach and servants."

"No, Kemp. To tell the truth, I want you to stay here in case . . . in case anyone should arrive and . . . and . . . want to . . ."

"What Lady Alissa is trying to say, Kemp," Lady Ellen interrupted, "is that she wants you and the other servants here at Collington to hold the fort against my son, her uncle Gerald, the present Lord Withers." With fire in her eyes she told the butler, "If he and his unsavory employees should come skulking around, see to it that they do not enter this house!"

Alissa laughed. It was a sharp, discordant sound that bore no resemblance to her natural laugh. "Well that was certainly plain enough, Grandmother." She turned back to the astonished butler, and her travesty of a smile disappeared. "Unfortunately, that is precisely the case, Kemp. But I don't want you or any of the others to do anything that might put you in jeopardy. You are more important than a piece of property. Do you understand?"

Kemp frowned a little, and blinked hard. All of them knew how much Collington Park meant to their mistress. Silently he vowed to die if he had to to keep Lord Withers out. Finally he nodded. "I understand, your ladyship."

The instant the butler was gone, Alissa turned back to her grandmother. "I want us to be in residence in London this week. I have a feeling we'll be safer there with our friends around us." Her grim expression spoke of purpose. "I must keep us all safe until I can manage to bribe or co-erce someone into marrying me."

Her grandmother was startled. "But I thought that Sir Thomas Lane was . . ."

Alissa put a hand on her grandmother's arm. "Uncle Gerald just came to tell me that Thomas Lane is dead." In spite of her best efforts, her voice broke and tears filled her eyes.

"Ah, no!"

"Yes. Thomas ran into Uncle at their club and told him he was coming to marry me. He was killed on his way here, and, God help me, Grandmother, I firmly believe that Uncle Gerald caused it to happen." Her gray eyes were full of determination even as they spilled tears. "I intend to go to London and put the matter into the hands of the Bow Street Runners." Her voice softened. "Please forgive me."

Lady Ellen put a hand to her heart, and pain registered on her face.

Alissa put an arm around her. "Are you all right?"

Lady Ellen gave her a wan smile of reassurance. "Yes, dear. I'm as all right as a woman can be who suspects she has given the world one of its worst villains."

Alissa hugged her tight. "You also gave it my father."

"Yes." Lady Ellen straightened. "Richard was special. One of the very best. I suppose that will balance the scale for me somewhat when I meet my Maker."

Seeing Alissa's continuing distress, Lady Ellen reached out and took her hands. "Oh, my poor darling. I can see you are blaming yourself for Thomas's death."

"I killed him."

"No. That's not true, Alissa." She gave the girl's hands a little shake. "I know you. You'd have warned him there was danger, I'm sure, and Thomas chose to come despite it. Besides, no one has brought in his body. There may still be hope." She grimaced as she felt her granddaughter flinch, and added, "But if he *is* dead, Alissa, then he is with his beloved Elaine, and I feel rather certain that Thomas might even thank you for that."

There was a sound in the doorway.

Both women turned to see a slender boy with a troubled frown on his handsome face. "Is everything all right?"

"Robin. Hallo, darling. Come and give me a kiss." Lady Ellen held out open arms and began to hum softly.

Robin grinned, cocked his head, and homed in on the soft, tuneless humming to walk confidently into his grandmother's embrace. "There is a great deal of commotion going on, and Bester is packing a trunk in my dressing room."

"Oh? Really?" Lady Ellen teased. "Do you think Bester is planning a trip?"

Robin gave a shout of laughter. "I think they are my things my valet is packing, Grandmama."

Alissa had used this pleasant interruption to regain control of herself. Now she said a little too brightly, "We are going to London for a while, dearest. Will you like that?"

Robin gave her question his earnest consideration. "It will be splendid to hear all the new sounds, and to have you describe the sights to me." He thought for a moment. "I'll probably even like the different smells." He laughed. "Though you always say they are awful. But I shall hate having to use my cane to get around. It's so easy here where I know where everything is," he said matter-of-factly. "I do think a change would be nice, though."

"Good. Run along and get dressed for the trip. We'll be leaving very soon now. It's cold out, so dress warmly,"

"Why such haste, Cousin Alissa? Has something happened?"

"Go!" Alissa ordered. "We can talk on the way."

As the child rushed from the room, she turned to her grandmother and said, "See how quickly he goes. He's so able that I forget sometimes that he's blind. And it's because he's so familiar with everything here." Her expression was troubled. "How dreadful it would be for him if I were to lose it all."

"Well, my dear," her grandmother said bracingly, "we'll admit just this once that it would be quite dreadful for all of us, the servants included, if you lost Collington Park. Then, having said it, we will put that thought aside and concentrate instead on your efforts to keep it, shall we?"

"Yes, of course. And I *shall* keep it! But there is something of equal importance that I must do first. I must bring to justice those who are responsible for Thomas Lane's death."

"Of course, you must," Lady Ellen said very quietly.

"Oh, Grandmother, I'm so sorry Uncle Gerald is your son!"

"No sorrier than I am, I assure you," Lady Ellen said drily. "However, that is not the problem at hand. We do what we have to do, my dear, and your cause is just. Murder cannot go unpunished. You must report this to the Bow Street Runners. There is no other course."

With regal calm, Lady Ellen turned away from Alissa to look out a tall window. After a moment, she frowned. Beyond its panes, the silver-gray sky was pregnant with snow. "Before you can do that, however, we have to reach Town, and the weather looks as if is going to make that rather difficult."

Alissa closed her eyes momentarily at the hurt she knew she had inflicted on her beloved grandmother. Then she stifled her guilt-filled pity and turned her attention to the sky outside. She was quiet as she studied it with the eye of someone used to living in the country. Finally, she said resignedly, "Not that we really need another obstacle, of course, but quite obviously it is going to snow."

Chapter Four

Michael Mathers clenched his jaw to keep his teeth from chattering in the brutal cold. As the ever-rising wind whistled through the trees lining the road and played sharp, treble tunes on the icicles hanging from their branches, he found himself almost yearning for the dry, life-sucking heat of the Iberian summers—dust, flies, and all.

As if he could read his rider's mind, Gladiator gave a low nicker and shook his great head. The violent movement sent a shower of snow over Michael.

Gritting his teeth to keep from cursing the snow that his four-legged companion had sent past his collar, Michael urged his mount on. If he were going to save the horse, he'd have to find him shelter, and since night was rapidly falling, he'd have to find it soon.

Suddenly, in spite of the fact that the white wall surrounding him muted everything but the whispering howl of the storm, he heard the flat, snow-deadened sound of a single shot up ahead of him. A pistol! He knew the sound

too well to mistake it. It was no poacher shooting to procure meat for his family while gamekeepers stayed close to
their firesides. You didn't hunt game with a pistol.

Was there some poor fool out in this blizzard signaling
for help? God knew no highwayman would be crazy
enough to venture out in this.

He pushed Gladiator into a trot, praying he wouldn't
lame the horse on a hidden patch of ice, and headed him in
the direction of the shot. Peering hard through the curtain
of snow, he looked for some sign of the person who had
fired the pistol.

Around the very next bend, he came upon the carriage.
It was an elegant affair, made more for driving in the parks
of London than for traveling the rougher roads of the countryside. Its very elegance had led it to its present pass.
Even with the weight of too much baggage, it had not been
heavy enough for its iron-rimmed wheels to cut through
the ice-covered surface of the bridge it had just crossed and
gain sufficient purchase to keep it on the highroad. Slewed
sideways into the ditch just past the bridge, it was firmly
resisting the efforts of its well-matched team to extricate it.

Michael rode toward the distressed vehicle. There was
a man at the horses' heads, and two others sheltering from
the wind behind the carriage. Just before he got there, his
attention was pulled away from the efforts of the snow-
covered coachman to encourage his horses by the sudden
opening of the carriage door.

His hand must have tightened on the reins, for Gladiator came to an abrupt halt in the swirling snow. Michael
didn't notice. He was aware only of the vision before
him—the graceful woman who stood in the door of the
coach trying to nudge down the folding step so that she
could alight.

She was beautiful. Her dark blue cloak's ermine-
trimmed hood framed a perfect face. When the capricious
wind tore open that cloak, Michael saw she had a figure

that matched her face's perfection. Then, the wind caught her hood and threw it back from her head, and he saw that great gray eyes illuminated the pale oval of her face and a riot of short, glossy, dark curls framed it. It was when he saw that her face held none of the fretting he expected from a lady in her predicament, that he became completely fascinated. What was such a jewel doing stuck in a road-side ditch in a blizzard?

Thanks to the fact that he rode a gray horse, she hadn't noticed him in the veil of swirling snow, and he was at liberty to sit there enjoying the sight of her, amused that a mere encounter with a woman in a snowstorm could make him forget the punishing cold. As he watched, the winged brows above her glorious eyes were pulled down in a light frown, and her soft lips set firmly with determination as she concentrated on forcing the frozen iron of the folding step to her will.

Michael dismounted. He did it without grace, clumsy from the cold in addition to the fact that he had but one arm to use. "Stand, Gladiator," he told his mount, then sloughed through the deepening snow to put down the step for her, glad she had not seen him get off his horse.

Obviously surprised at his sudden appearance in the middle of nowhere, she looked at him in faint astonishment for a second, then smiled and extended her hand for his assistance. Enchanted by her smile, Michael carried the hand she'd offered to his lips and kissed it, his gaze locked with hers.

The wind dropped as he kissed the slender gloved hand, and it almost seemed as if the very elements abated so as to miss nothing of this meeting. In the hush, Michael heard her take a quick breath and saw her eyes widen, and knew that she had felt the current that passed between them, too. Then her brows snapped down in a frown.

Michael laughed exultantly, the freezing weather forgotten. She was no simpering miss. This Snow Goddess had spirit! Furthermore, her frown did nothing to mar the perfection of her forehead. Suppressing the first real grin he'd felt in months, he offered casually, "May I be of any assistance?"

Her smile returned instantly. "I most sincerely hope so. I believe we seem to be . . . stuck."

Michael noted her pleasant voice with satisfaction. It matched the rest of her. Bowing, he told her, "Then I must insist that instead of getting down, you go back into the carriage and attempt to keep warm."

She looked at him a long moment, obviously deciding whether or not to obey him—whether or not to let a perfect stranger take, even temporarily, the reins of her life from her. He felt she was assessing him as a man, and her frank perusal brought him back to reality. Though his cloak hid the useless arm strapped to his side, he nevertheless felt himself color at her appraisal, and cursed the fact that she was evaluating only half a man.

As she acceded to his suggestion and reentered the coach, Michael closed the door a little too firmly behind her. Then, his smile gone, he turned away abruptly to begin the task of rescue.

"Ho there," he called to the footmen. Marks in the snow showed him they had already been attempting to push the carriage out of the ditch. "You two."

The pair who'd been sheltering behind the carriage came forward immediately. Michael saw they were dressed in rich livery, their greatcoats more than adequate for the severe weather in which they were presently caught. The lady was no pinchpenny, he decided, so what was she doing with this outdated carriage, and what the devil had made her decide to take such an ancient and un-suitable vehicle out in treacherous weather? If she had a man at home, then he was clearly remiss in protecting her from folly. If she had none, Lord knew she needed one to instruct her in the choice of a proper traveling coach that was certain.

"Unload the baggage," he told the footmen. As they obeyed his order, Michael went to the coachman. "Are the horses all right?"

"Aye, sor. Thankfully, they be right as rain. Just a bit nervous."

"What happened?"

The coachman accepted Michael's authority without question. " 'Twas a young fool in a curricle trying to get home out of the storm, I 'spect. Rushed 'round yonder curve mostly out of control, and it was try ta miss 'im or crash. So we ended up in the ditch."

"I see." Michael had to raise his voice just as the coachman had, because the storm had returned to its former strength. "Good man. A crash would have been far more serious."

The coachman relaxed. "Thankee, sor." He touched the brim of his hat and murmured, "Not ever'body woulda seen it that way."

"The shot you fired brought me. That was a smart move."

" 'Twasn't me as fired it, sor. 'Twas Lady Alissa."

So she was intelligent as well as beautiful. And she had a lovely name. Alissa. He tried it in his mind. *Alissa*. A name to whisper in the night . . .

Blast and damn! All of a sudden he felt as if the fates were conspiring against him.

Glancing back to where the two footmen stood, Michael told the coachman, "The baggage is off. Try your team again as soon as the men and I get behind the carriage to push."

"Ay, sor. Jus' you gimme the word."

Michael nodded and leaned into the wind as he strode to the rear of the carriage.

● ● ●

Inside, Alissa looked at her grandmother and smiled as they listened to the shouted conversation of the men. "It seems," Alissa said, "that we have a rescuer."

"Yes. His voice sounds like a gentleman's." Lady Ellen watched Alissa closely as she asked, "What is he like?"

"Tall. Dark. Broad-shouldered. Blue-eyed." Alissa cocked her head. "Handsome." An impish smile softened her face. "Possibly very handsome."

Lady Ellen hid the twinkle in her eyes by pretending to look out the window. While her face was turned away, she permitted herself her own small smile. Her granddaughter had noticed a great deal about a man who'd appeared for only a brief moment in the middle of a snowstorm. "Hmmmm," she said, "can't see a thing. The window is iced over." When she turned back, Lady Ellen's face was bland. "Are you warm enough, dear? That was quite a chilling breeze when you stood there in the doorway."

"I'm fine. I didn't notice the cold."

"Ah," Lady Ellen said with a great deal of satisfaction.

They could hear movement outside around the carriage. Before Alissa could ask what her grandmother meant, a deep-voiced cry, "Yo!" came from the back of the vehicle, the coachman shouted encouragement to his team, and the carriage lurched out of the ditch with a rocking jolt.

"He's done it!" Alissa's smile was radiant. "He's got us out of the ditch!"

Lady Ellen's smile matched her granddaughter's. Alissa hadn't said, "They've done it" even though the two footmen, the coachman, and certainly the horses had been involved with freeing them from the ditch. She'd said, "He's done it!" with more enthusiasm than her grandmother had seen in her for days.

Lady Ellen's smile became a little sly. After a moment, her expression was quite speculative, and when the thump of the luggage being restowed on the roof had ceased, and the carriage door opened again, she was ready.

The stranger stood framed in the coach door, enveloped in swirling snow. He touched the brim of his hat to them and said, "You're all set to go, ladies. Your coachman assures me that the horses were uninjured in the accident, and that there is an inn no more than two miles ahead. You'll be safe there until the storm passes." He turned to go.

Her grandmother saw the way Alissa involuntarily reached out, as if she would stop their rescuer from leaving them, then quickly withdrew her hand. "Young man!" Lady Ellen cried in her most imperious voice.

He turned back, a tight, lopsided smile on his face. Evidently he didn't consider himself a young man, but was too polite to ignore her.

"Surely," Lady Ellen told him, "you are not going to desert us!"

Her wording had the desired effect.

"Desert you!"

With that slightly outraged comment, one of his eyebrows lifted, and even an overprotective grandmother couldn't deny that he was a handsome devil. But Ellen knew she wasn't simply an overprotective grandmother anymore. Right now, her role had changed. The protection she felt for her precious granddaughter had become a little predatory where possibly eligible males were concerned. She was now a grandmother on the hunt. And she scented prey.

"Yes," she asserted. "*Surely* you will be kind enough to ride with us to see us safely to the inn?"

He hesitated only an instant. Then he bowed, smiled tightly again, and said, "Certainly."

"Well, then, get in, get in!"

Alissa was regarding her grandmother with open astonishment, but Lady Ellen didn't mind. She'd gladly play the part of an autocratic grande dame if that was what it took to get this young buck who'd so caught her granddaughter's interest into the carriage with them.

"I can ride beside you, madam."

"How very foolish that would be in this weather. It's freezing out there! Tie your horse behind," Lady Ellen ordered. Her manner and tone brooked no refusal.

The man regarded her steadily for a moment, one eyebrow raised again, and Lady Ellen wondered if he were going to insist on riding his horse. Why in the world would he want to? Then suddenly, he capitulated. Swinging his tall frame easily into the carriage, he leaned back out and called, "Gladiator! Follow," then closed the door.

He was obviously confident that his Gladiator would follow him to the ends of the earth if need be, that was plain to see. And Alissa was right. He was handsome. Very handsome. Seeing him safely sitting across from her next to their faithful—and probably shocked—abigail, Button, Lady Ellen had the oddest feeling that she knew exactly how it felt to be the cat who ate the canary.

Chapter Five

Michael sat beside their abigail, a round little woman with a pleasant smile, who'd been called Button when asked to make room for him. They sat with their backs to the horses with hardly a hand span of space between them.

Across from him, in the lantern-lit carriage, sat the Snow Goddess and the Dragon—as he'd whimsically dubbed the two ladies—and between them, a handsome lad of about ten. The boy was intently staring in Michael's direction, but his eyes failed to focus accurately on him.

Michael had seen that stare too many times not to recognize it. He hated to see it, here, like this. He'd seen it enough in the army. Obviously, tragically, the child was blind. And it was all the greater pity because the boy had his whole life before him.

Pity, however, was useless. Pity was an enemy to be despised. His thoughts turned to something more profitable. Assistance might not be as useless. Perhaps the doctor he'd gotten to help some of his friends who'd been blinded in the Peninsular War could help this child. He'd have to see to it.

Next to the child, the tartar who'd commanded his uneasy presence held tight to the lad's hand. She was a slender, straight-backed woman with the vestiges of a great beauty, handsome in her old age. Even in the dim light of the carriage lamps he could see that she had a twinkle in her eye. He could also see that she seemed remarkably pleased about something.

"I am Lady Ellen Collington," the tartar informed him. Her manner and speech were a great deal softer now that she'd successfully bullied him into the carriage, Michael observed. And evidently she'd decided she could smile. She did so with pride as she introduced her companions. "These are my grandchildren, Lady Alissa Alana Collington and her cousin, Robin. And that's Button, our abigail, beside you."

Michael flashed a smile at the round little woman beside him, then bowed from his place, a subtle, elegant movement of his upper body. "How do you do. I'm Michael Mathers."

The women smiled back. Both smiles were pleasant, but Lady Alissa's was reserved now that he was so close. In the depths of her eyes, he saw a sadness that intrigued him. Something stirred in him. Something that urged him to discover the cause of that sadness—and make it go away. He sternly suppressed the feeling. He was not one to play knight-errant. Not anymore.

Watching closely from her place on the opposite seat, Lady Ellen's curiosity was rampant. She wondered if perhaps there might not be more to this gentleman's name than simply "Michael Mathers." Unless she missed her guess, there was a great deal more. He had the posture of a military man, certainly, and that would give him a military rank in front of the "Michael," of course, but there was an additional, almost casual, arrogance about him that made her wonder if he hadn't a title as well.

Lady Ellen prided herself on being an accurate observer of the people around her, and she was ready to swear in court that there was more to the young man across from her than he had told them in his brief introduction. Putting aside her curiosity in the interest of good manners, she told him, "We are on our way to London, Mr. Mathers, and we are grateful that you came by at so propitious a moment." She smiled warmly at him as she confessed, "For a while there, I was afraid my grandchildren and I were destined to freeze." She watched Michael carefully, and saw that he was amused. Clearly, he knew that she was more interested in him than in what she was saying.

Smiling, he replied, "I'm certain your men would soon have thought of unloading the luggage if I hadn't happened along."

Lady Ellen smiled back, keeping the smile small to express polite disagreement. "Nevertheless, we are thankful for your assistance." Her gaze sharpened perceptibly as she added, "I wonder, though, what on earth you were doing riding out in this blizzard."

"I'd left friends on the coast, where the weather is milder. I'd hoped to make London before the storm caught me."

"Were you going to ride your Gladiator the whole way?"

"I was."

"He must be an extraordinary horse."

Michael's smile twisted, and Ellen suspected he was remembering feats his mount had performed in their past. "He is indeed."

Ellen went fishing. "And since the storm did break sooner than you expected?" She saw what she thought was a blush suffuse the man's cheeks. Then he threw up his chin and told her in a level voice with steel behind it, "The storm made it necessary to seek shelter for him."

"And," Ellen probed, "for yourself of course?"

The fact that she had made the statement a question sent one of their rescuer's eyebrows soaring toward his hairline. His voice was flat and cool as he answered, "Of course."

Ellen smiled and turned away then, pretending to look out her window as if he were no longer of any interest to her—as if her comments had been those of a hostess being hospitable and no more. But her curiosity was far from satisfied, and she was disturbed.

There was a pause in the conversation as Lady Ellen fought her curiosity. Then, "Alissa?" The boy's voice was clear and sweet, and Michael wondered what had blinded the child and whether there was any chance of helping him.

"Yes, dear?"

"Would you tell me what the gentleman who rescued us looks like, please?"

Michael seized on the excuse the child had given him to fasten his gaze on Lady Alissa's lovely face. Regarding her blandly, as if he were merely helping her to see him more clearly, he took advantage of the opportunity to study her.

She had a perfect oval face with a flawless complexion. Her huge gray eyes were surmounted by winged brows and surrounded by long, thick lashes. The sadness in their depths made it so that he could hardly take his eyes from them to consider the rest of her features. He smiled to see that even in this cold, the tip of her perfect little nose wasn't pink like that of the child's and the grandmother's—and his own, no doubt. The only color in her face was in her delicately tinted cheeks and in her rosy lips. Clasped over the lower lip as she studied him were white, even teeth.

"I believe," the vision said, "that the gentleman has blue

eyes." Her own eyes flashed to his for confirmation. When he nodded, she said firmly, "Yes. They are blue."

"Is he clean shaven, Alissa?"

"Yes."

The boy sighed. "Oh, dear. I'd rather hoped for a dashing mustache. Not a pencil one. A nice big one like a grenadier, or a dragoon."

Michael couldn't help grinning. "I shall begin growing one immediately."

"How very nice of you!" the child exclaimed. "What else, Alissa?"

"He has nice, white teeth, a square jaw, and a patrician nose that looks rather like it has been broken at some point." Her words tumbled over each other as if she were embarrassed, but she was obviously determined to satisfy the child and was looking at Michael with her lips pressed firmly together and a challenge in her eyes.

Was she daring him to resent this innocent survey of his person? He didn't. Though he'd long ago become accustomed to women taking interested stock of him, rarely had it been in so noble a cause. Usually they had been assessing him as an eligible *parti*—or a lover. That that would all change now because he was no longer whole, and would therefore be of no interest to the shallow belles of the *ton*, made this particular cataloging of his physical attributes bittersweet. He was determined, however, to focus on the sweetness of a sister helping a younger sibling to "see," rather than the bitterness that sought to overwhelm him.

"And he is tall?"

The lady Alissa raised an imperious eyebrow.

"Six feet," Michael supplied helpfully.

"And broad-shouldered, and," she peered hard across the carriage, "of medium build?" She'd made it a question, as he was covered by his cloak.

"Slender just now," he replied, then could have bitten his tongue.

Her eyes were full of the curiosity she was too polite to voice.

Michael mentally cursed himself for his careless remark. There was no way in hell he was going to tell this lovely young woman that he was "slender just now" because he'd spent several months hanging in chains against a damp cave wall!

She seemed to sense that there was something sinister behind his reluctance to explain, for her eyes widened for an instant when he frowned. When they met his calmly, however, he knew she was content that he posed no threat. He supposed it was nice she hadn't leapt to the conclusion that he'd been in some English prison.

The boy called Robin asked, "Is he a soldier? Is he wearing a uniform?"

"No, dear, I don't believe he is," Alissa answered.

"But I'll wager he has," Lady Ellen interrupted, watching him sharply.

Michael smiled a crooked smile, "Quite right, Lady Ellen. A great many of us served during the Peninsular War." He inclined his head. "Major Michael Mathers, at your service."

Robin burst out, "Oh, that is splendid! I do so love a soldier, don't you Alissa?"

To her surprise, Alissa's face flamed, but she managed to say calmly, "We all admire our brave fighting men, dearest."

"Well?" the boy pressed eagerly, "Do go on and tell me more about him."

"I rather think I've told you all that I'm able to perceive."

"His hair, Alissa. You've not told me the color of his hair."

"Black."

"Actually, it's merely dark brown," Michael corrected. "And not even that when I was out in the Iberian sun."

The boy cocked his head. "I suppose that's all right."

"Thank you," Michael said in a voice touched by laughter. "I'll try to stay out of the sun for a while."

Lady Ellen gestured toward the frost-veiled window. "That shouldn't be difficult." She smiled gently in the direction of her sightless grandchild. "Not for a while, anyway."

Chapter Six

"Inn, ho!" The coachman shouted with all his might from the high driver's box to bring out the inn's ostlers, then grumbled to the footmen who huddled beside him under his fur-lined, waterproofed robe, "Little chance they'll come out in this lessen we drag 'em out."

Inside the coach, Lady Alissa sighed with relief. An inn meant safety. She was acutely aware that her desperation to reach London might have ended in disaster for the ones she loved. Indeed, it probably would have done so if not for the handsome man seated opposite her. She owed him a debt of gratitude that she was at a loss as to how she might repay.

Lady Ellen broke into her thoughts as she said to Michael, "I know that you will want to see to your horse. I shall bespeak rooms for us all and a private parlor, and order dinner." She lifted her chin and narrowed her eyes at him. In her best tartar manner, she ordered, "For which you will join us."

Michael laughed and nodded compliance. "Are you certain you do not wish me to escort you into the inn?"

"There is no need. I am perfectly capable of informing the innkeeper that you, as well as my own party, will need accommodations. He will oblige me, I'm certain."

"I've not the slightest doubt of it, Lady Ellen." A quick glance at the Snow Goddess told him she was both perplexed and annoyed. If any of his former comrades-in-arms, the "Lucky Seven," had been present, he'd have bet them she wasn't used to seeing her grandmother behave in such a high-handed manner and was puzzled by it. As for the annoyance, he was forced to wait and see. Lady Alissa hadn't seen that his left arm was strapped to his side, so it couldn't be that she was sorry to see him join them at dinner. . . .

He broke off that thought with bitter laughter in his mind. Obviously, in spite of his handicap, his flattering estimation of his former charm for the ladies seemed to be intact. Ah, well, an appearance or two in London society would no doubt change that. The *ton* had no tolerance for the maimed.

The coach rocked to a halt at the inn door. Blown by a bitter cold wind, snow swirled into the carriage as Michael opened the door next to him and got out. Seeing that the two footmen had leapt down from the box and were attending the ladies, he went straight to his horse. "Well, old boy, I've found you shelter. I'll have you rubbed down in a few minutes, and with any luck, they'll have a deeply bedded stall for you."

Gladiator nickered and shoved at his master's shoulder, eager to get in out of the storm. Together they found the way to the stables, Gladiator leading.

Michael kicked snow out of its way and pulled open one of the tall double doors. They entered a dimly lit haven that smelled of horses, leather, and hay. This time, Gladiator's low nicker was one of approval and content.

An ostler unwrapped himself from his blanket at the sound and rose from his bed of straw. "Sorry, Gov'nah. The weather like it be, we didn't expect nobody. I'll take 'im."

"Thank you, but I see to my own mount." Michael smiled to take the sting out of his refusal and added, "Besides, the coachman will be here in a moment with his team, and you'll have your hands full."

The man pulled his forelock in the usual gesture of respect for his betters and went to kick at an inert bundle still in the straw. "Up with ya, Alfie. A team's comin'." The second horse handler jumped up and ran to the door, knuckling sleep from his eyes, a bit of straw in his hair.

The ladies' coachman entered then, a horse in either hand and fire in his eyes. "Get out there and get the rest of my team, ya lazy bastards!" The ostlers fled out into the blizzard, yanking their coats on as they ran. Cursing fluently under his breath, the coachman snatched up a handful of straw and twisted it into a tool with which to groom his horses.

Michael was grinning as he fashioned a straw whisp of his own and started getting the snow and wet out of Gladiator's mane and off his coat. Working to rub warmth into the gelding brought back his own.

On the other side of the barn aisle, the coachman was crooning to his horses as he worked over them. Now that the ostlers had brought in the rest of the team, his mood was vastly improved, and he ordered the horse handlers about almost cheerfully.

Michael missed the man's cursing. It had reminded him of happier days in the cavalry with Harry and Bly, Stone and MacLain all working beside him to see to their mounts before they saw to their own needs. Smiling, he turned to the man. "It's good to see the way you care for your cattle."

"Thankee, sor. I've a fondness for them, don't you see."

He grinned at Michael. "Besides, if I didn't take the best care of 'em and then some, Lady Alissa would have the hide off me an' tack it to the barn wall."

Michael stopped grooming Gladiator. "Is that so?" The remark was pensive, not a question, but the coachman answered it.

"Aye. Ye can count on it."

Michael dropped his head against his gelding's neck for an instant. When he looked back at the coachman, the expression on his face was grave. "I don't know your name,"

"Floyd Green, I be, sor. At yer service."

"Well, Floyd Green, I'm Michael Mathers, and this is Gladiator." He swept his hand down the satin length of his horse's neck. "I feel much about him as your mistress feels about her horses, and if anything should happen to me and you come to know of it, I would like you to add him to your stable." Michael ignored Green's start of surprise and went on. "He is steady and wise, and has always proved himself more than capable to look after me. Though he is quite large, his gaits are easy, and he would make a fine mount for the boy. All boys should be able to ride. Perhaps your young Master Robin most of all."

The coachman was finding it hard to come up with words. Finally he swallowed convulsively. "Sor, I'd be honored to do as you say if we still have a stable." He ducked his head then, as if he'd given away something that was not his business to tell. "At any rate, Heaven itself forbid that anything befall . . . your lordship." He blurted out the form of address as if he had no right to have guessed it, and regarded Michael as if he dared him to deny it.

Michael put him out of his misery. "Aye, Floyd Green, I'm Viscount Kantwell right enough, but don't let it trouble you. I've been too long in the army to let such things stand in the way of making a new friend." He extended his hand to the coachman.

After a long hesitation in which he fixedly regarded

Michael's hand, Green seized it and shook it heartily, "An honor, sor, an honor."

"I feel the same, Mr. Green. Exactly the same." Michael clapped the astonished man on the shoulder and left him standing there open-mouthed as he turned away to lead Gladiator into a stall.

Leaving the relatively warm safety of the barn, Michael plowed through the drifting snow to the back door of the inn. Curiosity about the man's hint that there might not be a stable belonging to the ladies at some time in the future filled his mind. He realized, however, that the faithful retainer would say no more on the subject to an outsider, so it would have been pointless to have stayed in the barn to ask.

He fully intended to find out, however. Though the coach in which he'd found the little party was ancient, the horses were of the finest quality, as were the liveries of the men.

Michael smiled broadly at the way he'd assigned ownership of the equipage to the Snow Goddess without even thinking, and flinched as the freezing cold hit his front teeth. Deciding the quick discomfort served him right for getting thrown off subject by the remembrance of Lady Alissa's spirit and beauty, he closed his lips firmly and returned to his speculations. Her men's liveries were not only of the finest quality, but extravagantly comfortable with their heavy, caped greatcoats and the fur-lined rugs to keep them from freezing that he'd noticed on the coachman's box.

The ladies had been richly gowned, as well. Their cloaks were lined with the most expensive furs. The boy was expensively clad, and the quality of the abigail's cloak was excellent. There was no lack of funds, he could easily see.

Neither woman had the restless, slightly voracious eyes of a gambler, so he didn't consider that they might have gambled away their home—with their stables. Therefore, he could come to but one conclusion. Obviously trouble was brewing because there was no man to look out for them. That it was serious trouble was just as obvious. Why the hell else would two women—three, if he counted the abigail—drag a blind child out in the midst of blizzard?

As he reached for the latch on the inn's kitchen door, he made up his mind to discover the facts behind their coachman's careless comment. And in doing that, perhaps he'd discover the reason for the sadness in Lady Alissa's eyes.

Where better to do it than at dinner with the Dragon and the Snow Goddess?

Chapter Seven

Ducking his head to keep it from hitting the low lintel, Michael stamped snow from his boots just inside the inn's back door. He knocked it from the shoulders of his campaign cloak as best he could with one hand and shook more from the brim of his hat. He straightened as he emerged from the short, low-ceilinged passage into the large, roomy kitchen.

Wonderful smells were coming from the fireplace where two women tended steaming pots and a spit boy cranked industriously to turn a huge roast. A third woman basted the meat with something that, when drops of it hit the fire, sizzled and sent a tantalizing aroma to him from across the width of the room.

Suddenly, Michael was hungry. Very hungry. Funny, with all the tempting dishes that Regina and Kate had had prepared for him, he'd never been hungry enough to care whether or not he ate, but now he was ready to devour an ox.

He grinned and shrugged, refusing to give the matter more thought, and walked past the table where a girl no older than twelve was dicing carrots, her ruffled mobcap slipping down over her eyebrows. Led by the familiar clamor of men drinking, he headed for the common room.

Pausing in the doorway, Michael took in the clean white-washed walls, the highly polished bar on one side of the long room, and the well-scrubbed tables on the other. Noting the shine on brass and copper, he decided they had come upon a good inn.

There were eleven men in the common room, he saw, and at the moment, they were all staring at him. He lifted his chin and let them stare, meeting their curious gazes with a frank one of his own.

The occupants of the room saw a tall, athletic man with his cape still swinging from his broad shoulders, stirred by the length and power of his stride. He was a handsome devil, but the men didn't care about that—all their womenfolk were safe at home, after all. Home with the children, where they belonged.

The quality that arrested them, that kept them staring too long and then turned them away hastily when they realized what they were doing, was the expression of command that he wore as comfortably as he wore his old campaign cloak. This man was a force to be reckoned with, a man who was certain he'd be obeyed. The ex-soldiers among the group found it hard not to jump to their feet and salute him.

There was a long silence. Then the newcomer won them all by his manner of addressing them. "Gentlemen," he called them with a slight bow, and crossed to the bar. A chorus returned his greeting, then conversation started again as, the spell broken, every man spoke at once, their attention still on the stranger.

The innkeeper was busy at the bar, and Michael had need to talk to him. But not now. He would never ask the man to send a valet to help him dress in the morning with every ear in the room attuned to him. Just having to do it at all set his teeth on edge as he said, instead, "Ale, if you please, innkeeper."

"Certainly, sir." The innkeeper drew rich brown ale from a keg behind him and slid a tankard of it across the bar to Michael.

"I thank you." Michael placed coins on the bar and headed for the inviting warmth of the fireplace's inglenook. Right now, more than anything else, he wanted to toast the cold out of his bones and quench his thirst. When he could feel his feet again, he'd find out where his room was and wash up. Unless he missed his guess, the women would bathe and change and fuss over the boy, so he had time to thaw. Too soon, he thought, smiling, he'd have to cope with the problem of dinner with the Dragon.

He'd sensed that Lady Ellen wanted something from him, but for the life of him he couldn't fathom what it might be. Could her requirement have something to do with the expression that had puzzled him so? Was that unexplainable expression—almost of desperation—that he'd seen in the depths of her beautiful granddaughter's lovely eyes the explanation? And if so, what the devil could it be?

He was turning ideas over in his mind when suddenly he heard Lady Alissa's name mentioned. Well aware that a barroom was never the place to mention a lady's name, he nevertheless fought down any instincts of gallantry in the interest of gathering information.

"Aye, that's her. That's Lady Alissa Collington." A roughly clad yeoman with a ruddy face was the speaker.

"That beauty who just arrived is the Lady of Collington Park?" This man looked like a clerk.

"Coo. Who'd 'ave thought it?" The third man to join in the discussion looked as if he'd be more at home in the backstreets of London.

The first answered with impatience. "Well, why

wouldn't ya think it? You've got ears on ya, so you've heard what a flaming beauty she is. 'A diamond of the first water,' they call her. Every man in the aristocracy has been after her for the past eight years."

"Oh? Then why ain't any of 'em got 'er ?"

Another man brought his tankard over to the group discussing Lady Alissa Collington. This one looked a good deal more prosperous than the others and his voice and manner were those of a gentleman. "I think I can answer that," he told the three men. "It seems that Lady Alissa was never certain whether any of her suitors were asking for her hand because they loved her or her grandfather's considerable fortune. And, of course, she had the typical young girl's desire to marry for love."

With a sneer, the least appealing of them said, "Ah, ever'body knows them aristos marry ta add ta their lands er fortunes."

"Ah, yes." The gentlemanly one smiled his condescension. "That may well be, but Lady Alissa wanted something more, you see. And, unfortunately, as a result she may very well lose all."

Michael was careful not to shift his casual position, but he was suddenly intent on the conversation at the table not far from him. Was he about to learn the reason here, in the common room of an inn, for that sad expression he saw at the back of the Snow Goddess's eyes?

"Yes. If Lady Alissa does not wed before her twenty-fifth birthday, she'll lose Collington Park and the extremely impressive fortune her grandfather left her."

"Lose it 'ow?"

"By the terms of her grandfather's will she must forfeit it all to her uncle, who inherited the title." He paused for effect, then added, "And her birthday is next week."

"Lord a'mighty. That's close on us, that is."

"Serves 'er right, I say." It was the man Michael had mentally labeled "the gutter rat" who spoke. "If'n she's been too proud to make up 'er mind and take one of the gents what offered for 'er, then let 'er pay the consequences, I says."

"Aye," the first man said. "You have a point. Seems to me like she's too proud of being in charge of all that money. Why shouldn't a husband have the spending of it? A woman's no proper person to manage a fortune."

They rambled on, but Michael had ceased to listen. There must be more to it than these gossiping men knew. What they'd said would certainly give rise to concern in the mind of the lady in question. She'd lose control of her fortune, of course, but she'd still be well provided for by her uncle. He was, after all, as head of her family, responsible for the whole coachful of them.

So the problem wasn't that there was no man in Alissa's life.

No, there must be something more to this. There had to be in order to give rise to the quiet desperation he'd sensed in Alissa Collington. She wasn't the sort to care that deeply about mere money. Something else was afoot, and he was more than curious to learn all there was about it.

Rising slowly, he went to the bar to make his galling request for assistance to the innkeeper. If he were going to get ready to join the ladies for dinner, there was no way he could waste any more time.

Upstairs, in spacious, low-ceilinged rooms that adjoined one another, Alissa was trying to coax Robin to let her scrub his back so he could get dressed for bed.

"Please, dear. Your valet isn't here, so someone else will have to wash your back for you. If not me, will you let Button?"

"No! I'm too old now for ladies to help me with my bath. That's why you got me a valet in the first place."

"Robin!" Alissa was close to losing her patience. There was so much to think about, so much to guard against to keep her loved ones safe. She was tense enough already. She didn't need to argue back-scrubbing with Robin.

Suddenly, Lady Ellen was there. She took the sponge from Alissa and told her calmly, "Go and see to your own bath, I'm getting hungry."

"But *you're* a lady, too," Robin wailed.

"Nonsense. I'm your grandmother. Bend forward so I can get your back."

Robin complied.

Alissa threw up her hands, laughing in spite of herself, and went into the adjoining room she shared with her grandmother. There she found Button rummaging through a trunk for yet another gown for her to choose from; there were already three laid out on the bed. "Button, don't trouble yourself further. I'll wear one of those you've already found."

"I was looking for the one with the . . ."

"Button, dear, Grandmother is getting hungry."

"Oh, dear. Oh, my." Lady Ellen's hunger settled the matter instantly. "Then we shall have to hurry to get you bathed." She all but pushed Alissa toward the copper hip bath in front of the fireplace, untying the tapes of her gown as she pushed. "Good thing I bathed Lady Ellen before we started out."

"Good thing indeed," Alissa murmured as she was shoved into the tub. "Otherwise you might have drowned her!"

Button answered by pouring a pitcherful of warm water over her and asking *very* sweetly, "What was that you said, my lady?"

"Not a thing, Button, not a thing."

A few minutes later—minutes during which Button washed her mistress with more than her customary vigor and Alissa vowed not to snipe at her abigail in the future, sotto voce or not—Alissa was wrapped in a drying sheet and Button was toweling dry her curls with unaccustomed roughness. "All right, all right!" Alissa surrendered. "I apologize. Of course you'd never drown Grandmother."

Button put on a greatly astonished look. "Why, wherever did such a strange, unkind thought come from? Of course I'd never drown Lady Ellen. The very idea!" The toweling of Lady Alissa's curls became far gentler now that Button had received her apology.

"What's that?" Lady Ellen bustled back into the room. "Who's planning to drown me?"

"No one, Grandmother. I misled Button with a rather facetious remark."

"I can just imagine." Lady Ellen laughed. "Hurry and dress. Robin's ready for bed, and his and Button's dinner will be here in a minute."

Alissa went over to the bed and spent a moment choosing which gown she would wear. She finally settled on a long-sleeved, blue-gray silk gown with a gathered lace flounce at the wrists and around the low neckline. "This one, Button. I'm sure the private parlor will be warm, and I'll take a shawl for walking through the corridors."

Button dropped the gown over Alissa's head, and turned away to look for a suitable shawl. Almost instantly she came back with a paisley one in shades of blue trimmed with a satin ribbon that matched the blue-gray of the gown almost exactly. "This one is lovely with that gown. Sit, and I'll put a ribbon through your curls."

Alissa sat and tried not to wonder how much longer she would be permitted to enjoy this pleasurable luxury, but the effort was in vain. Her anxious mind still asked how long would it be before she would no longer be dressed and fussed over by her faithful abigail. She knew that if her uncle Gerald had his way, it would be for precisely one more week. But what of her own efforts? *Would* she succeed in finding a husband before the week was up?

The query started ice flowing in her veins again. What if she failed to find someone to marry her? What would become of dear Button? And all the others—all the faithful servants who peopled her life and gave it safety and comfort?

Button finished dressing her, and, fleeing the questions for which she had no answers, Alissa went to get her young cousin. She brought Robin back into the women's room to settle him at the tiny table there for his dinner.

"I say, Grandmother, I was really looking forward to dining with Major Mathers."

"I know, Robin. I am." Lady Ellen watched Alissa closely as she asked, "Aren't you, Lissa?"

Alissa's face colored. She was indeed looking forward to seeing their enigmatic rescuer again, but she wasn't exactly certain why she was doing so with such breathless anticipation. He'd appeared out of a blizzard and sent her senses swirling like the snow from which he'd emerged. After tonight, however, they'd probably never see each other again. She would be too busy fighting her uncle, and their rescuer would no doubt be busy with his wife and family. Men as handsome as Major Mathers were always married. Some were even happily married, she thought, hating the empty feeling that came from imagining him surrounded by a family.

That feeling was born of envy, she knew, and not of any ill will directed against their hero. It came because she was fairly certain that that sort of happiness would be beyond her grasp now. She'd sought it for so long in her desire to love and be loved by the man she eventually married that she felt sure she'd never attain it now that she must marry in haste in order to save her family.

Her very bones went cold as her mind added, *If, indeed, you can marry at all.*

Desperation swept down on her like a black cloud. She must—she just must—marry in time to save Collington Park and these precious people she loved.

Striving to hide her distress, she kissed Robin and told

him, "There will have to be another time, dearest. You need your rest."

Robin frowned but surrendered. "It's just that I like him so. And he sounds really splendid."

"He's very handsome," Lady Ellen offered.

"Hmmm," Alissa responded.

"Major Mathers, I mean."

"Hmmm." Alissa made a business of arranging her shawl to suit her.

"And he seems very capable."

"Yes, he does."

"I wonder if he's married." Lady Ellen's gaze was fixed on her granddaughter's face. She was rewarded by a blush and a touch of irritation.

"I should think so," Alissa managed after a moment. "Most of the men one admires are."

Lady Ellen was more than pleased with the results of her probing. She was almost content enough not to ask any more questions. Almost, but not quite. There were some things one simply couldn't help. With a purr she queried, "So do *you* admire him, Granddaughter?"

Alissa turned a face toward her grandmother that would have turned a lesser woman to stone. Even as she drew a deep breath to answer her beloved grandparent, she was saved from doing so by her cousin.

"Oh, I do, Grandmother. I *do* admire him. Excessively."

"So do I, Robin," Lady Ellen answered softly.

Alissa, thankful for the reprieve, started for the door. "Shall we go down, then? That way you can admire him at closer quarters."

Chapter Eight

With a heavy heart, Michael waited in the private parlor Lady Ellen had reserved for their dinner. This was the moment of truth. This was the moment when they would see him as he was. See the half-man to which he'd been reduced. Steeled though he was, he dreaded it. To pretend otherwise was to be a liar as well as the coward he knew himself to be. For coward he was. He'd rather face a salvo of French cannon than the shock and pity he knew he'd see on the faces of the two women to whom he had been, briefly, a hero.

He heard their voices in the hall as they approached the room. He drew himself up to his full height, turning to face the door with his face set like that of a prisoner awaiting sentencing. Bracing himself, he watched them enter the parlor.

Lady Ellen was first, of course, and he gave her top marks for her reaction on seeing him. "Ah, there you are, Major Mathers. We . . ." She had started to greet him be-

fore she saw the useless arm bound to his side. Her hesitation was hardly noticeable, and he had to give her points
for not staring. "We were afraid we'd taken too much time
changing from our travel clothes. Ladies inevitably do, of
course. Have you been waiting long?"

Alissa, just behind her grandmother, hadn't missed the
slight pause in the older woman's greeting. She was instantly alert. What was the matter? Lady Ellen was never
at a loss for words, and certainly not in so simple a matter
as a conventional greeting. Then Lady Ellen moved on
into the parlor, and Alissa saw. Major Mathers wore his
left arm strapped to his side, obviously useless.

Even though she'd thought herself prepared for whatever had startled her grandmother, Alissa felt as if she had
received a physical blow. She caught her breath at the pain
of it. That this man, a truly magnificent man, should have
sustained such an injury tore at her heart.

Against her volition, her eyes were drawn to the heavy
belt that snaked around his wrist, encircled his arm above
the elbow, then passed behind him to come forward again
to meet and buckle under the long-fingered hand the
arrangement held close to his body just above his waist.
Somewhere in the back of her mind she noted that it was
cleverly planned and neatly done. It marred only slightly
the appearance he made.

Alissa's gaze rose to meet his and found him looking at
her sardonically, challengingly. The scorching glance he
sent her stopped her where she stood. Its message was obvious. He dared her to pity him.

Then he turned away to seat Lady Ellen at the table in
the center of the parlor, and Alissa could breathe again,
think again. Their rescuer was injured. From the casual
way he wore the belt that held his arm, she deduced that
he was quite familiar with the contraption, so he had probably been maimed—as so many brave Englishmen had
been—in the war against Napoleon. She'd always been

sorry for every one of them she saw, but she was deeply upset over this man. Was it because she was personally indebted to him that she felt such a depth of sympathy? Was that indebtedness the reason that her sympathy seemed to border on sorrow? Was the strength of her emotion caused by the seriousness of her own tangled responsibilities? Or did the confusion she was feeling signal something more?

Lady Ellen mercifully interrupted her thoughts. "Sit opposite me, Lissa." She smiled up at Michael. "And if you will sit at the head of the table, sir, we shall be able to talk comfortably."

Michael moved to the heavy, ornately carved Jacobean chair opposite Lady Ellen's and held it for Alissa.

Hating the color she knew was staining her cheeks, she came to him and sat, murmuring, "Thank you." What she really wanted to say was "I can manage. Don't help me. Surely this heavy chair is too difficult for you with only one hand." But she didn't, of course. Surely no one ever said such things. Surely. It would be an attack upon his masculine pride, and she would have to have been as blind as her own dear Robin not to see that Major Michael Mathers had an overabundance of *that* commodity.

There was a knock on the door, and the innkeeper himself entered bearing a roast of beef, its succulent aroma preceding it to the table. Michael eyed it as if it were an enemy, and Alissa knew he'd never manage to cut up meat with only one hand, much less to carve for all of them. Dare she offer to help him? Just the thought of doing so curdled her soul. He would hate her for life.

The innkeeper was followed by a serving woman with a tray of bowls filled with steaming vegetables and freshly baked bread wrapped in a spotless linen napkin. And there on the tray was a single plate on which the entire meal had been carefully prepared for someone who lacked the use of both hands.

Shocked, Alissa looked straight at the Major, something akin to horror in her eyes. Would he be insulted? Would he be hurt?

To her amazement, his eyes were laughing at her. Incipient pity turned to righteous indignation. She wanted to slap him! How dare he! It wasn't *her* fault he'd been injured. And it wasn't her fault that she hadn't been prepared to learn that someone as able as he was *had* a serious handicap. After all, he'd had on a cloak that had covered his left arm the only time she had seen him. Why was he surprised that his arm had come as something of a shock to her?

Restrained from slapping the smirk off his face by her own good manners, Alissa still wanted to strike out at him for laughing at her, so she said, stating the obvious, "Robin won't be joining us." She couldn't say the rest of the spiteful little speech that had crowded into her mind. Her heart wouldn't let her.

Michael said it for her. "No doubt, with his handicap he is sensitive about eating with strangers. He prefers to eat with Button, I presume."

Alissa was ashamed. She could feel her cheeks flaming. Never a coward, she looked the Major straight in the eye and said, "Yes. He is young and hasn't completely mastered his blindness. Nor," she said with a faint air of challenge, "has he the ability to arrange for his food to be served in a manner that enables him to manage gracefully, as you have done."

Lady Ellen sat back in her chair to watch them, both eyebrows raised. When she was younger, she'd have interfered, striving for peace at her table. Life, however, had taught her much, and she watched with interest, certain that with these two, things would work out well.

Michael laughed aloud. "Touché!"

"Well." Lady Ellen breathed a little sigh of relief. "That matter settled, may I ask you to carve, please, Mr. Hemmings?"

The innkeeper stepped forward immediately. "With pleasure, my lady." Gesturing to the serving woman, he galvanized her into action, and shortly all was in readiness. "Will that be all, your ladyship?"

"Another bottle of wine, I think." She looked toward Michael. "Burgundy?"

He nodded with a smile, and Lady Ellen dismissed the innkeeper with a wave of her hand. He left the parlor with the round-eyed serving woman close on his heels, and the door closed softly behind them.

In typical English fashion, those at the table began their conversation with the weather. "The wind has dropped," Lady Ellen offered.

"Yes," Michael agreed. "The storm seems to have either blown itself out or passed on by us."

"Let's hope it hasn't gone on before us!" Alissa said.

Michael smiled at her. "No chance of that. It was headed away from London."

Alissa smiled back, thinking how much younger he looked when he smiled—and, impossibly, how much more handsome. In the warmth of the room, his cheeks had more color than they'd had in the coach and the cold, and with his mouth more relaxed, his lower lip was a little fuller. She caught herself staring at his mouth and applied herself hastily to her plate, a blush forming.

Lady Ellen fought down a smile and looked from her granddaughter to Michael. She lost her battle with the smile when she saw that he was as absorbed in staring at her granddaughter as Alissa had been a moment ago in regarding him.

And Michael *was* staring. In the warmth of the parlor, Alissa had discarded her shawl, leaving the low neckline of her gown fully visible, and Michael was enchanted. Everything about the Snow Goddess was lovely in the candlelight.

He was doubly glad now that he had lighted every candle in the room. True, he'd done it so that the women could see his handicap clearly and get that behind them all, but now the extra light gave him a very good look at Lady Alissa. It was only due to the large number of candles he'd lighted that he could see that her blush started low enough to tint the porcelain smoothness of the tops of her breasts before it reached her cheeks. His gaze lingered on those breasts an instant before he recalled his manners and tore it away to look higher. She had superb shoulders and a slender, graceful neck. The soft blue-gray of her gown complimented the alabaster of her skin and brought out the gray of her eyes. As the men in the common room had proclaimed, the Lady of Collington was a diamond of the first water. Michael even found himself in agreement with the gutter rat, whose simple admiration had named Lady Alissa "a flaming beauty," for she was undeniably blessed with a beauty that burned its way into a man's very soul.

In spite of himself, Michael was moved by that beauty, never mind that she was as unobtainable as the sun for him now. He had no right to look on her as anything but a pleasant—and surely temporary—acquaintance. Since his residence in the caves below Cliffside, he was only fit to play Beast to her Beauty, and he had never believed in fairy tales.

Lady Ellen asked brightly, "Do you think it will clear?"

Michael gave himself a mental shake and added a silent curse for good measure. He'd all but forgotten his hostess was in the room. "Very probably, Lady Ellen. I can hear no wind now. I'll check outside to see if snow is still falling if you'd like."

"No. Heavens, let's enjoy our dinner and the wine. We can peek out when we decide to go up to our rooms." She sipped her wine then asked, "Tell me, Major, do you go to London on business, or is your family there?"

"I have no family other than an uncle who lives in

Northumberland." He grinned. "Needless to say, we seldom see each other."

Alissa smiled and pretended a delicate shiver. "I don't blame you for that. I'd certainly not go to Northumberland often. I think it's a desolate, craggy place." She considered the harshness of that remark and qualified it. "It might be because the family property there is almost in ruins that I feel as I do, however."

Michael chuckled. "Well, my uncle's property is excellently maintained and sinfully luxurious, and I still feel Northumberland is a desolate, craggy place. Whenever I'm there, I can never be at ease. I'm always too busy being careful not to lame Gladiator, the blas . . ." He caught himself and, in deference to the ladies, changed *blasted* to "the blessed terrain is so unfriendly to both man and beast." He grinned again. "Fortunately, my uncle is a reclusive sort who considers my every visit to check on how he fares an impertinent invasion of his privacy."

Alissa smiled at him and said, "Well, I think it's good of you to go. Neither of us would set foot up there for all the tea in China." She turned toward her grandmother, "Would we, dearest?"

"Indeed not. I wouldn't have to worry about the treacherous rocks underfoot. The cold, alone, would finish these old bones off in short order." She looked from one to the other of them with an expression of quiet satisfaction and said, "Speaking of the cold, Major, won't you join us in our coach for the ride to London?"

For a moment Michael was tempted. Then he realized that to spend any more time with these people, especially with the delectable Alissa, would only make the loss of them more noticeable when they had parted. So he answered, "Thank you, no. Gladiator would stop speaking to me if I forced him to trail after us all the way to London."

Alissa turned her head away so that he couldn't see her smile.

"Does my refusal please you so much, Lady Alissa?" Michael inquired instantly.

She was startled by his stiff remark, but recovered herself quickly. Looking at him over her shoulder she said, "Well, you *are* rather large, and you *do* take up a great deal of space . . ."

"Lissa! You naughty puss! You stop that this instant!"

Alissa laughed merrily. "Very well, Grandmama." Smiling broadly at Michael, she told him, "I suppose I should explain my smile." Her eyes warmed, and her voice took on a hint of shyness. "I smiled because everyone at home is always teasing me about the way I talk to my horses . . ."

"And her dogs," Lady Ellen intoned in a level singsong. "And the barn cats and the vicar's pony, and . . ."

"Oh, hush!"

Lady Ellen subsided with a chuckle.

Michael's face lit up with a grin. "So you were glad to hear there is someone else who talks to their animals."

"Exactly."

Everything seemed to stop as they smiled into each other's eyes. Seconds ticked by unnoticed.

Michael experienced a tearing remorse that he would never see this exquisite beauty after they said their goodbyes in the morning. He understood now, after all he had overheard about her in the taproom this evening, why she had risked her dangerous journey. She was obviously rushing to London to marry one of her suitors before her birthday next week. And who could blame her? It was, again, obvious that she cared a great deal about her grandmother and her cousin. Since she had them with her, she must feel herself responsible for them. Without her fortune, Lady Alissa would have to put that responsibility in the hands of the head of her family. That thought brought another. Alissa must be reluctant to give him the reins of her life, or she would have done so by now. Was there some very good reason for that? He fell to mulling over that possibility—and cursing the fact that he'd been away from England so long that he had lost track of who was who. He had no idea who'd inherited old Collington's title and become the new Lord Withers. And, worse, he'd no idea whether the heir was an honorable man or a rotter.

Gazing at Michael, Alissa felt a breathless sense of loss as she, too, thought of saying farewell. If only she knew him better, or had time enough left to get to know him before her birthday next week.

She hadn't time, of course. The anniversary of her birth was charging down on her with the speed of a runaway mail-coach. Duty to those she loved and to those dependent on her at Collington Park loomed on the immediate horizon, and soon the pleasure of any man's company other than the one to whom she was wed—whoever that turned out to be—would be denied her. She herself would deny it. She would have no choice, because she would fear being led into some shameful indiscretion by the strong attraction she felt where this man was concerned. She took a deep breath and clenched her fists to keep from reaching out to touch his arm in a bittersweet caress of repudiation.

Across the table, Lady Ellen regretted Michael Mathers's refusal to share their coach to London, more than she had thought possible. His determination to ride had put a period to her hopes that, with a little more time together, something might come of the obvious feelings he and Alissa were experiencing for each other.

How she wished that this gallant young man could be the husband that her granddaughter so desperately needed. They would be safe in his hands, she knew, and she knew, too, that with him, Alissa would find the happiness she had longed for all her life. It caused Ellen pain to know that it was all slipping from their mutual grasps, but she was wise enough to admit defeat.

Finally, after sadly watching the play of emotions on the faces of her young companions, Lady Ellen said very softly, "Tomorrow will be a long, eventful day, children. I think we should all seek our beds."

Chapter Nine

As they were leaving the cozy parlor, Alissa remembered, "We must see what the weather is doing."

"Indeed, yes," Lady Ellen agreed. "I hope we will be able to continue our journey without further mishap. I've no wish to end in the ditch again without Michael accompanying us." She smiled up at their escort. "I do wish you'd reconsider, Major."

Michael shook his head. "I'm sorry. I must get to London quickly." That was true. For his own safety, he must distance himself from these wonderful people before his heart became further engaged.

They went to the front door of the inn, Michael closing the first set of doors that sealed off the vestibule before they opened the second pair to the frigid outside air. When he had thrown the tall double doors wide, Michael stepped aside for the two ladies to precede him.

The view awaiting them was enough to quiet them all, and they stood simply looking out at the snow-covered inn yard and the moonlit landscape beyond. The scene was magical. Their whole immediate world lay silent before them, all of it as far as the eye could see painted a cool blue by the reflected light of the moon.

Alissa half-turned and smiled back at Michael, and he was assailed by a longing he'd thought he'd successfully suppressed for good and ever. It was so strong, he'd no choice but to acknowledge it, but that yearning was a luxury he could no longer permit himself. Why the blazes must it turn up now?

The night was peaceful—clear and still. Hanging among bright stars in a cloudless sky, the moon mocked the idea that only a few hours ago Michael had hardly been able to see his horse's ears through the hard-driven snow. The shining silence of the night denied the fact that they'd been encompassed by the roaring winds of a blizzard that very afternoon.

Gone as if it had never been, the storm had passed, leaving on every tree ice-laden boughs that drooped to touch the snow-covered ground. Deep-piled drifts, pale blue in the cold light of the moon, sheltered vibrant blue shadows—shadows that contrasted sharply with the wind-smoothed slopes glittering like diamond dust above them. Over them all, stark trees cast bold, contouring outlines on their pristine surfaces.

Alissa stood quietly with her back almost against Michael, as if for warmth. And Michael stood silently behind her, reveling in her nearness and this chance to gaze down, unobserved, at the subtle lights on her lustrous hair and the gentle curve of her soft cheek.

Unable to stop himself, he bent down to catch the sweet scent of her, and a sudden urge to place just one gentle kiss on her shoulder where her shawl had slipped away from her slender neck almost overpowered him. His nostrils flared as he breathed in as much as he could of the womanly perfume that was Alissa's alone, storing it in his senses, foolishly making a memory—torture for now and treasure for later. A treasure to savor when this lovely woman with so much sadness in her eyes would be gone from his life forever.

With a jolt, he became aware that Lady Ellen was watching him. But when he glanced her way, it was only to find her serenely regarding the scene before them. Michael, with an effort that surprised him, stepped back away from Alissa, and Lady Ellen turned to look at him. In the light reflected off the snow, he thought he saw tears in her eyes.

After a moment, she said quietly to him, "Sometimes I think that even the most beautiful things can make us sad, don't you, Major?" Her smile was faint. "Especially when there is such magic in the moonlight."

Michael found he needed to clear his throat before he could answer her and decided to settle for a nod and a gruff "Aye, your ladyship." Unbidden, his gaze went to Alissa.

All through their exchange, Alissa had been lost in contemplation of the peaceful landscape, unaware of the tension behind her. "Are you thinking of the poor, ice-broken trees and the hardship the snow will make for the horses, Grandmother?"

Her voice infinitely sad, Lady Ellen said, "Of things broken, and of hardships, yes, dearest." Then she smiled up at Michael. "May I have your arm, sir? I find that I am suddenly very tired,"

Alissa was all concern as they entered the inn proper. "I'm so sorry, dearest. My haste has worn you out. Will you stay here at the inn and rest until I have gone to Bow Street to the Runners? I shall return for you as soon as I finish my business with them."

Michael was startled at her mention of the Runners. *What the devil? What could a gently bred female want with the Runners?* He could hardly ask for an explanation if neither lady offered one, but he was shocked. And he wasn't the only one whom Alissa's statement surprised. The clerk who had been in the taproom earlier that evening was passing through the foyer to the stairs at just that instant. He stopped dead to stare at them, then bowed to the ladies before hurrying on up to his room.

Eaten alive by curiosity, Michael escorted his two companions to the door of their rooms and bade them farewell, all the while mentally cursing the good manners that kept him from asking any questions.

"It has truly been a pleasure making your acquaintance. Thank you for my dinner, and please tell Master Robin"— he smiled and added—"and Button good-bye for me."

Lady Alissa held out her hand to be shaken. Instead, Michael raised it to his lips as he had in the heart of the blizzard when they'd met.

Ellen opened the door and, turning back as she entered, told Michael, "We shall never forget you, Major Mathers. Never."

Alone with him, Alissa rose quickly on tiptoe and breathed a farewell kiss beside his mouth with the same whispered word, "Never."

As Michael stared, staggered by her action, the door closed softly behind her with the finality of a guillotine blade dropping. "And just as well," he muttered as he turned away a long moment later. Better to cut off the acquaintance before it . . . developed further.

Michael thought of going to the taproom for a brandy. God knew it would be welcome. Somehow, though, he wanted to be alone. So he went to his own room, let the inn's valet assist him out of his boots and clothing, and spent a miserable night tossing and turning. When at long last he slept, he spoke one name aloud in his fitful sleep. And the name he sighed was "Alissa."

In the morning, his temporarily hired valet grinned from ear to ear over the half crown he'd gotten for his services as he bowed himself out of the room. Finally alone, Michael relived the previous evening's interlude. He doubted he would ever forget. How could he? And why should he, when memories were all he intended to permit himself for the rest of his life?

When he got to London, he'd send servants to watch for the Collingtons' coach—men to guard them while they were at Bow Street and to follow them to their London residence. Men to see them safe. He might want nothing more than to do it himself, but he couldn't risk it. No woman had ever affected him as Alissa had, and he wasn't going to put himself any further at hazard in what was clearly a no-win situation. Alissa was not for him.

He refused to dwell on it. It was enough that he was forced to acknowledge his infirmity—to bow to it and to the changes it made in his life. He'd be damned if he was going to wallow in it!

With more than necessary force, Michael stuffed his things back into his saddlebags by the simple expedient of shoving the bags against the headboard of the bed to hold them still enough to pack. He'd gotten used to these little adjustments to accommodate the fact that he had but one hand he could use, and generally, he hardly noticed them anymore. Today, in the early dawn, he did notice, however, and his clumsiness annoyed him. Today, too, he had good reason for haste. He wanted to be gone from the inn before Alissa and her family awakened.

Last evening, as they had said their good-byes, he'd realized that he'd better put as much distance between himself and the beautiful Alissa as possible if he didn't relish something akin to torture at never being a part of her life. She was like a drug to his senses—like some sorceress unconsciously casting a spell on him.

"And you're a lackwit," he muttered to himself disgustedly as he hurried down the stairs.

"Oh, I sincerely hope not, Major!" She was there in the foyer at the foot of the stairs, her eyes bright with mischief.

Michael stopped dead on the last step. Staggeringly beautiful in a crimson traveling suit topped with a matching ermine-lined cape, the Snow Goddess stood looking up at him, and all he could manage was a wooden "You've risen early, Lady Alissa."

"I must reach London as quickly as I can. The innkeeper says that the roads must be fit to use as a gentleman who departed last night said he'd be right back if they proved impassable."

"That's good news." The length of her speech had given him the time he needed to recover himself, and he was even smiling at the absurdity of having been turned to stone for a moment by her beauty.

"Yes, isn't it? I'm particularly glad to know it as I've been unable to convince Grandmother that I would not in the least mind returning for her later this evening."

Lady Ellen swept into view from the hallway to the parlor, where the family obviously had breakfasted. "Indeed not!" she informed them both. "There is no way I'll have you traipsing around the countryside unnecessarily in this weather." She smiled brightly at Michael. "I'm certain the Major agrees with me. Don't you, sir?"

Michael bowed with a smile of his own. "Quite right. Even if the roads are passable now, there's no guarantee that they would be in the evening." His gaze engaged Alissa's. "Usually there's a bit of thawing in the sun, then when the afternoon temperature drops, the roads ice over, and are more treacherous than ever."

"Ah, see, Alissa." Lady Ellen was triumphant. "You know the Major is right."

Alissa laughed. "I wonder if you would say so if he'd thought it wiser for you to remain behind and wait for me?"

"Of course not!"

They laughed there in the early morning light that filtered through the windows beside the door, bound in the comfortable web of their newly formed friendship. Michael could actually feel the pull these two made on his heart.

Their carriage arrived then, and the inn servants bustled past them carrying their luggage. Outside on the cobbled inn yard, the horses stamped and blew in the cold, their warm breath making a small cloud before them. The coachman had his hands full making them stand still as the baggage was loaded.

One of the footmen put down the iron step of the carriage, and Michael handed Lady Ellen in. Robin and Button followed. Alissa hesitated, her gaze fixed on Michael. The expression in her eyes would have startled him. Turning back to assist Alissa, Michael took her hand. At her touch, he felt his breath shorten.

Alissa turned stricken eyes to Michael. "This is goodbye, then?"

The question cut him like a saber slash. She wanted him to deny it. She wanted him to tell her he would call, that he would further their brief acquaintance. She wanted him to show her that he wanted to do so. He could see it in her face. But Michael's decision had been made. There was no doubt in his mind that to see her again would be to court a pain he wasn't certain he could bear. Taking great care to keep his voice even, he told her, "Yes, it is, unfortunately. I shall only be in London for a very short time. Then I must see to urgent business in other places as soon as possible."

"I see." Her gaze held him.

With all his heart he wished . . . But that was impossible now. He was a cripple, and she was . . . She was the Snow Goddess. That capricious thought brought a genuine smile. He took her hand to raise it to his lips. His eyes darkened. "May the rest of your trip be uneventful, Lady Alissa." His voice deepened and he added as he kissed her gloved fingers, "It was a greater pleasure than I can express to meet you." Belatedly he added, ". . . all."

Alissa made a little, involuntary sound, quickly suppressed, and entered the coach, averting her face. Michael turned from her then, and said his good-byes to the others.

"Good-bye, sir," Robin said.

"God keep you, Major," Lady Ellen told him. "God keep you well."

Michael's voice was strained as he said, "Thank you." Trusting himself to say no more, not even her name and title, he turned away, his cape swinging from his broad shoulders in his haste.

Robin listened to the sound of Michael's boot heels striking the cobblestones as the Major headed for the stables. "He's gone, isn't he, Grandmama?"

"Yes, dear." Lady Ellen put her arm around his shoulders, hugged him and sighed. "Yes, I'm afraid he really *is* gone."

Alissa tossed her head, then pulled the hood of her cloak over her shining curls and called briskly, "Get along, then, John Coachman! We don't have forever, you know."

Lady Ellen slipped her other arm around her proud granddaughter. Tactfully, she didn't say a word about the tears she saw glinting in her lovely gray eyes.

Button, fussing to settle Robin from her place opposite them, said, as she reached across to tuck the lap robe around him, "Well, I certainly hope we don't end up in a ditch this time!"

Chapter Ten

Heading quickly to the stables, Michael knew each stride carried him farther from where he longed to be. Had he been a whole man, it would have been simple. He'd have tied a disgruntled Gladiator to the back of her carriage and accompanied *her* to her destination. To both her destinations.

Bow Street was nowhere for Alissa to go alone. The very thought that she might do so twisted his gut. Even so, he knew from the deep concern he saw in her eyes whenever she looked at her grandmother that she'd never let Lady Ellen go there with her, no matter how much Lady Ellen insisted. No, it was up to him. If she were to be watched over, then he had to reach London in time to send his secretary out to meet and accompany them. He could trust Lewis Hanford to accompany them, to settle Lady Ellen and Robin comfortably, and to escort Alissa safely to Bow Street. Her abigail, Button, would have to go with her for propriety's sake, of course, and he trusted his secretary to treat her with all consideration as well.

His plan was made, and it was sound. So why in blazes was he so blasted uneasy?

Driven by a nameless anxiety, he wanted nothing more than to vault onto Gladiator and ride for London as if all the fiends of hell were chasing him. That was impossible on two counts, of course. First, since the act required two hands, his vaulting days were over. They had been ever since that shattering blow to his shoulder had left him a one-handed cripple. Second, he could never risk Gladiator at a neck-or-nothing pace in the kind of footing the storm had left. The roads were barely passable. The possibility of ice on them was a genuine threat to both horse and rider.

Calling for his horse, Michael tossed the ostler a coin and led Gladiator to the mounting block at the edge of the stable yard. At least by using the block he could spare the groom the sight of his clumsiness. And himself the galling shame of it.

He walked faster. The sooner he was in the saddle, the sooner he'd pass the coach that carried *her* and the sooner he'd get to London. Once he'd set his plans for her safety in motion, he could immerse himself in his long neglected business affairs and attempt to forget the beautiful young woman with the sad gray eyes.

He made a rude sound that perfectly expressed his opinion of how likely it was that he could ever forget the Snow Goddess or, for that matter her family. They had captured his heart in a way that . . . Suddenly he stopped, and the horse beside him threw up his head in surprise and nickered at him.

Something wasn't right. If he hadn't been immersed in thoughts of *her*, he'd have noticed sooner. The cadence of Gladiator's strides was off just slightly. In the packed snow, Michael hadn't been able to tell that one of his mount's hooves was bare, for none of them rang with the iron of a shoe since they were on snow. The little difference in the way Gladiator moved and handled his off fore-foot told the tale.

"Blast it!" He checked quickly for signs of damage to the hoof itself and was relieved to find none. Smoothing Gladiator's foreleg as he replaced the hoof gently on the snow-covered ground, he told the big gelding, "Now we need the blacksmith to replace that shoe, Glad." Frustration welled up in him. There was no chance that he'd pass the carriage that carried the woman he feared seeing again, as he'd hoped. No way he'd get beyond them to arrange for their safety and be able to go on to the business of putting together, somehow, the pieces of his life, for now he'd be delayed. Again.

In the carriage Alissa blew her nose violently.

Lady Ellen patted her granddaughter's knee and tactfully said nothing. Tears always made her nose want to drip, too.

"Well," Alissa said at last, "I hope he gets his business done easily."

"And quickly?" Lady Ellen asked.

There was a long hesitation, then, "No," Alissa said with a sigh. "Even if he completes all he has to do, he won't come to London. He won't call on us." She bit her lip, then lifted her chin and said firmly, "I doubt that I shall ever see him again."

Lady Ellen went back to patting Alissa's knee. She knew what her granddaughter was suffering. She'd seen the looks that had passed between the two young people. It was obvious that they were strongly attracted to each other. And it was just as obvious that they were meant for each other.

Sighing, she admitted that they would probably never see the Major again. He was young and handsome, and obviously well off, or he wouldn't have had business in several places to use as his excuse to be gone from them. But he was maimed, too, and therein lay the problem, for what seemed a tiny flaw to them evidently was a monstrous disfigurement to him.

It was one of life's major aggravations that the young always seemed to think they had to be perfect in body to be worthy of love. Never mind that he was intelligent, cultured, handsome, and all the rest. He would fix his mind only on his disability. By the time he was reconciled to it, Alissa would already have married—forced to it by her responsibilities and the dastardly behavior of her uncle, Lady Ellen's only remaining son.

When Lady Ellen glanced surreptitiously at her granddaughter, she saw that her eyes were glistening again with tears. Her own eyes filled, and she turned away to pretend to look out the window on her side of the coach.

The next instant, there was a cry from the box. "Whoa! Whoa! Easy there, lads!"

Alissa lowered her window and called, "What is it, Mr. Green?"

"Naught but a tree down, my lady. 'Tis a small one. We'll have it cleared in a few minutes." He ordered the footmen, "Down ya go, lads!"

Alissa felt the carriage bounce as the two footmen jumped down to move the tree. Then everything turned to confusion.

A strange voice shouted, "Leave that tree alone and stay very still if you want to live!"

Who'd said that? Alissa was indignant. How dare someone threaten her men! Were they to be robbed in broad daylight? The very idea! They'd been gone from the inn for only half an hour, and snow or not, this was a public highway.

The next moment, concern for her loved ones overcame her indignation. How frightening this must be for Robin. What a shock it must be to her grandmother. She heard the

sound of horses being ridden out of the trees that bordered
the road and real fear hit her. The man wasn't acting alone.
She could see three men joining him, and heard others who
were out of her line of vision. Suppose the Major were to
overtake them now? He couldn't be far behind. He'd be in
danger!

Alissa leaned out her window to see who'd stopped
them. There were six of the miscreants. She could see them
all. Those she thought of as henchmen had their faces hidden by bandanas and mufflers, the cowards. Not so their
leader. The order to leave alone the tree that blocked the
road had come from the man Alissa had seen in the foyer
of the inn last evening. He was unmasked and she could
see his face clearly.

Instantly she recognized him as the very man the
innkeeper had told her had left the safety of the inn last
night but would return if the roads were impassable. How
ironic that it had been that promise, made by this man, that
had given her hope of a safe journey.

Four men came up to the coach. Three of them led
Alissa's two footmen to the edge of the road at gunpoint
and proceeded to tie them back to back to a tree. The fifth
kept his pistol leveled at her coachman where he sat on the
box, the driving reins clenched in his fists.

Robin cried, "Grandmother! Alissa! What is it? What's
happening?"

Lady Ellen lied smoothly. "We are being robbed by
highwaymen. Just be calm, Robin." The look she shot toward Alissa over the boy's head held anything but the calm
she recommended to her grandson. It was clear she thought
this anything but a simple holdup. Alissa could see that
Lady Ellen suspected something infinitely more dangerous.

Alissa stared back at her grandmother. The expression
in her own eyes echoed the panic in Lady Ellen's, but her
face was calm. In her mind there was no doubt that these

men had been sent by her uncle and that knowledge struck fear in her heart. She was determined, though, that it would be a cold day in hell before she let these men see it!

"Please get down from the carriage, Lady Alissa."

Alissa stalled. "Why? What do you want with me?"

The man moved nearer. "I'm under orders to deliver you to the asylum in . . ." His glance flashed to Lady Ellen's white face as she gasped, "Asylum!" and he thought better of announcing their destination. "Never mind where you are going, Lady Alissa. Your uncle's plans for you have been made, and I have been sent to carry them out, so let's get on with it." He offered her his hand to help her dismount from the coach.

Alissa slapped it away. "I have no intention of going with you! My uncle has no jurisdiction over me!"

"Oh, but there you are wrong, my lady." He smiled at her. It was an evil smile. "Lord Withers is the head of your family, and you are only a spinster. He has every right to dispose of you as he sees fit."

"Dispose of me is right! Dispose of me as if I were a troublesome burden. *Dispose* of me with no thought given to my wishes or inclinations in the matter!" She spoke only to give herself time to feel for and procure the pistol in the holster beside the door inside the carriage. Her fingers brushed the firm wood of its brass-bound butt, and hope surged through her. This man had said too much, and had let them see his face. Even if she were incarcerated in some insane asylum and unable to identify her abductors to the authorities, she was nevertheless a threat to him. Lady Ellen and Button, too. It was plain to her that the other occupants of the carriage would not be left to tell this tale!

"You are right, of course," the man behind the gun told her. "You are merely to be locked away for the rest of your life so that you can cause his lordship no trouble. It's a foolproof plan, you must admit. Escape from a lunatic asylum is quite impossible."

Alissa knew then that her family was doomed. This man would leave no one behind to tell what had happened to her. To send agents searching for which asylum she was buried in. She would be helplessly entombed in an insane asylum, and her grandmother and Robin would be . . . Dearest God, she must stop him!

As her hand slid in to grip the butt of the pistol, triumph filled her. She'd shoot him down like the dog he was and . . .

But her kidnapper had seen the flash of triumph in her eyes and the stealthy movement of her hand. His false affability dropped away and he snarled, "Oh, no you don't!" Seizing her wrist, he savagely twisted her arm and yanked her from the carriage. Only his bruising grip kept Alissa from sprawling headlong into the snow.

Lady Ellen screamed.

Michael paid the blacksmith. "Thank you. My apologies for disturbing your breakfast."

" 'Twas no trouble, sor." The blacksmith grinned. "But I got to tell ya, 'tis surely rare I have the chance to shoe a horse for one o' the Quality so early in the day when it's not huntin' season, and that's God's truth."

Michael grinned back at him. "Yes, well you see, I'd hoped to overtake and pass some friends who started out even earlier to London."

"You gentlemen are always racing, one way or t'other. Your gelding throwing his shoe is apt to make you the loser this time though, sor."

Michael mounted a restive Gladiator and smiled down at the smith. "I'll just have to live with it." He settled his hat firmly and turned Gladiator toward the road. "Again, my thanks, and a good day to you."

"And a good day to you, too," the blacksmith told thin

air. He shook his head and added, "Aye, and good luck to ye, as well, for ye've a kind way about ye."

Unaware of the smith's benediction, Michael concentrated on the road. The surface wasn't thawing yet, and there didn't seem to be ice under the snow as he was certain there would be later, when the warmer temperatures of the afternoon had melted snow to water that the evening cold would freeze. He counted himself lucky that the footing was not treacherous at present. It meant that he could press on a bit. He allowed Gladiator to canter. Surely, with the carriage more apt to slide than a horse would be, Coachman Green would be taking it easy. At this rate he'd catch and pass the Collingtons' carriage in time to beat them to London.

The landscape through which he rode was not as magical as it had been the night before. Now instead of rich blues and darker shadows, the world was aglitter with the sparkle of sunlight on snow. And, of course, *she* wasn't there, standing almost in his embrace to add her sorcery to the magic of the night.

"Damn you, Kantwell!" he snarled aloud. "It isn't night. It's the broad light of day and damn well past time for you to get the cobwebs out of your blasted head!"

Gladiator flicked a nervous ear back at him.

"Sorry, old boy. Just talking to myself." He scowled and muttered, "*And* to my horse, by all that's holy. I must be going 'round the bend."

Michael knew that wasn't his problem, however. He was far from mad. He was only, he thought with a deep inward sigh, exceedingly foolish. He wasn't mad—oh, no, he was just grasping for the moon.

Giving himself a mental shake, he settled down to ride, watching the road ahead to be sure to keep his mount out of the ruts left by coach and wagon traffic. They'd be hard enough in this cold to form traps for a horse's hooves, and a twisted pastern was the last thing he wanted to have happen. Satisfying himself that his mount was watching the footing even better than he was, Michael began to plan all that he had to accomplish when he finally reached the capital. It was true, after all, that he had neglected his estates. Neglected them shamefully, with only the war as an excuse. It was equally true that they were ably looked after by his secretary and his stewards.

It was past time he paid them a visit, however. There were only three properties, not counting the town house in London, but he intended to make hard work of inspecting each of them. He needed to in order to distract himself from the only subject he seemed to be unable to keep out of his mind. Alissa. Her very name was a sigh. She would be difficult to forget.

Gladiator's long strides ate up the miles. The footing was not as bad as Michael had feared it might be, and they were making good time—much better than a coach would be making. No doubt he'd soon pass the Collingtons.

When they were some twenty minutes from the inn, he decided it was time to give Gladiator a breather and pulled the big gelding down to a walk. As he did, Gladiator lifted his head high and pointed his ears straight ahead so firmly that they quivered at their tips.

"What's up, Glad?" Michael asked his mount, smiling. "Have you caught sound of the coach?" An instant later the smile was wiped from his face and his blood chilled as he heard, not far ahead, a woman's piercing scream.

Chapter Eleven

Michael clapped spurs to Gladiator. The big gelding threw up his head in shock at the unaccustomed treatment, gave one outraged buck and tore off in the direction of the woman's cry. Almost immediately they arrived at the halted Collington carriage.

In a flash, Michael took in the scene. There were six rough-looking men holding up the Collingtons' coach, three with pistols. Alissa's footmen were helpless, bound to a tree, and her coachman was under the gun of one of the masked men. All that disappeared in a blur of fury when he saw that the man who'd so politely bowed to the ladies last night was now grasping Alissa's arm in a cruel grip and dragging her through the snow.

Rage engulfed him. With the blood-curdling battle cry he'd used to lead his troops through deafening cannon fire, Michael charged to Alissa's aid. Drawing the pistol from the right-hand saddle holster, he fired and killed the man holding the gun on Alissa's coachman. He flung that gun away to snatch the pistol from his other holster on the left. When he'd discharged that, another of Alissa's armed attackers slumped to the snow. Now only the bounder holding her had firepower.

Keeping his grasp on the second pistol, he reversed it in his hand and charged the man holding Alissa. Guiding Gladiator with his legs, he ran the man down, staggering him. As the villain fought to recover his balance, Michael leapt from his saddle and struck upward the barrel of the gun the man was leveling at him. The man's shot went high. Passing close to Michael's head, it blew his hat off and clipped a curl from the hair at his temple.

Alissa screamed, "Michael!" as his hat went flying.

The leader of the attackers scuttled backward, crabwise, away from the danger of Michael's fist, and climbed to his feet. "Get the girl," he yelled to his remaining thugs.

Straddling Alissa where she lay in the snow, Michael snarled, "I'll see you in hell first!"

The three remaining underlings spread out in a loose circle surrounding Michael. Slowly they began to close in on him.

"Shoot him!" the leader ordered.

One of the men ran for the pistol his confederate had dropped when Michael's ball had killed him.

"I want him dead, damn your eyes! Then we'll take the girl."

Unarmed, Michael stood his ground.

Alissa tried to rise to put herself in front of him. Michael pushed her roughly down out of the line of fire as the attackers closed in.

On the turnpike up ahead of the melee, two gentlemen were discussing the trip they'd embarked on that morning.

The smaller of the two, a well-built, medium-sized blond, tilted his head back to address his companion. "London *was* getting dull, Stone. You have to admit it."

The almost-giant beside him regarded him calmly for a moment. "MacLain," he said patiently, "London is *always* dull."

"Not for most of us. And it's only dull now because everyone's gone home to their country estates for Christmas. You're the problem, Stone," he complained. "You simply refuse to make the effort to enjoy Almack's and the rest of the pleasures the capital offers. Why, for the rest of us, just to see the newest crop of lovelies from the schoolrooms is always an exciting . . ."

"What the hell was that!" Stone was already gathering his reins as he urged his mount to plunge forward.

"Sounds like one of our own regiment!" MacLain shouted as they tore off in the direction from which the shout had come.

Two shots rang out, followed by a third and a scream of "Michael!"

They rounded the bend with both horses racing, leaning hard into the turn. There before them they saw their friend Michael Mathers poised to fight like a one-armed demon, straddling a female who'd fallen in the snow.

Stone yelled, "Kantwell! Hold on!" drew his pistol from his saddle holster and fired. The man closest to Michael dropped without a sound. MacLain drew at almost the same time, and winged the man who was holding a club and creeping up behind his beleaguered friend. The third assailant turned tail and fled.

Their leader looked straight at Alissa and threatened, "There'll be another day, milady. This isn't over yet!" He whirled away from them, ran to his horse, vaulted on and was gone.

Michael lifted Alissa from the snow, his arm tight around her. "Are you all right?"

Alissa threw her arms around his neck and buried her face in his throat. "Oh, Michael!" Now the crisis was past and the danger over, she was a little shaky, but she had conquered her fright and was really quite capable of standing on her own. She had no intention of doing so, however. This might be the last time she would have the chance to cling to him, to breathe in the warm, masculine scent of him. The last—no, the *only*—chance she would ever have to hold close this wonderful man she knew would soon leave her life forever.

Pressing her body against the hard one that held hers, she could at last permit herself the shudders of awful fear for the safety of her loved ones that she'd been holding back.

"Alissa." Michael murmured her name, and she felt the tightening of his arm and the quick pressure of his lips on her forehead. Alissa pulled away far enough to put her head back so that she could look into his eyes. What she saw there stopped her breath and filled her own eyes with glory.

Then, snow flying up from the skidding hooves of their mounts, Michael's friends arrived beside them. The blond one demanded, "What the dev . . . What was that all about, Kantwell?"

"Yes, Michael," the tall one asked quietly, "what was going on here?"

"An attempted abduction of her ladyship."

The short, blond man spoke with enthusiasm, "Tarnation! Too bad we didn't get here in time to get in a lick or two."

"I'd say it's a good thing you got here when you did." Michael turned Alissa toward their rescuers. "Permit me to present my friends Stone and MacLain, Lady Alissa. This is Captain Adam Stone." He gestured to the tall, solemn man. "And the other is Lieutenant Justin MacLain." To the two men he said, "Gentlemen, Lady Alissa Collington."

The men bowed, MacLain staring as if moonstruck, and Alissa was forced to relinquish her hold on the man she had hither to thought of as Major Mathers. "Gentlemen," she acknowledged them quietly. She felt Michael start as he realized how closely he was holding her, then, with the deepest disappointment, felt his arm drop away from her. Glancing up at him from the corner of her eye, she saw that he was blushing slightly—and was pleased.

But there was something nagging at the edges of her mind. In the excitement of the moment she had almost missed it, but she was remembering now. When the two strangers had arrived, she could have sworn they called Michael a name she was unfamiliar with. Cantrell, wasn't it? Whatever it was, it was not Mathers.

Surely the Major hadn't misled them by giving them a false name? Lady Ellen, Robin and her? Or *had* he lied about his identity? Was he *that* anxious to avoid further contact with them? The idea was almost more than she could bear. Turning to the two new arrivals, she asked, "I believe I heard you call the Major 'Cantrell.' Was I mistaken?"

"Yes. And no," MacLain told her. 'Twasn't Cantrell. Stone here yelled 'Kantwell! Hold on!' all right. Kantwell, not Cantrell."

Holding her breath, Alissa waited for clarification. The blond seemed to have finished all he felt required to say, though. Exasperated, Alissa looked to the giant beside him. Stone's eyes held quiet amusement. Alissa wondered if he sensed that she was dumbfounded by his friend's denseness. Then Stone answered her question. "Major Mathers is also Guy Michael Mathers, Fifth Viscount Kantwell."

Alissa felt a flood of irritation. Her eyes flashed at Michael. Why had he neglected to tell them his title? When one introduced oneself, one did not leave part of one's name off. At best it was a rude oversight.

Michael felt as if he'd been caught in a lie. "I am more a major than a viscount, Lady Alissa," he offered.

She pursed her lips in displeasure. Her stare told him in no uncertain terms that she was angry with him.

Michael felt his ears warm and knew he was blushing. "Blast it. I didn't think it mattered."

She regarded him steadily for a long moment. The beast knew very well that everything about him mattered to her. And if he didn't, she'd be angrier still. Her chin rose.

Stone held his breath.

MacLain watched with open interest.

Finally, Alissa told Michael in a quiet voice, "And of course, it wouldn't matter." She left a pause before adding, "because you never intended to see us again." She made it a flat statement, spoken in a voice dead with disappointment.

Before Michael could answer, she turned away to Stone and said, "Forgive me, gentlemen. My feet are so very cold. Mr. Stone, would you be so kind as to help me to the carriage?"

Stone tossed the reins of his horse to Michael and with a challenging glance, spread his hands. To Alissa he said, "If you will permit me, Lady Alissa?"

Alissa understood that he meant to carry her to the coach, and she saw that it was a deliberate attempt on Stone's part to annoy Michael. She didn't usually join in these silly masculine games, especially those that bordered on impropriety, but she was annoyed at Michael. So, holding out both arms in a gesture of acceptance, she told Stone, "Of course you may carry me, Mr. Stone. Thank you."

Instantly she was swept up into the large man's strong arms and borne effortlessly to the carriage where her anxious family waited. Only as she went did she look back over Stone's broad shoulder at Michael and see his stricken face. Seeing it, something deep inside her curled up into a tight little ball of pure misery.

Michael could not have carried her. Michael had the use of but one arm.

Instantly, Alissa was so ashamed she could have wept.

She stammered her thanks as Stone put her into the carriage, leaning effortlessly in to deposit her on the bench beside her grandmother. Her slight weight was in no way a threat to the balance of so large a man.

Alissa managed to murmur some kind of introduction, telling those in the coach that Captain Stone was a friend of the Major's—or at least she thought she did. From her grandmother's warm reply, she imagined she had.

But what had she *done*? The pique that had followed hard on the heels of her panic at thinking Michael had deliberately withheld his full identity from her was no excuse for the callousness of what she had just done. No excuse at all.

She wished she could blame Stone's obvious desire to tease an old comrade-in-arms, but she couldn't. It had been she who had lifted willing arms to Michael's large and able friend, pettishly hoping to show Michael that she was displeased with him.

Instead she had wounded him. Deeply. Inexcusably.

"Stone!" The cry came from in front of the coach. "We could use your bulk here, old ox."

Stone grinned ruefully. "I apologize for my friend MacLain's elegant turn of phrase, ladies, but I suspect I am needed to help move that fallen tree so that you may continue your journey." He bowed and closed the carriage door.

Alissa sat back with tears in her eyes.

Quietly, Lady Ellen took her hand.

Robin asked a little querulously, "Is everything all right, Lissa?"

After a moment Alissa answered him firmly. "Yes, dear, everything is fine."

She couldn't remember ever in her life having told a bigger lie.

Chapter Twelve

The rest of the journey to London was uneventful. *If,* Alissa thought, *you could count repressed tears and a heart that felt as if it would break at any minute uneventful.*

At any rate, her footmen, chagrined but immensely relieved, were again on the box with her coachman, and they were rocking along on the vastly better road nearing the capital at a good clip. They'd be in Town in no time.

Looking out the window on her side of the carriage, Alissa could see MacLain acting as outrider. Stone and the man she now knew was Viscount Kantwell rode on the other side. Even thinking of Michael as Kantwell failed to bring her the irritation she sought to help her through her misery. Soon they'd reach London, and then he'd be gone from her life, and there was nothing she could do or think that would give her comfort in these circumstances.

So she spent the rest of the trip watching him. Storing in her mind the picture he made, riding as if he were part of his horse, straight and tall and completely at ease in the saddle, gave her as much pain as pleasure. But much of life was pain, and she was aware that there was a great deal more coming. She would have to marry. There was no other course open to her. And the man she married was not to be the one she wanted. One day soon the lips that would claim hers would not be Michael's. The hands that touched and caressed her would not be his long-fingered hands.

Hand, she corrected herself. And that was the whole problem—that he could use but one hand, and that it mattered to him just as much as she was indifferent to the fact. It was Michael for whom she had such shattering feelings, not his physical perfection or lack of it.

Furthermore, she was no idiot. No, nor a girl fresh from the schoolroom without the ability to read men. Michael Mathers—*Viscount Kantwell,* she corrected herself acidly—was as attracted to her as she was to him! She'd stake her reputation as a "diamond of the first water" on it. Indeed, she had no reason to be so silly as that. She knew. She simply knew. With her heart, with her spirit, with every fiber of her being she knew. But it didn't matter. There wasn't anything she could do to change him, to make him see that they belonged together. There simply wasn't time.

With a heavy sigh Alissa settled back against the velvet squabs of the carriage. Feeling her grandmother squeeze her hand, she turned to her and smiled bravely. "I'm all right." Her smile wavered, and she dropped her gaze.

The grip her grandmother had on her hand tightened.

After a moment, Alissa raised her gaze again to meet her grandmother's. Her eyes were aswim with tears. In a tight little whisper she admitted, "But it would have been easier if I had never met him."

By the time they arrived at the huge mansion that had long served the Collingtons as a town house, Alissa had herself back under control. When the footman opened the carriage door and let down the step, she was completely composed.

MacLain was right there and offered her his hand. Stone assisted Lady Ellen. Michael, who had deliberately hung back until Alissa was safely escorted, handed the reins of all three horses to one of the grooms who had come running and helped Button and Robin down. With grave courtesy, he took them to the door where an austere butler and several other members of the staff waited.

Lady Ellen said, "I do not know how we can ever thank you, but you must call and let us try."

MacLain grinned hugely. "Rather! Nothing could please me more, Lady Ellen. Stone would like that, too. Wouldn't you, Stone?"

Stone ignored his impetuous friend. "I feel my duty here is not done yet, Lady Ellen. Kantwell tells me that Lady Alissa requires an escort to Bow Street. I stand ready to accompany her whenever she wishes to go."

"What?" MacLain had not been privy to Michael's confidence to Stone. "Bow Street? Hmmmm." He was eaten alive by curiosity, but manners had finally come to the fore and forbidden him to ask. Instead he offered, "I'd be happy to lend my services as well, Lady Alissa."

Alissa's glance shot to Michael, who stood quietly off to the side with Robin. She caught a look in his eyes that left her breathless. Instantly, it was gone as if it had never been. He bowed stiffly and said, "I regret that I am not at liberty to join you, Lady Alissa. You could not, however, be in better hands." He turned to Lady Ellen. "It has been a great pleasure meeting you, Lady Ellen. Thank you for all your kindness. I shall never forget you." The next words seemed torn from him. "Any of you."

Lady Ellen rose on tiptoe and placed a kiss on his cheek. "God keep you, Michael."

He turned abruptly and left them. His voice no longer under his command, he refused to say more.

As the sound of Gladiator's hoofbeats faded, MacLain burst out, "Oh, I say. Kantwell's never been *that* rude before!"

Stone was staring after Michael. In a pensive voice he said, "I think he must have a great deal on his mind. And he has been . . . under a great strain."

"Huh! As if we ain't seen him under strain in battle more times than enough. No, it must be something else. Deuced odd, though."

Lady Ellen blinked back tears and said briskly, "Come, gentlemen. Let me offer you tea." She cocked her head and considered the two ex-soldiers. "Or perhaps something stronger, while my granddaughter prepares to go to Bow Street."

Several streets away, in a square of sedate but elegant town houses, Michael rode Gladiator down the mews that separated it from its almost identical neighbor. He stopped and stood for a long moment just looking at the neat stable yard at the end of the alley. He knew then that he'd never expected to see this place again, and was startled at the depth of feeling that swept over him as he viewed it and smelled its familiar odors of good leather and fresh hay.

A silver-haired man came out of the stables, alerted by the sound of Gladiator's iron-shod hooves on the cobblestones of the mews. He stopped dead when he saw Michael. "Master Michael! You're home."

Palmer addressed him as he had when Michael was only an eager lad begging him to teach him about horses. The expression on his open face gladdened the weary traveler's heart. Someone had missed him other than his former comrades-in-arms. Someone from his childhood had remembered and cared.

By the time Michael went on to the house, he was smiling again.

•　•　•

The next morning, Alissa was back to pacing the floor.

"Do sit down, Alissa, you'll make me dizzy. Tell me what transpired last evening at Bow Street. You were so reticent when you got back, I felt there must be more to tell."

"Actually, Grandmama, there wasn't a great deal to tell. I just didn't want Michael's—I mean Viscount Kantwell's—two friends to know how disappointed I was."

"Weren't they any help?"

"Of course, they were. Having two such men with me gave a great deal of weight to what I'd gone to say. It's just that, no matter who was with me, nor how strongly they supported me, it was still the same old story. I am a woman, and as such could hardly have my facts straight. They promised in the calmest sort of way that they would look into the matter, but it was obvious they had no real interest in pursuing it. Especially when it came to accusing someone as illustrious as my uncle!"

"Oh, dear, surely not!"

"Oh, yes. I promise you it is true." A smile broke out. "The one really splendid thing was that Captain Stone offered, in the calmest voice ever, to break the runner's scrawny neck for him if he continued to treat me as if I didn't have any idea what I was talking about."

"You don't tell me!" Lady Ellen's eyes were shining.

"Oh, yes, I do. And furthermore, Lieutenant MacLain told him he belonged in the asylum my uncle's agent had threatened me with."

"Good for him!"

"Well, yes." Alissa frowned a little. "But I'm afraid his comment only confused things. After all, I want the Runners to prove Uncle Gerald responsible for Sir Thomas Lane's murder. I don't want them to go off on a chase after the men who tried to abduct me."

"Yes. Yes, I can see that, but surely . . ."

From the doorway of the drawing room, the butler cleared his throat.

"Yes, Quillen?"

"A messenger has come, Lady Alissa."

"What did he want, Quillen?"

"He wanted to give you this, milady, but I insisted on bringing it myself." He lifted his hand and showed her a slim package tied with a dark ribbon.

Alissa raised an eyebrow.

Quillen had known her since she'd been born, and he had no trouble interpreting her look. "He was cheeky, milady," was his reason for not permitting the messenger to accompany him into her presence. "I saw no reason to expose you to him."

"Very good, Quillen." She reached for the package. "Thank you." She saw her uncle's seal on the papers in her hand and took a steadying breath. "Please bring us tea."

She didn't want the butler in the room when she opened the package. She had the oddest feeling that she might not behave quite as well as he would expect her to, and she hated disappointing faithful servants. Almost as an afterthought she added, "And please close the door, Quillen. I'm certain I feel a draft."

"Of course, Lady Alissa." The butler bowed himself out, closing the door behind him.

Alissa turned to her grandmother.

Lady Ellen watched her with bright interest in her eyes. "Is it from Gerald?"

"Yes." Alissa stared down at the packet.

"Well, my dear, you must open it to see what is inside, you know."

"I can almost feel what is inside. A spate of malice, at the very least."

"Open it, Alissa," her grandmother ordered.

Alissa sat on the edge of the settee her grandmother occupied and pulled the ribbon from around the fold of papers. Perusing them quickly, she snapped, "How very like my uncle. He has sent yet another copy of Grandfather's will and a letter of instruction with it."

"Well?" Lady Ellen wanted to hear more, but the thunderous look on her granddaughter's face kept her from urging her more strongly to hurry with the information.

When finally she spoke, Alissa's voice was bitter. "Whatever we may think of this situation, Grandmother, the letter accompanying this copy of Grandfather's will says that Gerald is sending his solicitor here today to go over its terms with us"—she changed her voice to the pompous tones of her uncle—" 'so that we shall have no excuse to delay complying with them.' "

"Delay complying?" Lady Ellen's voice was indignant. "The very idea! How a son of mine could have turned out to be such a . . ."

Alissa was saved from hearing what her grandmother thought of her second son by the reappearance of their butler. Quillen stood in the doorway of the morning room, his posture stiff and his expression one of acute disapproval. Seeing that he had their full attention he inquired, "Are you at home, your ladyships?"

Alissa and her grandmother exchanged a glance. As usual, her grandmother deferred to Alissa. Being able to do so was one of the comforts of her old age—one she intended to enjoy. After all, Collington Park was Alissa's now. So were all the duties and responsibilities that went with it. She only hoped the girl would be able to keep it.

Alissa told the butler, "Yes, we are at home, Quillen."

"Since that is the case, my lady, there is a person asking to speak with you." He held out the small silver tray he carried, as he moved toward her.

Alissa took the visiting card from the tray and read to her grandmother, "Josiah P. Clodpole. Clodpole, Penney, Penney and Caton, Solicitors, Threadneedle Street, London." Her gaze locked with Lady Ellen's. "Well. It seems we are important enough to command the senior partner in the firm." Alissa's eyes flashed. "The size of my inheritance commands it, rather." Forcing herself to master her rising anger, she told the butler, "Show Mr. Clodpole to the blue drawing room, please, Quillen. Lady Ellen and I will talk to him there."

The butler left to summon the waiting solicitor, and Alissa and her grandmother walked down the hall to the blue drawing room and settled themselves to wait. A few minutes later, Quillen reappeared and announced, "Mr. Clodpole, your ladyships."

The solicitor hurried over to them, clutching a folder of papers and looking acutely embarrassed. "I am sorry to bother you in your home, your ladyships, but I thought you might find it more comfortable than having to come to my office."

They let his words hang in the air a moment, then Alissa hated seeing him look so uncomfortable. "That is very kind of you, Mr. Clodpole. I'm sure both my grandmother and I appreciate your consideration." She gestured to a chair opposite the settee she and Lady Ellen occupied. "Please sit down."

"Thank you." He placed his folder carefully on the small table beside the chair indicated, flipped the tails of his coat up out of the way and sat. Having done so, he looked from one of them to the other. After a frowning perusal, he cleared his throat and asked, "Lady Alissa, forgive me for asking you so personal a question, but can you tell me you are betrothed?"

Alissa hid the fact that she was offended. After all, that was the crux of this whole matter. If she weren't married by her twenty-fifth birthday, everything she had would become the property of her avaricious uncle. His solicitor had every right to ask whether or not she was betrothed, so she curbed her annoyance and answered quietly, "No, sir, I am not betrothed."

Mr. Clodpole gave a great sigh and pulled out his handkerchief. Mopping his forehead, he told them, "Lady Alissa, I wish with all my heart that you could have answered that in the affirmative, for an affirmative would have spared me this very unpleasant duty." He reached for the papers, cleared his throat, and said brusquely, "Lord Withers has bidden me inform you of the provisions he has made for you, in light of what will soon be your . . . straitened circumstances." He scowled down at the paper he'd selected as if he'd rather have had a snake in his hand.

When he seemed unable to begin, Alissa told him, "It's all right, Mr. Clodpole, my grandmother and I have a very good idea of what is in the paper you must read to us."

"Oh, I'm certain you cannot have," the little man burst out.

Seeing his pained expression, Lady Ellen raised her chin. "Sir, we are both aware that my son is a monster of greed and that he possesses not one vestige of the milk of human kindness. So do go on. I assure you, we will in no way blame you for what you have come to tell us."

Clodpole shook his head and murmured, "Most kind, ladies, most kind."

Passing his handkerchief over his brow again, he looked at them with pity in his eyes, then began. His voice registered his reluctance to read Gerald Withers's unfeeling words. Clearing his throat again, he began. " 'Since my late brother Richard's daughter, Lady Alissa Collington, the only one of them who is whole enough to work at anything, is not qualified for any position that would enable her to support an old woman and a blind child, I, Lord Withers, head of the Collington family, have made the following provisions for my mother, my niece, and the son of my late sister Blanche, my nephew Robin. I will expect these provisions to be adhered to on the day of my niece's twenty-fifth birthday.' "

Clodpole chewed his lower lip, then read on. " 'My

mother will receive a small allowance for food, coal, and candles, and will repair to my estate in the north of England known as Caderfield, there to spend the rest of her days.' "

Alissa cried out, "Caderfield is a ruin! That house is not habitable. Grandmother would be neither safe nor able to maintain her health there!"

Seeming to shrink into himself, Clodpole took refuge in his papers and read on. " 'My nephew, now being ten years old, will accompany and care for her, obviating the need for servants.' "

Alissa leapt to her feet, fury struggling with horror for mastery in her voice. "Robin is blind!"

The solicitor closed his eyes for a moment, as if he'd like to blot out the next words before he had to utter them. Taking a deep breath, like a diver about to enter the water, he read, " 'And for my niece, Lady Alissa Alana Collington of Collington Park, I have arranged her betrothal to the Earl of Wanemoor. The wedding is to take place one week after her birthday.' "

"Wanemoor?" Alissa cast about in her mind. Who in the world was Wanemoor? Could there be an earl of whom she had never even heard?

Lady Ellen had heard of him, however, and there was no confusion in her reaction to the name. Her face as white as the handkerchief Clodpole again passed over his face, she clutched at Alissa's hand and drew her back down beside her. Her accusing eyes met those of the man sent to read this dreadful news to them.

The solicitor dropped his gaze rather than face hers. Lady Ellen's voice was a horrified accusation. "Wanemoor is an abomination, Mr. Clodpole. A pervert. No decent house receives him! In fact I doubt that anyone receives him at all! The man has already had three young wives. He has driven one to suicide and one to madness." Her voice shook with loathing. "No one knows what happened to his third wife!"

Alissa, her face stony, her head held high, rose again. She told the solicitor firmly, "I think, Mr. Clodpole, that we understand the plans my uncle has made for his family. I believe you can leave those papers for us to read at our leisure. Now that I am aware of the care"—her voice dripped with sarcasm—"that my uncle has taken for us, I wish to utilize every second of this final week before my birthday to do whatever I can manage to do . . . to thwart him."

Mr. Clodpole rose instantly, glad to be free of the matter. He bowed, and said with feeling, "I sincerely thank you for relieving me of a truly onerous duty, Lady Alissa." Then he gathered and neatly stacked the papers he'd brought, leaving them on the table. As he did, he wrestled with his professional ethics . . . and lost. Twisting his hands, he blurted, "Though I am your uncle's, not your, counselor, Lady Alissa, I must tell you that you would do well to marry as quickly as you can."

His face twisted with distaste as he took a final glance at the stack of papers. He hurried away across the room without even taking proper leave of his two hostesses. At the door he paused, an agitated little man who was clearly uncertain about what he should do. Suddenly, he turned back and cried to Alissa, "Hurry, milady." His eyes beseeched her. "Hurry and wed. You must! Marriage is your only chance!"

Chapter Thirteen

"*Marry, must I?*" Alissa swept her uncle's papers off the small table on which the solicitor had left them so neatly stacked, and stamped on them. "As if we hadn't been racking our brains for days as to how I might go about doing just that!"

"I'd think," Lady Ellen offered gently, "that the first thing to do would be to get out and see who is in Town, and thus let everyone know you are back."

"Oh, dearest, it will be days before we get the first invitation. You know that, Grandmother. No one even knows we are in residence yet."

"No, that is not completely true, dear. Fortuitously, I'd written my old schoolmate, Anne Arbester, that I might see her soon, as we might be coming to Town to look for Christmas presents for Robin. She must have taken it for gospel, because this morning, I found a card of invitation to a soirée she and the Marquess are giving this very night."

Alissa was taken aback. "Tonight!" She threw a glance at the mantel clock and wailed, "It's already almost tonight, now. And we have no escorts. We can't trail in without escorts, we would be pitiable. Impossible. We simply can't be ready to go out so soon."

Lady Ellen recognized her granddaughter's reluctance for what it was. "Alissa," she said bracingly, "you are having an attack of what your grandfather would have called cold feet, and it is quite unlike you.

"I know you have chosen your course, though God knows neither of us likes it, and both of us abhor the necessity that has forced you to it. You *have* made up your mind, however—I know you have—and I admire you for it. Keeping Collington, its servants and its pensioners from your uncle is a worthy endeavor, and you are a courageous girl to undertake such a monumental task. Especially since that task has proven to be fraught with danger. Now that all that is said, I must add, however gently, Lissa, that you have only one week left."

Alissa's shoulders sagged for an instant, and tears came to her eyes. She blinked them back, then stood tall again and answered her grandmother with simple dignity. "You are quite right, of course." She turned to leave the room. "I'll go and see what Button can put together for me to wear." She paused in the doorway, and some of her old impishness shone in her eyes. "I'll leave it to you to conjure up an escort."

Lady Ellen watched her granddaughter's graceful exit until she could see her no more, then she hurried to the writing desk and pulled out a sheet of her late husband's crested stationery. She was smiling as she wrote to "conjure up" an escort for herself and Alissa.

At Kantwell House, Black, Michael's butler, was harassing his staff to make rooms ready for the master's two army friends, and to prepare them a suitable dinner. His comment that a little notice would have been nice, he kept to himself. It was bad enough that Cook went straight up the wall when she learned that she had three gentlemen who had appeared out of nowhere for whom to fix dinner. The fact that one of them was her beloved master was the only thing that had kept her from giving her notice then and there.

Water was heated and lugged upstairs for baths for all three of those gentlemen, and maids and footmen scurried to unpack and press evening clothes that had spent two days crammed into saddlebags so that the guests could go out. With no valet in residence—due to Michael's long absence—Black had to give all the instructions for the proper dressing of gentlemen guests to his two most intelligent footmen and hope for the best. He consoled himself that Captain Stone and Lieutenant MacLain were used to battlefield conditions and would probably not be as difficult to please as town beaus.

Dinner went off without a hitch, and Captain Stone and Lieutenant MacLain were groomed to a fare-thee-well by the competing footmen, each hoping to outdo the other—with an eye to the chance of promotion to the vacant post of valet.

At long last the guests were ready to be on their way. "Are you certain you won't come with us, Michael?" Stone asked quietly.

MacLain chimed in, "Yes. Devil take it, Michael, you can't hide in here forever, you know. You'll have to go out sooner or later."

"Then it shall be later." The expression on Michael's face closed the discussion.

Michael stood in the doorway as they left, bidding them good night and assuring them he'd be more than glad to hear of their adventures in the sacred halls of Almack's *over breakfast coffee*. He looked hard at them to be certain they understood his emphasis on a *morning* discussion. He was ready to sleep long and hard after the events of the last two days, and had no desire to be awakened at their return.

Stone got the point, and grinned.

MacLain frowned, looked down at himself and asked, "What's the matter? Something on m'cravat?"

Michael and Stone exchanged looks, and both shook their heads.

"Later, then." Stone clapped his host on the shoulder and walked out. "Come, if you insist on dragging me to the marriage mart, MacLain."

MacLain shrugged and surrendered. "Oh, all right." He followed Stone, then turned and said to Michael, "Don't wait up."

The butler sighed as he closed the door behind them. Michael laughed. "It's been quite a day, hasn't it, Black?"

Black permitted himself the tiniest hint of a smile. "Yes, your lordship, it has, indeed."

"You've handled it well. I thank you." Michael turned to go to the study. "Please convey my appreciation for their efforts to the rest of the staff." Suddenly he grinned. "I'll make peace with Cook tomorrow after breakfast."

"Oh, sir, I'd go before then if you don't want your toast burnt." Black looked as if he'd shocked himself with the comment.

Michael laughed. "I'll be sure to follow your suggestion."

Black hurried to open the study door and to pour a glass of brandy for his master. Then he bowed himself out and Michael sat alone in his study, the glass of brandy in his hand, the decanter on the table at his elbow.

Now that the flurry of getting Stone and MacLain off to Almack's, to "look over the latest crop of lovelies," as MacLain put it, was past, the house was silent. Without the enthusiastic MacLain around, Michael could take stock.

He smiled, remembering the pleasant hubbub his arrival had caused, and the sincere pleasure his head groom,

Palmer, had expressed at his safe return. It was good to see familiar faces and to know his servants were pleased to see him, but now the greetings were over and his guests had gone out for the evening, and Michael was left alone.

The quiet wrapped around him like a blanket. All was peaceful and calm. With Stone and MacLain out on the Town and his own wants attended to, the house had settled back into its usual smooth routine, and Michael was even more solitary than he had been the last time he'd come home to the capital.

Perhaps this was the reason he'd enjoyed his army life. There had always been someone around—to play cards with, to argue with, to share a joke with. Here at Kantwell House, there had never been anyone. His parents and grandparents were long dead, and he was an only child.

If he'd married instead of going straight out of university to fight for his country against the French, there would have been a wife waiting for him. There might even have been children. But fate in the form of Napoleon Bonaparte had decided the matter differently, and now it was too late for all that. Now he was maimed—though he could hardly blame that on the War, and certainly not on The Little Colonel—and it was too late to start a family. He was a cripple.

He drank deeply of his brandy. His mood darkened as he admitted that it was more than too late for him now. Doubly too late. For now he'd met the only woman he'd ever wanted to ask to share his life, and she was perfect. Damning himself for a fool, he further admitted that, with all his heart, he wanted someone just as perfect *for* her. Not a man with but one useful arm. She deserved . . .

A knock at the front door mercifully interrupted his thoughts. He heard Black heading down the hall to answer it. A moment later, his curiosity was satisfied as the butler came into the study bearing a heavy vellum missive neatly folded and sealed.

Michael discovered the sealing wax was still soft as he ran his thumbnail under it, while Black sucked in his breath in disapproval, and returned the letter opener to the desk with elaborate—and extremely obvious—care. "Will there be any reply, your lordship?"

Michael was distracted. "No," he muttered, "no reply. No, wait. Don't send the messenger away yet. I must think."

Black watched as, instead of quiet thought, his master leapt to his feet and began pacing, cursing with admirable fluency.

"Is it bad news, my lord?"

Michael turned toward his butler, saw the concern on his face, and stopped turning the air blue. "No. Not bad news, Black. Just . . . just a difficulty." He glanced at the clock on the mantel and snarled, "That late already, is it? Blast and damn!"

Looking down at the note in his hand, he read it again.

> *I truly hate to inconvenience you, Michael, but as you know, there is no one else to whom I could possibly apply at this late hour. Knowing you have not had time to accept an engagement, I take the liberty of throwing myself on your mercy to beg for your escort tonight. For serious reasons that I am not at liberty to divulge, we must attend a soirée. As I am certain you will realize, to do so without an escort would be unthinkable. I regret infinitely this further imposition on you, Michael, but I have nowhere else to turn.*
>
> *Please rescue us once again.*
> *Fondly,*
> *Ellen*

The signature started another round of curses. How the devil could he refuse her when she signed herself so intimately? Blast it! She knew he could not. Nor could he pass this responsibility on to his now absent comrades.

He turned a face to his butler that would have petrified a lesser man. As it was, he saw Black pale a bit. "Tell the messenger that I will come within the hour. Alert my coachman, if I still have one here . . ."

"Palmer is more than able to serve as your coachman, my lord."

"Good. After you've alerted him, find someone to dress me for a—" He bit back his unique and colorful description of the event to which he had been summoned, and said merely, "a soirée," but he snarled the word.

Black was already upset that there was no valet available, now Michael's attitude made matters worse. He'd absolutely no intention of letting one of the footmen he'd permitted to dress their guests touch the master—especially when it looked as if he might explode. With offended dignity he intoned, "I shall see to the matter of your toilette myself, my lord."

"Very good." Michael's temper was cooling. After all, he wasn't angry with Lady Ellen. His anger stemmed from having to face society before he was prepared to. Or rather, before he had prepared society, by means of a few judicious visits to his club and a ride or two in Rotten Row, for the shock of seeing his disability. To just appear at a large gathering was asking for problems. Problems he was in no way willing to face so soon.

Seeing Alissa again was both benediction and torment. He wasn't prepared for that either.

Standing around in his study wasn't going to accomplish anything, however, so he grinned at his butler and said in a far gentler tone, "Let's get at it, Black."

Together they left the room.

The soirée was, as Michael had feared, a real crush. Their hostess, Lady Anne, would be positively in alt over the huge attendance. It seemed to him that the world and his wife were present, and that every one of them turned to stare as he entered the spacious room just behind the famous beauty and heiress, Lady Alissa Collington, and her grandmother. Whispers began behind hands and fans, and there were even a few comments made aloud about her escort.

"Look. Isn't that Kantwell with her?"

"Why so it is! I thought I'd heard that he'd been killed someplace or other. Handsome dog for a corpse, ain't he?" The speaker laughed at his own humor.

His wife struck him with her furled fan. "Be silent. Can't you see he's been injured?" Her tone changed as she turned to another woman and spoke with a honeyed venom. "I wonder what dear Lady Lydia will think of *that.* She's always bragged so about his physical perfection."

"Margaret!" gasped the woman, leaning closer to her. "I can't believe you said that!"

Margaret threw her an arch look. "Oh, yes you can. We've both long known that Lydia took him for her lover. And you'll be just as interested as I will to see her reaction."

Alissa had heard, and was more angry than she had been in a long time—and Heaven knew she'd had enough bouts of anger lately. A glance at Michael's carefully controlled face made her angrier still. Her expression haughty, she lifted her chin and gazed around the room as if deciding whether or not she would deign to stay.

"Oh, dear," Lady Ellen told Michael, "Lissa is about to mount her high horse. We must do something."

Michael leaned down to her and asked, "Shall I give her an assist into the saddle?"

Lady Ellen turned and glared at him. "Behave, Michael. I already have my hands full with Alissa."

Michael grinned and bowed his acquiescence. "I shall endeavor to be on my very best behavior, my lady."

The situation was saved by their hostess. "Ellen! I have been watching for your arrival."

Lady Ellen smiled with genuine pleasure, and the two elderly women embraced. "I'm sorry we were too late for the receiving line. We are only just this afternoon arrived from the country, and are not yet organized."

"Then I am doubly honored to have you!" Lady Anne kissed her friend on the cheek and beamed at the three of them. "Lady Alissa, it is wonderful to see you again." She added with softly voiced pride, "You are more beautiful than ever, my dear. As lovely as I have always known you would be."

Alissa smiled affectionately at this kindly friend from her childhood, and Lady Ellen started breathing again. Alissa asked, "Is your niece, Rosalynda, here this evening, by any chance, Lady Anne?"

"No, I'm sorry. I believe Rosalynda is still at her grandmother's until tomorrow. She will be certain to make getting in touch with you the first thing she does on her return, now that I can tell her you are here in Town. She counts you her best friend, you know."

Alissa smiled. "As I do her. I shall be glad to see her again."

Lady Anne turned to Michael. "How do you do, your lordship. I'm so very glad you have come. My husband has watched your battlefield exploits in the dispatches with a great deal of interest. He has been eager to meet you in person for some time and was so happy to learn from Lady Ellen's note that you would be here this evening." She linked her arm with her old classmate's then slipped her other hand gently into the crook of Michael's crippled arm as if she had noticed nothing odd about it. "Come. Permit me to take you to him. He is full of questions and is absolutely anxious to make your acquaintance. There he is, just over there with . . ."

"Michael!" A beautiful redhead in a stunning gown that

showed rather more of her perfect shoulders and bust than Lady Ellen thought proper, rushed up to them. She stopped short and stared in horror at Michael's bound arm and black-gloved hand. "Oh, Michael," she said again, this time in a hushed voice full of repugnance, "is it true then? Are you *maimed*?"

Alissa, close beside the Major, sensed, more than saw, him stiffen. Quietly, she took his good arm, aligning herself with him in the eyes of everybody watching. And it seemed to her as if every soul in the room possessed eyes that stood out on stalks! She could feel her chin lifting again and didn't care. If ever there was a woman who deserved being looked at down one's nose it was this exquisite nincompoop. How dare she be so careless of Michael's feelings! How dare she make such a dreadful remark in public! How dare she make such a dreadful remark at all?

Even as Alissa glared at the gorgeous redhead, the woman said in breathless tones of revulsion, "Oh, Michael, I could not bear to have you touch me with *that*!" Her gaze was locked on Michael's black silk gloved hand.

Very softly, Michael told her, "I can assure you, Lydia, that you need have no fear of it." He bowed slightly. "I trust you will excuse us." Then, with his head high and his cheeks stained with an angry flush, he walked away from her, Alissa still on his arm. Ladies Anne and Ellen followed, a shocked but determined rear guard.

As they passed, Alissa glared at Lady Lydia, reached down, grasped her skirt, and pulled it quickly aside to keep it from coming in contact with that of the despicable redhead. A gasp at the insult this gesture of disdain offered Lady Lydia escaped those closest to the little group. Alissa smiled sweetly and inclined her head toward them as if accepting applause for her action.

Feeling a tremor along her arm where it pressed against the Major, she shot a glance at his face, her eyes full of quick sympathy. She found the wretch trying not to laugh!

And here she had thought him dying of public rejection by the beauteous Lady Lydia. When he looked at her, however, his eyes were warm with humor. "Well done, Lady Alissa. That was a very telling parting shot."

Alissa wasn't certain whether she was being praised or made fun of. She *was* certain, however, that she was piqued. She didn't like being caught between the Major and the woman who quite obviously had been his lover. Not one little bit.

At any rate, she knew she had certainly not begun her reentry into society in a fashion designed to make friends.

No, that wasn't true. The decent people there wouldn't hold her actions against her, she knew. The only problem was that she wasn't at all sure that she had the option to be choosy about whom she befriended. She had a week left. Only a week.

Her stomach knotted, and she fervently prayed that somewhere here or at the next party she would be able to find one decent man who could be persuaded to chance agreeing to marry her. Looking around the room, she wasn't encouraged.

Their little party arrived at the group in which their host stood talking, and Lady Anne introduced them. The process took several minutes because she had to work precedence out in her mind. Then conversation started up again.

A man said, "By Jove, I've always wanted to meet one of 'The Lucky Seven'!" You men cut quite a dash in the War on the Peninsula. Brave lads, all of you!"

"Ashley Stoddard was one of you, wasn't he?" another of the men asked.

"Yes," Michael said very quietly. "One of the best."

"Murdered on the battlefield by a man who wanted to steal his horse, wasn't it?" This from another, older man.

"Yes," said a third. "But he was brought down by several of the famed 'Lucky Seven' led by Blysdale and Task-ford. You were one of them. Isn't that so?"

Michael nodded.

"Hallo! Kantwell!" A young man in rather untidy but expensive evening clothes bustled up to the group with a friend a few paces behind. "By Jupiter, you *are* a crip. No offense. Just had to see for myself if it was the truth. Couldn't believe it when m'sister Lydia came caterwauling to me about it." He pulled a falsely sympathetic face. "Too bad, too bad." Then he brightened. "But at least now some of the other whips among us will have a chance in the cur-ricle races. Can't beat us one-handed, can you, now?" Suddenly, he yelped, "Ouch!" and jumped away from Alissa. "I say!"

"Oh," Alissa said sweetly, "did I tread on your foot? So careless of me."

"Yes, yes, you did, and it was." The young man scowled at her. "You should be more careful."

Michael said, "I don't think I can permit you to speak to Lady Alissa in that tone, Murray."

The younger man was too busy rubbing his instep to be fully aware of what he was doing. "Oh, really?" His voice was spiteful. "And just what do you think you can do about it?"

Softly Michael inquired, "Shall we step out into the garden and see?"

Murray's companion spoke. "Come away, Murray. Surely you won't descend to fighting a cripple. It simply isn't done." Tugging at his friend, he pulled him away.

Lady Ellen was stunned at such behavior. The rest of the group stood in polite silence, as thoroughly shocked as she, then everyone began talking at once. Of one accord, they pretended the scene they had just witnessed had not taken place. Michael conversed pleasantly with the men, playing his part adroitly.

Alissa was shaking with rage. Rage against the pain she

knew the last half-hour had caused the Major. She could feel his tension, though no hint of it showed on his voice or manner. Only the heightened color in his cheeks told her he was distressed.

When she thought Michael had succeeded in convincing the assembled company that he was unaffected by the cruelty shown him, Alissa could stand it no longer. Smiling wanly, she asked him, "Lord Kantwell, I am so sorry to ask you to leave when you are enjoying yourself so, but I have a devastating headache. Could you please take me home?"

Chapter Fourteen

After she'd managed to talk Alissa into going to bed, Lady Ellen went down to the study. There she stood for a long time in the light from the flickering flames of the failing candles, and stared down at her granddaughter's desk. On it lay the list of possible suitors Alissa had worked so hard on. Running her eye over it, she found she could not be glad of a single one of them. For each name, she could have penned a fault that made the man unacceptable.

It pained her to see that one name was conspicuous by its absence. Major Guy Michael Mathers's name did not appear.

"Ah, my poor darling." She sighed. "It is worse than dreadful that you should be forced to this to save little Robin and the servants . . . and me, too, no doubt." She twisted her hands in an unfamiliar gesture of anxiety. Never in her life had she felt so helpless. And so totally *useless*. And oh, how she hated it!

"What shall I do?" she asked herself in an agonized whisper. "How can I help her?"

She bent her head over her clasped hands and prayed for guidance as she had never prayed before. After long minutes, peace settled over her. She moved to the tall window of the study and looked out over the moonlit garden under its sparkling blanket of snow. "Yes," she whispered, her breath adding to the frost patterns on the panes. "Yes, of course!"

A solution had been presented to her, her decision about it had been reached, and she felt as if the weight of the world had been lifted from her. She glanced across the room at the tall clock. It was a preposterous hour for a call. A ridiculous hour, and rude as well, but she didn't care. She smiled, straightened, took a deep breath, and walked quickly out into the hall.

Almost immediately she ran into Quillen. She suspected he'd been lingering nearby deliberately, looking after her as he always did the family members. Lady Ellen smiled at him and ordered, "Quillen! Send for John Coachman, your strongest footman, and my cloak. I'm going out."

"Surely not, your ladyship! It's past midnight."

"I'm well aware of the hour, Quillen. My business won't wait. Please hurry. And *quietly*. I don't want my granddaughter to be awakened."

"No, I shouldn't think you would," the butler muttered as he went off, shaking his head, to do as he'd been told.

Lady Ellen grinned. Suddenly she was not half so weary as she'd been just moments ago. Nor did she feel as useless.

There was a loud knock on the front door of Kantwell House.

"What the devil? Who the blazes could that be at this hour?" Michael rose as he heard his butler hurrying to the door. He was too curious to wait to be told who had come calling at such an odd hour.

Black rushed past, shrugging into his coat and re-buttoning his vest as he went. Then Michael heard the butler open the tall front door and step hastily back from it. For an instant he wondered if he should get the pistol out of the nearby drawer where it had been since his grandfather's day and go to Black's defense. That action proved unnecessary as he heard a male voice announce, "Lady Ellen Collington to see Viscount Kantwell."

Black sounded as if he had choked on something, then managed, "I shall see if he is in," in a weak voice.

"Well, of course, he's *in*, man." Lady Ellen sounded annoyed . . . and very determined. "Just see if he's still *up*!"

"I'm up, Lady Ellen." Michael made his own announcement around a broad smile. Long, eager strides took him to her side. "What in heaven's name brings you here? Why didn't you just send a note to summon me to you?"

He watched his startled butler take her cloak, then offered her his arm and led her toward the drawing room.

"No, no," she protested. "I'll be more comfortable wherever you were when I arrived." She glanced up at him. "And *you'll* be more comfortable wherever you've left your brandy."

He grinned at her. "So I'll be needing brandy as a restorative when you've finished your midnight visit, will I?"

"It's not midnight, Major, it is past one in the morning. And yes, I'm afraid you will."

He frowned. "Nothing has gone wrong, has it?" What *could* have happened? None of the men he'd secretly posted around Collington House had come back to report anything unusual to him. Even so, the bottom dropped out of his stomach.

"No, dear boy." She patted his hand soothingly. "Nothing *more* has gone wrong." With a heavy sigh she told him, "Everything that could have gone awry, had already done so before we met you. With, of course, the addition of the attempted abduction of my dear Alissa. But you had a first-hand view of that little episode!" Her eyes twinkled at him. "And you were a splendid hero through it all, I might add.

"But no, nothing has gone wrong since that. The reason I've come to you in the middle of the night and without my granddaughter's knowledge is that I have every intention of enlisting your help in putting things right."

"I think perhaps," Michael said after looking hard at her, "that I *shall* need that brandy!" He led her down the hall to the study, calling over his shoulder, "Black, please bring tea for Lady Ellen."

"Very good, your lordship." Black hurried off to see to it. His dignity was, after all, already marred by the fact that his vest was unevenly buttoned, so undue haste wouldn't make matters any worse.

Lady Ellen settled into the chair to which Michael led her with a little sigh. Michael sat opposite her in the one he'd previously occupied and watched her more than a little warily. When Lady Ellen had arranged her skirts to suit her, a gesture that told Michael she was not at ease with whatever mission had brought her to him, she folded her hands in her lap and considered him gravely.

When she continued to regard him steadily without speaking, yet with a decidedly speculative light in her calm blue eyes, Michael could bear it no longer. "And just what is it I am to put right, and just how am I to do it?"

Lady Ellen smiled and relaxed a bit. "Major, I watched you fight off Alissa's attackers from my relatively safe place in the coach, and I was able to see everything very clearly." She paused and sat watching him. "Fear for the safety of loved ones sharpens one's powers of observation, don't you agree?"

Michael frowned slightly, but didn't answer.

"Yes," Lady Ellen said pensively. "It also lets one see what happens with surprising clarity. I'm sure you've had the same experience in battle, haven't you, Major?"

It wasn't a real question, and to Michael it acted like a goad. He sensed Lady Ellen's proximity to the truth, and it was touching a nerve. He rose and began to pace. "Many times," he finally admitted in a tight voice.

"Then you'll understand that I couldn't help seeing the total disregard *you* had for your own safety."

"My primary concern was for your granddaughter's."

"Michael, there was more to it than that."

"Was there?"

"Can't we stop this fencing and speak with one another honestly?"

Michael stopped in front of her, his good hand fisted behind his back, as if he were a soldier standing at ease. Ease, however, had nothing to do with the way he was feeling.

Ellen broke the protracted silence between them. "I think you did not care whether you lived or died."

Michael made no answer.

"I was hoping you might answer that, Major."

Michael heard the desperation just under her words. Throwing his head up, he forced himself to tell her, "Very well, since you must have it. My life is of very little value to me, Lady Ellen. With this useless arm I can never aspire to the life I had dreamed of." He continued to look at a spot over her head, refusing to meet her eyes.

"Michael . . ." It was a whispered rebuke.

"Yes," he finally ground out, "I'll admit it, if you insist. I would not only have counted it an honor to have lost my life in your granddaughter's defense, I'd have counted it . . . a relief. To have rid myself of the burden of life while performing a rescue would have been at least honorable. More to be desired than the outright committing of suicide, wouldn't you say?" He turned his tortured visage away from her. "Don't go on thinking me a hero. There's no heroism in sacrificing that which one no longer values."

"Oh, Michael." Lady Ellen couldn't stop the soft cry of pity.

Michael fixed her with a glare. "What! Is it so unusual to want to be rid of a life that has become tedious?" His tone gained anger. "Do you really think I look forward to being treated with the same pity *you've* just shown me for the rest of my life?"

Ellen recognized that his words were a cry from the heart. Her own heart quailed to hear them. She wished with every fiber of her being that she could comfort him. But she wasn't here to comfort Michael. She was here to win safety—yes, and comfort, too—for her granddaughter. And maybe, just maybe, true love for her precious Alissa. And in the winning of it, the same for this magnificent young man. Resolutely, she set about it.

"I'm sorry if you think that was pity for you, Michael. It was, instead, sorrow—deep sorrow—at seeing one so young, with so very much to live for, ready to throw it all away."

Michael continued to glare. "Please spare me all the platitudes, Lady Ellen. Good friends have spent the last few months drumming into me that I am young, I am handsome, I am rich. All that is true. I am not *able*, however, and that is what is most important to me. I, not only a cavalryman but a horseman of some fame, cannot mount a horse without great effort. I must *lumber* up onto the beast. I can no longer sail. I cannot drive, for I have no whip hand. I therefore cannot win the races for which I had gained some small fame among my peers. Blast it, Ellen"—he dropped her title in his earnest desire to *make her see*—"I—" His face twisted sardonically as he threw all propriety to the winds. "I, who was rather more than simply a proficient lover, can't even hold a woman in my arms—can't make love to her without my weight crushing the life out of her. I can't have a life! Damn it to hell, it's too late for me. It's *gone*!"

Ellen stared at the hands she clasped fiercely in her lap. When finally she spoke, she asked mildly, "Are you acquainted with the Earl of Wanemoor?"

"What!" Michael was rocked by the sudden change of topic.

"Wanemoor." She studied the flaming contempt in his face. "So you do know him."

"I know his reputation. If but half of what is said of him is true, the man wants killing."

"Yes. I fear I agree with you."

"Fear?" He was quick to interpret the note in her voice correctly.

"Yes, my dear, fear. You see, Alissa's uncle has arranged for her marriage to Lord Wanemoor at the end of the month."

"He can't have." Michael's expression was one of profound disbelief.

"Oh, but I assure you that he has."

Michael was pale under his tan. "Then the story I overheard at the inn was true? Alissa must wed or turn her inheritance—and thus her independence—over to her uncle, Lord Withers?" Michael spoke the man's name with the distaste he felt for him.

"Yes. And you have seen what he can do. Those were his men who attacked our carriage."

"What was their intent?"

Ellen raised her chin in that gesture that so reminded Michael of his Snow Goddess. Carefully watching his eyes, she told him, "They were sent to take Alissa for confinement in an insane asylum."

"My God!"

"I think that God had very little to do with it. The idea came straight from the Pit, I've no doubt." Ellen weighed his reaction, then said very softly. "Clever of him, actually.

Alissa could hardly be expected to find a man to marry her there, could she?"

Michael didn't answer her. He was still wrestling with the horror of the beautiful Alissa in the hands of the brutish warders and the frequently violent inmates of an insane asylum. His blood had run so cold at the thought that he felt as if it had frozen in his veins.

Chapter Fifteen

Several squares away in Collington House, Alissa wasn't asleep. Try as she might, she was unable to sleep for the myriad worries that haunted her. At least that's what she told herself as she tossed and turned in her bed.

It wasn't true, of course. The problem of her inheritance and her responsibility for her servants and loved ones rested heavily at the back of her mind now, for something else had pushed it there. That something else was Major Michael Mathers—not Viscount Kantwell but Major Mathers, for that was the way she would always think of him.

She could see him now in her mind's eye, a tall, militarily straight figure who'd appeared magically out of the swirling snow mounted on an all but invisible gray horse. She smiled dreamily at the recollection. He had seemed to ride the winter wind.

Her smile died and she turned restlessly onto her other side to stare at the firelight-dappled draperies on the window on the opposite wall for a change. Hopelessly she asked herself, *Why did I have to meet Michael Mathers now? Why did he have to charge into my life at just this point?* If he'd come later, she would already have been safely wed. And if he had come sooner, she would have had time to win him for her own. She knew she could have won him, had she been granted the time, because she'd felt the strong attraction that had flowed between them.

But no, he had to be all tangled up in the fact that he was maimed. She'd known instinctively that it would take months to convince him his disability didn't matter, to make him see that she loved him anyway.

Oh, why, in Heaven's blessed name, did he have to be so stupidly sensitive about his useless arm! *She* didn't care that he'd lost the use of his left arm. He could have lost the arm completely, and it wouldn't have made him any less a man.

She tossed onto her other side in a perfect fit of aggravation. What did it *matter* if he had the use of only one arm? After his heroic rescue of her from her uncle's henchmen, it was more than apparent to her that he did as well with but one arm as most men did with two.

She'd been half in love with Michael after that tender interlude in which they'd stood so close in the inn doorway, staring out at the moonlit landscape. She'd been almost overwhelmed by her longing to move back just half a step and lean against him as he'd stood so close behind her, but of course propriety had forbidden it. In her very soul she'd known that he'd longed to slip his arms—*arm,* she corrected her thought impatiently—around her and hold her. He hadn't, of course, for the same inane reason.

And the next morning—ah, dear God! Was it really only *this* morning? This morning, she'd fallen even more in love with him as he'd stood possessively over her in the snow and snarled that he'd see her would-be abductor in hell before he'd let her be taken from him.

Even then, with her heart soaring with pride in him,

she'd guarded what she had left of it fiercely against him, knowing the danger of giving it to him completely. She had held on, hoping to preserve as much as possible of her heart to give to whomever she was forced to marry in order to save her grandmother and Robin.

Almost from the moment she'd met Michael, she'd prayed fervently that she could retain enough of herself to someday find happiness in the marriage she must, of dire necessity, make. But she had hoped in vain. Tonight had proved her undoing. Helpless to prevent it, she'd been catapulted the rest of the way into love with her major by his magnificent behavior at Lady Anne's soirée.

The stoic dignity with which Michael had withstood the dreadful remarks of that young toad, Murray, had won her admiration. The quiet challenge he'd issued in her defense when Murray had spoken sharply to her after she'd deliberately stomped on the young moron's foot had thrilled her. But most and worst of all was that searing moment when she had felt the pain that radiated from him when his challenge had been refused on the grounds of his infirmity. That had torn her heart apart—and her last defenses down. From that instant, she'd known that she loved Michael Mathers with all her heart and soul and mind. She was his forever. She would never be free to love anyone else.

Now she was doomed to a loveless marriage of convenience, for she understood that it would take a very long time to convince Major Michael Mathers that he was all a woman's heart could possibly desire—especially *her* woman's heart—and she had only a week.

In one week, she would have her twenty-fifth birthday, and on that day by set of sun, she would either be married, and mistress of her fate and the fates of all those who depended on her, or she would be penniless and at the nonexistent mercy of her cruel and greedy uncle.

If she herself were the only one to be considered, she would gladly throw it all to the four winds and follow the

Major in rags until she won his heart. But that was not the case. Her uncle *would* send Lady Ellen and Robin to Caderfield, that awful ruin in the north of England, where they would be unable to survive without the servants he fully intended to deny them.

Furthermore, Collington Park would be his, and all the servants, her faithful servants, would be turned away. The pensioners would be told they would no longer receive their stipends, and the horse that had survived Sir Thomas Lane's fatal fall from the bridge would be shot—her uncle had promised it.

"Oh, blast!" Frustration twisted her stomach into a knot. With all her strength, she threw one of her pillows against the wall. It hit with a most unsatisfactory soft thud and fell harmlessly to the floor. She glared at it for a long minute, then threw herself down again and surrendered to the tears that had threatened ever since she'd finished writing that galling list of men she might marry—the list that Michael's name had not appeared on.

"Oh, God, why?" Alissa cried aloud in anguish. "Why did I have to fall in love now!"

Burying her face in the remaining pillow, Alissa surrendered to a fit of weeping. Worn out with worry and the monumental events of the past few days, she finally slept.

In the study at Kantwell House, Michael, every muscle tensed, faced Lady Ellen with the same attitude he'd use to face an armed enemy. He was beginning to get a glimmer of where she was headed.

Lady Ellen smiled to see the understanding dawning in Michael's eyes.

"Lady Ellen," he began, throwing out his hand to stop her from speaking. Then he dropped it to his side, shook his head and paced the rug in front of the fireplace. "Lady Ellen," he said in a much calmer voice, "what you are about to propose is impossible."

"Impossible?"

"Quite impossible."

"And why is that? Is it just because you have lost the use of one arm?" She rose and stepped in his way, battle flags flying. "Am I then to understand that you think that while it is impossible for my granddaughter to marry a man who is less than physically perfect, it is, in your opinion, quite all right for her to marry a sexual monster twice her age?"

He stood unmoving, still half on his toes because he had been forced to stop abruptly to avoid walking into her.

"Well?" she demanded. "Are you willing to condemn Alissa to such a fate?"

"Of course not!" He all but shouted his denial.

Lady Ellen didn't turn a hair. Thrusting a finger at him, she demanded, "Didn't you tell me you were ready to sacrifice your *life* for her when you stood over her like a colossus daring her attackers to take her from you?"

"Yes, but . . ."

"There are no 'buts' about it, *Lord Kantwell*. You were ready to give your life to save her then." Her expression softened, and she said quietly, "Michael, I'm asking you to *give your life to save her now.*"

Michael sucked in a breath and spun away from her. Going to the fireplace, he held tight to the mantelpiece as if he needed to connect to its stability.

To die for her was one thing. To *live* with the woman he loved as her husband, unable to touch her because he must save her for the man she would someday fall in love with—that was another thing altogether.

It didn't take the full power of his mind to determine that he'd be consigning himself to a torture that would make what he'd suffered in the caves at Cliffside seem as nothing by comparison. He wasn't sure he could bear it.

Long moments passed as Michael marshaled and considered his arguments. Lady Ellen stood waiting, praying that she would prevail. When Michael turned back to her, his face was calm. No hint showed of the near panic he felt at the thought of a lifetime of nearness to the woman he loved, but could never tell of that love.

He had his emotions under control now. His duty was clear. If he had to, he could endure the torture of Alissa's constant presence in his life. He'd have to. There was no way he would let Wanemoor near her.

On the positive side, he'd be able to protect her from her uncle from now until he handed her over to the man she'd someday love. He could eventually—God preserve his sanity—assist her in finding that man—a man worthy of her. Then, of course, he'd have to absent himself . . . permanently. Alissa could hardly have two husbands at once. It was only a question of his already chosen fate being delayed a bit.

Taking another deep breath, he told Lady Ellen in a firm, steady voice, "Very well. I will agree to marry . . ."

"Oh, Michael!" She hugged him fiercely. "Thank God! I was so afraid that she would have to marry someone that she didn't love—" She broke off abruptly, a hand across her mouth, her eyes wide with dismay. It wasn't her place to tell him that Alissa loved him.

He never noticed. His attention was on plans for the immediate future. "There is a condition." His expression stern, he told her, "The wedding is to take place on her birthday and not a moment sooner, and from now until that time, you must promise me to search for a more suitable bridegroom."

Oh, dear Heaven, she thought in exasperation. *They are all so dense.* Every single one who wore male attire. Dense and totally lacking in perception! A blind *woman* would be able to see that the two of them, he and Alissa, were not only meant for each other, but already were head over heels in love!

Michael couldn't, though. All Michael could see was

that he had lost the use of an arm. Ellen sighed. That loss had caused a far more important one, she saw, but she could hardly tell her future grandson that he had lost his *mind*!

She rose on her tiptoes and kissed him gently on the cheek. "Thank you, dear. You have greatly relieved my mind."

She could always tell him later that he'd lost his mind.

"I'm glad to be of service, Lady Ellen." His smile went crooked. "Though all I am doing is lending you something that no longer has any value to me."

She sighed inwardly, and vowed to dedicate herself to changing his attitude. Right now, however, she had to get back to Collington House and discover a way to break the news to, and to manage, Alissa.

Chapter Sixteen

Alissa was outraged. "How could you, Grandmother!" She'd be eternally grateful that Lady Ellen had come into her bedchamber and dismissed Button before she had broken her news. At least that had saved her a little humiliation, but she was still angry. "How could you do this to me? How could you go to him, hat in hand, and beg him to marry me? How could you!"

Lady Ellen regarded her calmly. "I could quite easily, my dear. Major Mathers is a gentleman of the highest order, and a hero as well. If I am forced by loathsome necessity to add a man to my family tree, I can see no harm in trying to add one I can be proud of." She cocked her head and added pensively, "Perhaps he will serve in some small way to balance your perfidious uncle in the sight of generations to come."

At her words, Alissa stopped charging around the room looking for something she might throw that would not distress either of them too much to lose. Her anger had almost evaporated at her grandmother's last remark, but she knew better than to let her off too easily.

Turning her reproachful regard on her grandmother, she demanded, "And that was your only reason for choosing him?"

"Well, Lissa, to be absolutely honest, I'd had the opportunity to peruse your list of, er, shall we say, candidates for your hand, after you retired last evening, and I must admit I could find no one on it that I cared to associate with for the rest of my life." She shrugged elaborately. "It seemed only prudent to attempt to influence the outcome in favor of someone whose company I enjoy."

Alissa stared at her suspiciously. Her grandmother was up to something more than finding her a husband, she was certain of it. But what?

Before the younger woman could speak, Lady Ellen added, "And he was closest and available. After all, no one else will want him with that maimed arm." She casually turned away, as if she had said nothing out of the ordinary, but Alissa caught her watching her out of the corner of her eye.

Still Alissa couldn't help her reaction, though she suspected that it was exactly what her grandmother hoped for. When it came to Michael Mathers, she seemed to lack the cool control she usually exercised over her emotions. In this instance it was a relief just to let go. Indeed, it was quite liberating. "How can you say such a thing? I've never heard you be so cruel and heartless! He is more wonderful than any other man I've ever met. Braver! More noble!"

She paused and pictured his solemn face in the moonlight, its sculptured planes accented by the shadows that night in the doorway of the inn, and accused, "Yes, and far more handsome, too, since you've decided to be so uncharacteristically shallow in your judgments." Her voice regained heat. "How can you point to so minor a defect and say that no one will have him! Any woman with half a brain in her head would count herself lucky indeed to marry a man like Michael Mathers!"

Lady Ellen turned back to Alissa, suppressing the triumph she obviously felt, her face guarded so that it expressed only a desire to convey a warning. "I'm certain his debility would be an embarrassment to anyone he married, dear. He is quite clumsy mounting a horse, I noticed." Ellen dredged her mind for more of the words Michael had hurled at her in the wee hours and remembered, "And he could never *drive* you anywhere in any style. After all, he has no whip hand. And . . ." But she stuck at the rest of what Michael had said. She simply couldn't tell her unmarried granddaughter the rest.

"And nothing!" Alissa rose to the bait and all but spat the words at her. "I can't believe this is *you* talking. How can you stand there and tell me any of this matters? It is the *man* one marries, not his physical perfection." Warned by the expression dawning on her grandmother's face, she gasped. Too late she saw the trap that had been laid for her.

"Exactly!" Lady Ellen pounced, triumph in every line of her body. "I'm extremely proud of you for finally saying so. It is precisely what I'd expect of you." She chuckled and said in a low voice, "Though it took you long enough."

Then Lady Ellen's entire attitude softened and she went to Alissa and took her hands. "Oh, Lissa. You think that I went to Michael because you were feeling so hopeless, caught as you are in the very awkward position you've been placed in by your uncle Gerald's shameful behavior, don't you, dear?" She shook her head in denial of that purpose. "But that was not really the reason—or at least not the *only* reason. Indeed, I'm not even certain your plight was the primary one. I went to the Major because *he* is the one who is so hopeless, Lissa."

Alissa stared, stunned. "I don't understand."

"It's quite simple. I firmly believe that the opportunity to save you from your uncle may very well be the saving of the Major's life."

Alissa frowned, speechless. She shook her head, bewildered.

Ellen said very softly, "I believe that the reason Michael resisted our best efforts to have him call on us once we got to Town was because he was purposefully distancing himself from life. He was withdrawing from it with the full intention of soon seeking an end to his own."

Alissa's eyes widened and filled with tears. "Oh, surely not."

"I'm afraid so. He admitted as much to me when he finally agreed to marry you."

Alissa's tears disappeared and a frown marred the perfection of her face. "No. Absolutely not! I can't believe that. You must have misunderstood. Michael Mathers would never commit suicide. Never."

"Of course he wouldn't put a gun to his head. But he *is* fully capable of putting himself at risk time and again until his purpose has been accomplished. And I fully believe he intends to."

"Oh, dear God. He mustn't. He is far too fine a person to be lost to the world."

"Yes, he is."

Alissa surrendered. "Oh, Grandmother, I have never felt so unsure of things in all my life. I've seen my whole world turned upside down in the last three days. I have caused a dear friend's murder. I am so distressed that I can't think what to feel anymore."

"Why, then, are you so angry because I have taken things into my own hands and gone to Michael to ask him to marry you? Can't you trust me to know what needs to be done, Lissa? This isn't just the first step toward solving the dilemma in which *we* find ourselves, this is the first step in saving Michael, as well.

"Don't you see? He will hardly be able to leave you alone to face your uncle after you're wed. He will have to be there to protect you. In addition, he will have a great many responsibilities to shoulder. All of this will require time. I am praying that *in* all that time he will forget that he ever wanted to be free of his life."

Alissa looked a question at Lady Ellen.

"Yes, my dear. It will be up to you to convince our splendid young hero that life is worth the living. And remember, too," Lady Ellen reminded her, "whomever you marry will have complete control of your finances. Complete control over your estates and your servants, you know. Who better to handle them than a man whom we both find so eminently trustworthy?" She gave Alissa's hands a little shake. "Especially when it will save his life."

Alissa pulled free and thrust her hands into her dark, well-ordered curls and pulled, hard. "What a complete simpleton I am! You've trapped me neatly."

"And?"

Alissa locked gazes with her for a moment, then smiled and admitted, "And I suppose I should thank you."

Both of them laughed their relief, then hugged each other tight and burst into tears.

Breakfast at Kantwell House was a little later than usual. The night before, Stone and MacLain had gone out on the town with gentlemen they'd met in Almack's, and Michael had spent the greatest part of the night rearranging his mind to accommodate this new position in which he found himself. As a result, all three had had too much to drink and too little sleep and all three had been slow to rise.

The hour was late for breakfast, so they had the unappreciated benefit of strong morning sunlight spilling across the table from the tall windows that made up most of one wall of the room. It caused MacLain to squint in the light reflected from the white damask tablecloth and reposition his silverware to eliminate the glare off the bowl of his spoon.

After the first cup of coffee, MacLain broke the silence. "How was your evening, Kantwell? You look as if you were up late. Did you read a book?"

Michael looked across the table at him with haggard eyes, weighed his news for shock value, and decided on revenge. "I got engaged."

Stone dropped his cup.

Rearing back in his chair, a startled MacLain announced, "By George! Now I see that you really *don't* have any reason to go out in society!"

Chapter Seventeen

Stone leaned back in his chair. "So how did this betrothal come about, Michael? Or would you rather not say?"

"Quite the contrary." Michael's haggard face was grim. "I have every intention—indeed, every reason—to bring you and MacLain into the picture. I anticipate that I'm going to need your help on this one."

"On getting leg-shackled?" MacLain was aghast.

Michael and Stone shot quelling glances at him and shook their heads at each other.

The butler was hovering, all ears, and Michael ordered, "Cigars, Black. And strong coffee. This promises to be a long discussion." Turning back to his friends, he told them, "Gentlemen, we have a damsel in distress."

Sunlight also brightened the cheery breakfast room at Collington House by the time the family had gathered there.

"Did you sleep well, Alissa?"

"Yes, thank you, Grandmother." A hint of mischief gathered in her eyes. "And you?"

"Yes, thank you. Why should I not have?" She deliberately played into her granddaughter's hands, waiting with a suppressed smile for the outcome.

"Oh, I just wondered. I've been told that people who have something on their conscience . . ."

The joke between them was interrupted by the butler's entrance with a letter borne on a silver salver.

"Thank you, Quillen." Alissa saw the Kantwell crest and the strong, angular handwriting and caught her breath. She turned the note over and over in her hands, strangely reluctant to open it.

Lady Ellen looked up from her embroidery and asked anxiously, "Is that from your uncle?"

Alissa smiled across the table at her grandmother. Quick to reassure her, she said, "No, dear. It's from Viscount Kantwell."

"Ah. Well? What does he say?"

"I haven't opened it yet."

"Spare me the obvious and get to it, Lissa. What does the man say!"

"Are you worried he's begging off?"

"Never! Michael would never do such a thing. It's just that I'm eaten up with curiosity about his next move."

"That's an odd thing to say." Alissa was frowning at her dear grandmother.

"Not at all. I wonder if he will simply play the suitor or mount a military campaign to keep you from further accident."

Alissa applied herself to opening Michael's note. She, too, was impatient to see what it contained. Two terse lines and his title as a signature—it was certainly no billet-doux!

Dear Lady Alissa,
    As the day is a particularly splendid one, I won-

*dered if you might enjoy a ride in the park this after-
noon.
Kantwell*

"Hmmm." Alissa looked across at Lady Ellen with a
twinkle in her eye. "Judging from the tone of his note,
Major Mathers seems to want to play the suitor in a rather
curt and militaristic manner. It cuts straight to the point
like a saber slash." She went on to read the missive aloud.

"My. That does seem a bit abrupt, doesn't it? He hasn't
even said when he'll call for you."

"I imagine that will be stated after I reply."

"Then reply, dear. Reply."

Alissa raised an eyebrow.

"Oh, no. Don't ask me how to do so. And don't think of
refusing because he hasn't made a fuss over you like one
of the Town beaus. He's a soldier first and foremost, I believe. And I think that is what I like about him." She sent
her granddaughter a quick smile. "I think that's what you
like best about him as well, isn't it?"

Alissa's responding smile cleared away the last of Lady
Ellen's doubts about what she had done to bring the two
young people together. "Of course you will accept. You are
betrothed, after all."

Alissa felt herself go a little fluttery at that thought. It
was an utterly new sensation. Betrothed. She was engaged
to the man she admired above all others. In fact, the man
she was head over heels in love with. However, the certain
knowledge that he would never permit himself to recipro-
cate her feelings marred any joy she might feel about it.
While she would revel in every moment they spent together, she would be very careful that no hint of the love
she felt for him was discernible. To let it show would be to
humiliate herself beyond bearing.

She sighed deeply. Why did life have to have taken such
a disconcerting turn in only the last few days? Only last

week, she had been happily at home in her wonderful Collington Park. Surrounded by the family she adored and the servants she held in deepest affection, she'd never imagined that it could all turn topsy-turvy in the matter of moments. Her whole world had been turned upside down! Her uncle's letter, her friend Thomas's death—and then the soul-shattering discovery that she was in love with . . .

She forced her thoughts away from the dismals that threatened her and asked her grandmother, "What on earth shall I wear?"

Lady Ellen took one look at her granddaughter's flushed face and shining eyes and bit her tongue. After all, it would be cruel to tell a girl so obviously, truly in love that if she were going for a ride in the park with her betrothed, the proper attire *would be* a riding habit.

She watched his approach in secret from her place beside her grandmother. Tall and straight without stiffness, he rode with the grace and ease of a man who habitually spent long days in the saddle. He seemed a part of his horse.

Alissa felt her heartbeat quicken. He was going to be hers! She had wept herself to sleep with hopelessness on the very night her grandmother had coerced him into marrying her. Deep inside, her pride writhed at the thought of him marrying her because her dearest grandmama had all but—indeed, even might have—begged him. After all, until her uncle started his campaign against them, she'd had more suitors than any woman had a right to. She'd been the belle of the ball, a diamond of the first water, the toast of London for more years than were to be expected. "An Incomparable," she muttered darkly .

Lady Ellen turned toward her. "What was that, dear?"

"That was absolutely nothing," Alissa stated firmly, her spirits soaring. For it *was* absolutely nothing. All of it. All the praise and adulation, all the false fawning and true admiration, all of it was nothing. A sop to pride, a boast to vanity. Nothing.

Now she had the real prize. The man she loved was to be hers. Being honest with herself, she admitted that, though she would rather, much rather, that he be in love with her, she was practical enough to take him any way she could get him. Once she had unlimited access to Guy Michael Mathers, Fifth Viscount Kantwell, she was going to take full advantage of it.

Using every feminine wile she possessed or had ever observed, she was going to win his love. Or, she vowed, take it by force, if all else failed!

The object of her attention dismounted awkwardly and walked to the door. Alissa was glad that she and her grandmother had stood hidden by the draperies. More than anything, she wanted to avoid his knowing she ever saw him at even the slightest disadvantage.

She turned and gave her grandmother a fierce hug, and all but ran across the room when Quillen tapped upon the drawing room door to announce their guest.

"Alissa!" Lady Ellen's tone was sharp.

"Of course." She gave a deep, self-disparaging sigh. "I'm behaving like a schoolgirl."

"Sit!" And then, "Enter," to the butler.

Alissa ran to the nearest chair and sat, picking up a book of poetry that happened to be there. "That was a pleasant line, don't you think, Grandmama?"

Under cover of Quillen's announcing the viscount, Lady Ellen hissed, "Book is upside down." Then she moved forward to greet Michael warmly as her granddaughter slammed the book back onto the little side table as if it had burned her fingers.

"Michael, dear boy. It is wonderful to see you."

Mischief lit his eyes as he captured and carried her hand to his lips. "And after so long a while, too."

Ellen took back her hand and tapped him reprovingly

on the arm with it. "Rogue," she said to him, sotto voce. "You look as if you could do with more sleep yourself."

He fought to repress a grin and lost. "We had a slight commotion at the house last night."

Alissa rose and joined them where they stood in the middle of the room. "Oh?" she queried, the expression on her face guarded. "I trust it wasn't an unpleasantness."

She watched him carefully, and Michael knew that she had been made aware of her grandmother's mission to Kantwell House. "Yes, it was." He refrained from looking her way as Lady Ellen drew a sharp breath. Continuing smoothly, he added, "Nothing out of the ordinary, however."

Nothing out of the ordinary! Alissa thought she was going to explode. *How dare he! Was he telling them he received proposals of marriage every night of the week? In his nightshirt, no doubt!*

Michael saw the outrage in his beloved's lovely eyes. Before matters got beyond his control, he grasped her hand and lifted it to his lips in spite of—and pretending he did not notice—her strong resistance. He kissed it gently and restored it to her, saying blandly, "Putting one's inebriated comrades to bed is not an occupation that is lacking in the experience of cavalrymen, my lady. It does, however, interrupt one's repose."

Lady Ellen's eyes were round as saucers. What a marvelous save that had been! Of course Alissa knew it for just what it was, but Ellen was certain she could hardly call her brand-new fiancé a liar.

"I think there may have been another reason you were sleepless last night, Lord Kantwell." Alissa's chin was high.

Michael turned a calm gaze on her flushed face and said in all sincerity, "I did lose quite a bit of sleep in thinking of my good fortune. And since I have the good fortune to address you as my promised bride, Lady Alissa, would you mind calling me by my Christian name?" He looked at her a little wistfully, as if reminding her of the times in the past when she had used it. "Please, I'd really like you to call me Michael."

She capitulated. She did intend to win his love, not this argument, after all. More flies with honey than with vinegar. Grandmother would have said it if she'd dared.

Smiling, Alissa took his arm, and excusing themselves from Lady Ellen, the two of them went out to the horses.

Chapter Eighteen

The day was splendid, just as Michael had said in his note. The temperature had risen and most of the snow had melted. It was as if nature had decided to make amends for the freak blizzard and grant an especially pleasant day. Riders and drivers alike were taking advantage of the unseasonable warmth and were headed for Hyde Park in droves.

Alissa was smiling as she went to the mounting block, giving Michael no time to offer to lift her into the saddle. Once mounted, she gestured unobtrusively for the groom walking Michael's Gladiator to bring him to the block, as she'd prearranged.

Michael looked a little startled, but mounted the block and stepped aboard his gelding with no comment beyond one eyebrow raised at her.

Alissa felt a blush coming and hastily turned away. Did the man miss nothing? It was going to be difficult to keep him from catching her taking care of him, she could see that clearly.

Fortunately, her mare was fresh and decided to take fright at the light reflected from a puddle, so Alissa could pretend to be more occupied with controlling her than she had any need to be.

Michael was beside her instantly, his big gelding blocking the mare's way. "Are you all right?"

Now that her heightened color could be attributed to her mare's misbehavior, Alissa smiled at him and relaxed. Laughing, she told him, "I'm fine. Firefly is just being silly. She'll settle down in a minute. Let's go on, shall we?"

They rode side by side through the busy thoroughfares to Hyde Park. The clatter of carriages and the rumble of wagons and drays made conversation difficult, so they rode to and through the gates of the park without speaking, each content with the other's presence, neither feeling the need to chat.

In the park it was quieter, and the scenery was much more enjoyable. There was sunlight on the bare branches of the trees, making them seem softer and less barren. Everywhere melted snow ran in gutters and drains and formed puddles that reflected the bright sky.

Riders on fine horses groomed to perfection rode in groups or pairs or alone, all enjoying this particularly pleasant day. Carriages of every design, most with the tonneaus open so that their occupants could more easily see and be seen, clogged the lanes through the park as they stopped so their owners could pass the time of day with acquaintances.

"Shall we head for someplace to really ride, or would you like to visit with any friends you might see?" Michael smiled as he placed himself at her disposal.

"I think I'd like to ride a bit first, if you don't mind. Visiting from the back of a fractious horse can be a problem, and I'm afraid Firefly has been without exercise for too long."

A twinkle appeared in Michael's eyes. "Well, we can't gallop on Rotten Row, of course. However, if after a sedate moment or two at the canter, your mare should run away . . ." He left the sentence trailing, knowing she would know what he proposed, believing she and her mare would enjoy a good run.

"You, of course would have no trouble catching me on that big horse you ride." There was a twinkle in Alissa's eye, too, but there was a wicked gleam behind it.

Michael lifted an eyebrow. "I trust I'm not going to regret this."

He was destined to discover the answer to that for himself.

With a shriek of dismay—suitably modulated to keep from sending every horse in the park into a breakneck race for home—Alissa spurred her mare and gave her her head. Firefly gave one monstrous buck to protest such unexpected treatment. Alissa pretended to be in danger of losing her seat, and deliberately dropped a rein.

Michael's heart almost stopped until he saw the grin on Alissa's face, and the firmness of her seat in spite of the wild gestures she was making to convince onlookers that she had lost control of her horse.

As Firefly tore off, Michael put his reins in his teeth long enough to settle his hat more firmly, took them back in his hand, and sent Gladiator charging after her. For added color, he shouted, "Hold on, Lady Alissa! I'm coming."

Purposely he didn't catch her, though the longer legs of his taller mount could easily have closed the entire distance between them. Instead, he let Gladiator run with his head even with her mare's flanks so that they could converse easily—and he could avoid the clumps of mud Firefly's hooves were throwing out behind her.

"You ride well," he told Alissa, absurdly pleased.

"I love it."

"You ride frequently at Collington Park, then?"

"Every day before breakfast."

"An admirable habit."

"Thank you." She flashed him a smile over her shoulder. "It keeps the cobwebs at bay and gives me the feeling of freedom when matters pertaining to the house and servants become too pressing." Alissa was gathering her mare as she spoke, preparatory to spinning away from him and off into the wooded area beside them. There her smaller mount would have the advantage of maneuverability, and she fully intended to wipe that superbly confident look off his face.

Wondering at the wicked gleam that had reappeared in Alissa's eyes, Michael glanced ahead to see how near they were to the boundary of the park. What he saw in addition to that boundary was a man with a fowling piece pointing right at them. "Down!" he shouted, and launched himself at Alissa, grabbing her around the waist, pulling her from her saddle. As they fell together, he heard the ball from the would-be assassin's fowling piece hiss by his ear. Again his hat went flying.

He twisted as they plummeted toward the muddy turf, making his own body a cushion for Alissa's.

"What on earth?" Alissa demanded as soon as she had caught her breath. She struggled to rise.

Michael rolled over and pushed her down again, under him, shielding her with his body as he frantically looked for the man with the gun. He saw a closed carriage speed away just outside the park, then his view was obstructed by a gentleman catching Firefly and starting back with her to where they lay. Other riders were rushing up from behind them.

Suddenly, Alissa began to laugh. "This is getting to be a habit with you, Major Mathers. Only this time, thank heavens, there is no snow. Will you always want to push me down under you?"

Michael's mind exploded with desire. He clenched his teeth to keep from telling her, "Yes! Yes, damn it, I *will* always want to push you down under me. In warm meadows full of spring flowers! In sun-kissed sand by the sea! On furs before a rough fireplace. And in my bed . . . oh, God, yes, in my bed!"

Alissa's eyes widened as she correctly read the expression in his. She tried to take a breath to say something, anything, but the weight of his body kept her from doing it. She must do something to break the spell that was spinning out between them. She must. . . . But it was so wonderful lying here half under his lean frame, so wonderful to look up and see his dear face so close to her own.

"Are you two all right?" The first of the riders had reached them.

"What the deuce happened?" The man leading Firefly arrived and stared at them, full of curiosity.

A third rider rushed up. "I say, old chap, that was an awful spill! Couldn't you have stopped the horses any other way?" The speaker's eyes widened as he saw Michael's bound arm and he stuttered, "Oh! Of c-course you c-couldn't. Stupid of me. So s-sorry and all that." In desperation he added, "I'll go catch your gray." He turned away, red-faced, and pretended to herd Gladiator, who had no need of his assistance, back to them.

They rose hastily from the grass then, Michael springing up with a mighty push of his arm and reaching back to pull Alissa to her feet. Alissa swayed, pretending dizziness, and leaned against him for a moment, reveling in the hard strength of his frame, glad to have this excuse to be held for just an instant.

"Are you hurt?" Michael's deep voice was even deeper with concern.

"No. I'm fine. Just had the breath knocked out of me and got up too fast."

Chagrined, Michael apologized. "I shouldn't have pulled you to your feet so quickly."

Alissa shot him a mischievous look. "No doubt you only did so to get me up before the next charge."

He frowned, not catching her meaning.

"You saved me being trampled by the rescue cavalry."

He grinned at her then, relieved and amused. Softly he asked her, "I don't suppose anyone has ever accused you of being a perfect minx?"

Their rescuers were mostly gone, having seen that the two of them were none the worse for their fall. Only the man holding Firefly remained. Alissa went to the mare and gathered up her reins. "Thank you very much for catching her, sir. She's quite flighty, and might have done herself some injury if you had not."

"You're welcome, my lady. May I assist you to mount?"

"That won't be necessary, thank you. My escort will see to it." She faced her saddle and bent her knee so that Michael could grab her ankle and toss her into the saddle as a jockey is given a leg up. It was the only possible way to aid her that did not require the use of two hands.

The man tipped his hat and rode away.

They were alone again. Michael threw her up into the saddle.

He had never loved her more than he did at that moment.

Sitting on Firefly looking down at him, she said as if nothing untoward had happened, "Your hat is over there by that tree. Don't forget it."

Michael retrieved the article in question, strode over to his horse, and, while Alissa carefully busied herself with arranging the skirt of her mud-spattered habit, mounted.

She picked up their conversation. "My grandfather frequently called me a minx. But he never called me a perfect one. Grandfather used to say that nothing here on earth is really perfect."

Michael looked hard at her, his eyes dark with banked passion. "Oh," he drawled, "I'm not so sure of that."

Blushing at the extravagance of his implied compliment, Alissa led the way out of Hyde Park and toward home.

"I suppose this would be a bad time to ask why you knocked me off my mare."

Relieved that the rush of their ride and the usual noise from the streets beyond the park's boundary had kept her from hearing the shot that had been fired at them, he said, "I just thought it was one way for us to get to know each other better."

Alissa stared at him in astonishment. Now his expression, so intense a moment ago, was perfectly bland.

She just hoped she could get her mouth closed before they got to Collington House!

Chapter Nineteen

"Grandmother will have a fit when she sees all this mud on my habit. She'll be certain I was thrown." Alissa chuckled. "She's convinced that Firefly is a dangerous horse." She turned the full battery of her smile on Michael. "I shall be very interested to hear you explain to her that you are responsible, not Firefly."

Michael grinned back at her, secretly elated that she had no idea he had thrown her to the ground, no idea of the mortal danger she had been in. "Shall I tell her I'm merely trying to establish a tradition?"

"Hardly! She was shocked enough at the way you shoved my face into the snow when our carriage was stopped by Uncle's thugs."

Michael could play her game. "I did *not* shove your face in the snow. I merely kept you from being shot."

"That's certainly an interesting 'merely.'" Alissa knew she was being silly, but she didn't care. She'd been so grimly hopeless such a short while ago—resigned to marrying the first man she could beg into it, and here God had given her the desire of her heart. He'd given her Michael. Michael, who was so unfailingly brave and who was strong enough to stand between her and her uncle. Michael, who had already amply demonstrated that he could keep her little family safe.

Her heart was singing, and she was as giddy as a schoolgirl. She didn't care if she seemed silly. What else could she be when she felt as if all her cares, as well as her own true heart, had taken wing?

"It seemed the least I could do."

"I *am* grateful, you know." The laughter had gone out of her face, though her eyes were still aglow. He had saved them all, but she was aware that he could very well have been killed instead.

Michael wasn't willing to let her laughter die. He'd seen too little of it, so he teased, "I strive to oblige."

Alissa's laughter came back, and they were both smiling as the grooms took their horse in the street in front of Collington House. One of them however, signaled to a footman, who ran, wide-eyed, back into the house to tell the Dowager Countess that her granddaughter had obviously had a fall.

"Oh, dear." Alissa stood attempting to shake some of the mud out of the folds of her riding skirt as she watched the footman disappear. "There goes the word of my fall to Grandmama."

"We'd best stand ready to catch the next footman then."

She looked up at him, frowning. "Catch a footman? Whatever for?"

"Unless I have misread Lady Ellen, I imagine that he will be running for a doctor. I don't think you want one."

Alissa laughed. "Indeed not. I shall leave the entrapment of that messenger to you."

"Come." He took her hand. And as he did, lightning leapt up both their arms. Only the fact that he had already framed his next words made it possible for him to speak them as they stared, thunderstruck, into each other's eyes. "We must head her off before she gives the footman his orders," he managed breathlessly.

"Yes." Alissa finally achieved speech when she got her own breath back. "We must." As the first to recover, she tugged at his hand and they hurried, a little distractedly, into the house.

Lady Ellen, looking every inch the Dowager Countess in spite of her diminutive size, came charging out of the drawing room to meet them. "Alissa! Darling! Are you all right? I shall have that terrible horse shot!"

"It wasn't Firefly, Grandmama." Alissa pulled off her stylish riding hat and tossed it onto a chair. With an arch look at Michael, she ran her fingers through her dark curls and said, "The Major pushed me off."

Shocked, Lady Ellen demanded, "He *what*!"

"I shall let the Major explain." Laughing, Alissa kissed her grandmother on the cheek and flung herself down on the sofa to watch the fun.

Michael hadn't relinquished his hat to the butler. He still had it under his arm as he'd carried it from the park. He flushed slightly as Lady Ellen looked at it quizzically. "Was Quillen so anxious to tattle that he neglected to properly take care of our guest?"

"N-no, Countess." Michael almost grinned to hear himself stutter like a schoolboy. He would have if it weren't so important to him that no one take any interest in his blasted hat. He did grin then, for that was the exact problem. His hat *was* blasted. High in the crown was a not-so-neat hole made by the ball from the fowling piece he'd seen leveled at Alissa. If she hadn't insisted, he'd have left the damned thing in the park where it had fallen.

"Well, then, Major?" Lady Ellen wanted to know. "Why in the world are you holding so tight to the dratted thing?"

Michael moved quickly to a side table and placed his

hat carefully on it so that the hole in the beaver did not show.

Lady Ellen watched him with interest.

"Well, Major," Alissa teased, "aren't you going to explain how we got all muddy?"

Michael took a deep breath. Like hell he was. He let the breath out again and said, "Simple. We fell off our horses."

"Wretch!" Alissa cried. "You know that isn't true." She looked at her grandmother. "Or at least that isn't exactly what happened."

Without speaking, Lady Ellen lifted an eyebrow. She wasn't smiling.

"True." Michael decided he might as well enjoy the tale. "The truth is I knocked her off Firefly."

"Oh?" Lady Ellen still wasn't smiling.

Michael thought her the coolest head he'd seen lately, and was doubtful he could distract her from learning what had really happened. He was going to give it a damn good try, however. "Well, yes, Countess. I was, er, that is, *we* were pretending that Firefly had run away so that we could have a bit of a gallop."

"Which is forbidden on Rotten Row, young man."

"Yes. That's precisely it. That was why we decided to have Alissa pretend to be run away with. I could follow to rescue her, and we'd get in one good run before we had to begin behaving again."

Lady Ellen strolled casually toward the side table. "I see. And you agreed to this, Alissa?"

Alissa sat up straight, her air of relaxation gone. "Yes, Grandmother."

"May I ask just why you did so?" Lady Ellen was looking down at Michael's hat. Idly she touched it.

Michael took in a sharp breath.

Alissa said, "It was harmless, and my mare needed it, dear. Firefly had been cooped up for so long. You know the grooms can't really give her any proper exercise here in Town. She really needed to run."

Lady Ellen gave Michael a cool, appraising look and said calmly to her granddaughter, "And your gallop ended with the Major throwing you both off your horses, is that correct?"

"Yes." Alissa sounded almost like a child again. She shook her head and said more firmly, "Yes, it's correct as far as it goes." She looked apologetically at Michael.

"I thought it went as far as the ground." Lady Ellen didn't sound as if she were making a joke, and her attitude silenced Alissa.

Michael cleared his throat in order to begin an explanation, but Lady Ellen threw up a hand to stop him. "Alissa," she said sternly, "I think it is time you excused yourself and went up to your bath."

With a rueful look at Michael, Alissa rose obediently and left the room.

There was a long silence in the drawing room. It was so quiet they could hear the door to Alissa's bedchamber close.

Instantly Lady Ellen turned on Michael with his hat in her hand. Poking a finger through the hole the ball had made, she demanded, "All right, Major. You will now please tell me how this happened."

"As we neared the park boundary, I saw a man aiming a rifle at Alissa. There was no time to waste. I dived on her and carried her to the ground. I held her there under me until I saw her assailant rush away in a closed carriage. By then, others had gathered or were coming to help us."

"So the whole world saw you lying on top of my granddaughter in Hyde Park."

Her dryly spoken words caused Michael's face to flame. Too well he remembered his lustful thoughts as Alissa had lain under him. He tried to answer as if he were as innocent as he should have been. "I saw no other way to ensure her safety, Lady Ellen."

She regarded him steadily.

"There, er, was no other cover nearby."

"I see." Still she regarded him without a smile. Finally she said, "I think it is time to get an announcement of your betrothal into the newspapers, Major."

Michael bowed. "I'll see to it at once, Countess."

"Good day, Major."

Michael was relieved to be dismissed.

When he had gone, Ellen permitted herself a smile. Not only had he saved her precious granddaughter's life, a matter for long prayers of gratitude later, but he'd blushed when she'd accused him of letting the whole world see him lying on top of Alissa without an apparent reason.

The very nice young man had not only had the good grace to be embarrassed by the impropriety of his action, but she'd detected a hint of guilt in that embarrassment. Unless she missed her guess, he had been prey to lustful thoughts as he lay with Alissa under him.

At least, she most fervently hoped so!

At that moment, Quillen came into the room. "May I get you anything, my lady?" His voice showed his concern.

"Yes, Quillen," she said with a smile. "I rather think you might. I've quite a desperate need for some sherry, please."

Chapter Twenty

There was another note from Michael the next morning. Alissa found it beside her place at the breakfast table. Opening it with her butter knife, she read it, smiling.

I trust you are no worse for wear after your "fall"
yesterday, and hope that you might be persuaded to
ride with me again this afternoon. I promise not to
throw you off your horse. You have my word on it.
Hopefully,
Michael

Alissa burst out laughing and passed the note to her grandmother. "It seems I am to ride with the Major again today."

"Does the prospect please you?"

Alissa pretended to consider the question, then gave it up. "Yes. Yes, it does. Very much."

Lady Ellen smiled. "I'm glad, dear." Her smile was a

forced one, however. Would there be another attempt on her granddaughter's life today? Please, God, she hoped not.

Suddenly Lady Ellen gasped as another possibility occurred to her. It took both a bride and a groom to make a marriage! Suppose the shot that destroyed Michael's hat hadn't been meant for Alissa at all? Suppose it had nearly killed its intended target?

Oh, dear God! Had they put Michael Mathers in dire jeopardy by enlisting his aid in their affairs? God knew Alissa already believed that she had killed Sir Thomas Lane.

Alissa grasped her grandmother's arm. "Grandmama, are you all right?"

"Yes, dear. I'm fine." She smiled to try to put the younger woman at ease. "Just a twinge. We have them at my age, you know." She cocked her head. "Isn't that the Major I hear arriving?"

The distraction worked. Alissa asked again, "Are you certain you're all right?" and when Lady Ellen assured her that she was, Alissa planted a kiss on her cheek and rushed to meet the Major.

Mounting was the usual flurry of Alissa trying to save Michael and Michael refusing to be saved. Now that he'd learned she'd accept being thrown into the saddle like a jockey, her slender ankle in his grasp, he was not to be denied. To humor her, however, he did use the mounting block, but his eyes told her plainly that he was aware of her subterfuge to save him embarrassment.

Each of them was in perfect charity with the other, and again they didn't attempt to converse over the din of traffic on the way to the park. As they entered the park, Michael turned to her. "By the way, Lady Alissa, I have placed the announcement of our betrothal in the newspapers, and there may be those who have seen . . ."

"I say, Kantwell, you sly old dog!" A pair of cavalrymen in their red-coated uniforms rode up to them. "We demand to meet your fiancée!"

A couple of Alissa's acquaintance rode up next, and introductions were made all around. Pleasant farewells and promises of later meetings were duly exchanged, and they rode on a few yards.

"Oh! There you are!"

Michael looked up at the cry to see a very pretty young woman with an unruly wealth of flame-red hair riding recklessly down on them. "Alissa, dear, what wonderful news!"

Alissa smiled and told Michael, who had shifted in his saddle as if he intended to catch the woman's horse by the bridle, "It's all right. She rides as well as I do."

"That's small comfort."

"What do you mean?" she demanded.

"You fall off."

Alissa burst out laughing. "Nevertheless, she's a magnificent rider, truly she is."

"Truly I am what?" the redhead asked, stopping her horse exactly beside Alissa's. She leaned over and gave Alissa a hug.

"A rambunctious hoyden!" Alissa teased.

The woman turned to Michael. "It's true. I am. But I'm also a Duke's only daughter with seven older brothers, so I get away with it. And I'm Alissa's oldest friend." She grinned and announced, "I'm Rosalynda. Lyn for short." She looked him up and down, then turned back to her friend. "I approve."

Michael bowed. "Thank you."

"Approve of what?" Alissa wanted to know.

"Don't play coy, Alissa. I approve of your fiancé, of course. Kenneth"—she looked at Michael again as she explained—"my middle brother"—then turned back to Alissa—"read us the announcement that was in this morning's *Times*." She laughed merrily. "It's going to spoil his whole day."

"Lyn! Haven't you forgiven poor Kenneth yet?"

"No, I haven't, and I probably won't. Laming my favorite horse is a serious matter. He'd absolutely no business riding him."

"Oh, dear, is Tanglefoot permanently lamed, then?"

"No. Jobson, our head groom, says he'll be 'right as a trivet' in a few more weeks. Though, frankly, I can't imagine why he thinks anyone would want to ride a trivet."

Mischief sparkled out of her warm brown eyes. "I suppose I shall forgive Kenneth when Tanglefoot is well enough to beat his precious old Zeus in one of our impromptu races sometime in the spring. Until then he can just suffer," she said airily. Then she told Alissa earnestly, "And I'm truly delighted that losing you to Lord Kantwell will make Kenneth all the more miserable."

Michael watched the two women, and decided that Lady Rosalynda had won a place in his heart. Thanks to her kind foolishness, Alissa was laughing. Impulsively he asked, "Won't you ride with us, Lady Lyn?"

"Oh, I like that 'Lady Lyn.' And yes, I'd love to. Thank you." To Alissa she said, "You really need me to anyway. You won't believe the questions all those quizzes up ahead are getting ready to fire at you."

Michael saw that, indeed, there seemed to be a prodigious number of riders milling around five carriages that were blocking their way. "I suppose it would be bad form to take off across country."

Alissa chuckled. "Yes, it would be. We can hardly be runaways twice in two days."

"Hmmm. Too bad. I think we're in for it."

"Here we go again," Alissa murmured as the first of the riders reached them.

"Kantwell! About time, old boy. Congratulations!"

"What great news!" The second rider was smiling as broadly as the first.

A third man beamed and told Michael, "Snabbled the best one of the bunch right out from under our noses. Well done!"

The next rider was a woman in a dark tan habit. Her expression was far less pleasant. So were her words. "Alissa, my dear. One must offer you best wishes for great happiness, of course, but isn't this a little sudden?"

Alissa took a breath to reply, her eyes flashing.

Lady Rosalynda stepped into the breach ahead of her. "No, Wanda, it isn't the least bit sudden," she said firmly. "Alissa and Lord Kantwell have known each other for absolutely dogs' years, and have corresponded for ages and ages. All through the war, you know." She turned to Michael, blatantly demanding support for her prevarication. "Isn't that true, my lord?"

Michael smiled broadly. He was hardly going to call this imp a liar, so, in for a penny, in for a pound. He told the assembled company, "Oh, yes, Alissa wrote to me every day."

Alissa fought down a gasp.

"And, I," he added hastily, "wrote at every opportunity." He turned a warm smile on his betrothed. "Our correspondence was all that kept me going."

Alissa's eyes showed him clearly what she thought of his comments, but there was laughter in them as well.

"And of course, the moment they saw each other again, they knew their love would last forever." Rosalynda sighed, observing a moment of rapture. Then she plowed back into the fray. Glaring at Michael she demanded, "Didn't you?"

Michael could have laughed at her performance, but he was onstage again, and this time his part took no effort. For this was no lie. He would cut out his heart if Alissa asked it of him. Why should he not lay it bare to this group of her friends to preserve her dignity?

Looking solemnly down into Alissa's eyes, he said softly, "Indeed. The moment our eyes met I knew that there would never be anyone else for me."

Three of the ladies in the barouche next to which they were all standing sighed audibly.

Alissa was having trouble breathing. Michael's words had taken her breath away. Even if she'd been willing to, there was no reply she could make. She was bereft of speech.

Wanda wasn't to be so easily deterred. "I wonder you didn't show up here last season to be with her."

Michael was beginning to dislike this woman. The smile he sent her was a tight one. "I was . . ."

"Lord Kantwell was detained on important business, Wanda." Lyn turned her horse in such a manner that its rump slammed into the shoulder of Wanda's horse.

"I say! Have a care. You nearly unseated me!"

"Oh, really? I'm so sorry. I had no idea you were such an indifferent rider."

It was the woman in tan's turn to gasp. She didn't hold hers back, however. She used it to show the depths of her exasperation. "I warn you, Rosalynda, you are your own worst enemy, and someday someone is going to put you in your proper place. You just wait and see!"

Lyn covered a yawn with her gloved hand. Unfortunately, it was her whip hand. Somehow the tip of her lash connected with the tip of the nose of the other woman's horse. The horse leapt backward. Lady Wanda sprawled forward out of her saddle and would have landed in the mud at their horses' feet had not two of the gentlemen riders caught her arms. They held her in the air between them, not quite certain what to do next.

Lyn spoke to her suspended enemy. "At least, my dear, when I am put in my proper place, I will still be mounted."

Rapidly backing her horse away from the group, she caused her mount to rear slightly. Thus creating a flamboyant exit, she left the park.

After a moment, Michael said, "We appear to be blocking the way." He tipped his hat to those surrounding them, smiled, and said, "I bid you good day." Alissa beside him, he rode on.

When they were safely out of earshot, Michael said to her, "Today, Lady Alissa, it seems we have shown the world how very glad we are to be betrothed."

Alissa shot him a rueful glance. As the first mention of their engagement in public, it had certainly been an interesting one. Recalling her friend's championship of her betrothal to Michael and the lies she had told, she couldn't help herself. Throwing her head back, she indulged herself in a burst of delighted laughter. When it subsided, she turned to her companion, and said, "You know, it is a very good thing that neither Rosalynda nor I are Roman Catholics."

Smiling, he asked, as he knew she intended he should, "And why is that?"

"Because after this day's work we would each be obliged to light so many candles that together we would probably burn the church down."

Before they had finished laughing together, a curricle with a couple she knew only slightly met them and pulled up as they approached.

"Lady Alissa!" the woman called. "How very nice to see you. We hadn't heard you were in London."

"I arrived only the day before yesterday." *Dear Lord! Could it have been just three days ago that she had met Michael, left the pleasant inn, almost been abducted and gone . . .* She yanked her mind back to the present, greeted each by name, and said, "I'd like you to meet my fiancé, Lord Kantwell."

More people spotted them and rode over. They went

through a new set of introductions and more wishes for their happiness. And, of course, the blizzard and the now unseasonably mild weather were discussed at length.

Alissa was ready to bolt before she got through the next few minutes of introductions and congratulations to Michael and felicitations and best wishes for their happiness. The enthusiasm of their well-wishers had drawn several others from the far corners of the park, and Michael handled them all adroitly.

"Yes, it was sudden." And "The announcement was in this morning's *Times*." Gracefully he ducked the question of how long they had known each other by smiling down at her and saying, "Not long enough, but now we are going to have a lifetime together."

By the time all the fuss over them had concluded, Alissa's head was spinning. Even so, she'd enjoyed admiring Michael's handling of both their friends and the merely curious members of high society who surrounded them.

Gladiator stood like a rock, but Firefly was beginning to fidget when Michael said in his deep, quiet voice, "I fear we are late for tea with Alissa's grandmother. I pray you will excuse us," causing all the laughing well-wishers to disperse.

Masterfully, Michael steered their horses toward a less traveled path, and eagerly Alissa rode off beside him.

"Heavens!" she said as soon as they were safely out of the park.

Michael laughed, a deep pleasant sound. "I'm afraid you must become accustomed to all the interest, Lady Alissa. It would seem that you are the latest news."

Alissa looked at him, and pretended to frown. It was far from a demonstration of her true feelings. Inside she was joyous. It was a beautiful day. No one had seemed to notice Michael's arm, though she was certain they all had. Because of their tact, her faith in her social class had been restored.

Michael had demonstrated to the world that he not only was willing to marry her but was looking forward to doing so—even though she knew the latter was not true. Seeing that he was more than able socially in his handling of what must have been an extremely trying situation for him pleased her. She had known that he was brave and noble. Today she had learned that he was inventive, humorous— and something infinitely more important. He was very, very *kind*.

But most of all, she was happy because today was the first time she had heard him really laugh.

Chapter Twenty-one

As *they approached* Collington House, Alissa looked ahead, cried, "My uncle!" and spurred her mare. Michael was close behind her as she reached the front door, slipped out of her saddle, and ran past the elegant equipage with the Collington arms emblazoned on its doors.

Cursing, Michael leapt from his own horse, commanded "Guard!" for all the world as if he spoke to a dog, and spared a single glance at Gladiator to see if the big gelding had successfully blocked Alissa's fractious mare. Muttering phrases he hadn't used since his army days, he took the steps three at a time. Charging past Quillen, who was bellowing for grooms to tend the abandoned horses, he caught up with Alissa just as she was entering one of the drawing rooms.

Lady Ellen stood in the middle of the room, a small, straight figure with a pale face full of defiance.

Looming over her, her son, the detestable Lord Withers, shouted down at her, "I read that bogus announcement in the papers. Foolishness! Lies! Nobody is going to save you by marrying my niece, you old fool! Get ready to . . ."

Thrusting past Alissa as she ran to her grandmother's side, a snarling Michael grabbed the Earl's shoulder and spun him around. Drawing his hand back, he smashed his fist into the Earl's jaw, sending him sprawling.

At that moment Quillen arrived in the doorway, breathing heavily. "Oh, miGod!"

"Haul this carrion out to his carriage and throw him in. If he comes to on the way, tell him I await hearing from his seconds!"

"No, Michael!" Alissa rushed to him and grasped his arm. "That is just what he wishes. He'd like nothing better than to kill you. He's a premier duelist!"

Now Michael was snarling at her. "Just how do you think he could best me? Do you think I've never fought off more than one man with no more physical ability than I now have? This cursed arm isn't useless for the first time just because this time its uselessness is permanent." Eyes aflame, his face was the face of an avenging angel. "God grant that he does challenge me. It'll be my pleasure to kill the bastard!"

Nervous laughter erupted from Lady Ellen. "Dearest Michael, what dreadful language! And I love every syllable of it."

"Loved language or not, you should *not* have done it," Alissa scolded. "We have only three days left until our wedding—two if you don't count what is left of today— and I think the time would be better spent planning *that,* rather than trying to find an opportunity to avoid it by getting yourself killed!"

Michael went deathly still. "Would you rather I had let his abuse of your grandmother go unpunished, Lady Alissa?" His voice was as cold as his heart. He was certain now that the only value he had for Lady Alissa Collington was that of a barrier to stop her uncle's enforcement of that unfortunate clause in her grandfather's will. And he had hoped . . .

Alissa had her arms around her grandmother. "No. No, of course not."

He stood just looking at her for a long moment. Then he tucked his hat under his arm like a military shako, clicked his heels together, and said, "Thank you for a pleasant ride, Lady Alissa." Turning to her grandmother, he bowed stiffly and added, "Good day, Lady Ellen," spun around, and marched out of the room.

Alissa stood in stunned silence, staring at his retreating, rigid back. She had never seen this icy side of Michael, and it was devastating. After their wonderful ride in the park, it was incomprehensible. It was a moment before she could get her breath. When she had, she asked her grandmother woodenly, her eyes still on the doorway through which Michael had departed, "You *are* all right, aren't you, Grandmama?"

Lady Ellen was watching her carefully. "Yes, dear. I'm all right." Then she asked very softly, "But are you?"

Alissa dissolved into tears. Flinging herself facedown on the settee, she wept as if her heart were breaking.

Ellen slipped carefully onto the sofa at her granddaughter's head and encouraged her to lift her head into her lap. When Alissa had complied, just as she had always done over the years when she was growing up, Ellen sat stroking her back and murmuring softly to her.

"No, I'm not. Today was wonderful. Perfect. Now, everything's all horrid." Alissa's muffled voice answered her grandmother's platitudes. "Everything is simply awful!"

Ellen waited for the next burst of sobs to end, then suggested quietly, "Why don't you tell me about it?"

Alissa lifted her head. "You *know* all about it."

"Yes, but you will be so much better if you sit up and tell me all that *you* feel about it."

Alissa shot upright. "What I feel? I feel dreadful. On

every account! I finally solved our problem by finding someone to marry us. I even finally found the man I love and long to spend the rest of my life with." Her eyes filled with tears again. "And then I have to see him killed in a duel with my uncle!" She threw herself back into her grandmother's lap.

Ellen began stroking her granddaughter again. "It isn't as bad as all that, you know."

Alissa turned her head and looked up at her with one eye.

"It really isn't."

"No?"

"You've seen him fight, remember."

"Yes." Her head was lifted and she was regarding Lady Ellen with both eyes.

"And he was quite fierce, wasn't he?"

Alissa sat up slowly.

"Wasn't he?" Ellen insisted.

"Yes. Yes, he was." Alissa's tears stopped falling.

"And quite able?"

"Yes." Alissa wiped her eyes with the back of her hand.

Lady Ellen handed her a lace-trimmed handkerchief and said, "And that was against many more men than just your uncle, wasn't it?"

Alissa sniffed. "There were six."

"And?"

Alissa sat up straight. "All right, Grandmama. I see your point. He is certainly a warrior. . . ." She paused to more fully feel the thrill that ran through her as she spoke the ancient word.

"And?" Lady Ellen refused to desist until she'd made her point.

"And he was victorious. At least he was as far as it went. I have to be honest and say that he was facing three men there at the end, and if one of them had taken time to reload one of their pistols . . ." She shuddered at that thought.

"But they didn't, and I think that he might have prevailed against them since they did not." Ellen watched her closely, glad the tears were over, then added briskly, "We'll never know, of course, as his friends arrived riding *vent-à-terre* before it came to actual hand-to-hand combat."

"Grandmother, surely he was at a disadvantage with but one hand."

"It didn't seem to bother him just now with your uncle."

Alissa frowned deeply. "Well, he did take Uncle Gerald by surprise."

"True. I think his temper got the best of him, don't you?"

"Indeed it did!"

Lady Ellen grinned. "I was quite flattered to see that a verbal assault on my person could rouse a gentleman to such violence in my defense. It was wonderful. Took me back to my girlhood."

"Do you mean to tell me that men actually fought over you with their *fists*?" Alissa tried to look shocked.

"Ours was a more boisterous day, my dear. Back in those days, we hadn't yet acquired all the manners we are constrained by now."

It was Alissa's turn to grin. "I've heard that elopements back then often took the form of abductions."

"Yes. Men were bolder. Less restrained by manners, as I said." She sighed. "One of my suitors planned my abduction to steal me from your grandfather shortly before our wedding."

"No! How exciting. Tell me."

Lady Ellen's brows snapped down in a frown. "Absolutely not! How can you ask me to put such terrible notions in the head of my favorite grandchild?" She smiled, glad to have distracted Alissa. "Besides, nothing came of it."

"What happened?"

"My brother John got wind of it and whisked me off to his house. Allen, my would-be abductor, couldn't find me. The next day, Papa told him what for, and I married your grandfather the next week."

Alissa laughed. "And were you sorry?"

"No." Lady Ellen laughed, too. "As it turned out, I much preferred your grandfather."

"Good thing for me!"

"Good thing for all of us, I think. It's been a good life."

Alissa's laughter died. "Yes. It *has* been a good life." Her face grew solemn. "And I have every intention of keeping it that way."

Her grandmother looked deep into her eyes. "Yes, I can see that you have, dear. So let's get to the business of doing just that, shall we?"

"Indeed, yes." Alissa rose and reached a hand down to help her grandmother. "Come, then. It's past time to plan my wedding."

Chapter Twenty-two

Michael's expression was thunderous as he rode back to
Kantwell House. Did Alissa really think he was so inca-
pacitated that he couldn't even defend himself against her
uncle? Couldn't acquit himself well? What, then, must she
think of his other abilities, mental as well as physical?

Would she think him incapable of managing her business affairs? Her estates? Of taking care of her pensioners—for surely Collington Park and Collington House had
pensioned off many a servant, and just as surely a number
of them must still be alive. If she couldn't trust him to take
care of himself in the little matter of duel, illegal or not,
would she be able to trust him to take care of them?

Damn and blast! Did she think him a complete incom-
petent?

Or was it that she feared that he'd get himself killed before he could marry her? That was probably the case. It all
came back to that, after all. He wasn't her *beloved*. He was
her *betrothed*—and he was that because she needed him to

marry her, *not* to protect her against the ugly piece of work that was her kinsman, as he would be proud to do. No, he was needed only to fulfill some condition of her grandfather's will.

His thoughts made him writhe, he found them so cursed uncomfortable. He wished he'd never agreed to marry her. Wished he'd left for his estates in the countryside as soon as he'd arrived. Wished he'd not tarried in London.

If he'd already been gone from the capital, Lady Ellen would have had to find another man to escort her to that fateful soirée the other evening. If he'd not been there . . .

Why engage in such futile thoughts? He *had* been in London, and if he were honest with himself, he'd admit that he had been glad to be there to smash the face of the man who'd been bullying Lady Ellen.

Ye gads, the bounder was her own son! *And* Alissa's dastardly uncle. So his thoughts had come full round again. This was the man he was to foil by marrying Alissa, and foil him he would—if he wasn't granted the pleasure of running him through first.

Still scowling, he rode Gladiator down the mews alley to the stables at the back. Stupid bastard that he was, he was about to marry the only woman in the world he would ever want, and he was grousing to himself about it!

At the stables, Palmer was waiting to take the great gray gelding from him. He chuckled to see Michael's frown and quipped, "Don't tell me ye're already feeling the pinch of them matrimonial bonds, your lordship."

"What?" Michael finally smiled. "No, Palmer. Not that. I was just thinking about one of my future relatives."

"I'm sorry to see what ye think of 'im. But remember, none of us gets to choose who we're related to, more's the pity."

"True enough, Palmer. True enough." He helped Palmer settle Gladiator, and by the time he left for the house, his black mood had lifted.

• • •

Back at Collington House, Alissa and Ellen were deep in plans for her wedding. "In spite of the fact that we're being married by special license, I want it to be lovely, Grandmama."

Lady Ellen's smile was warm. "Of course you do, dear. Every bride wants her wedding to be lovely and memorable."

"I meant that I want it to be lovely for Michael. I'm deeply aware that he is doing us such a good turn. And he'll never have another wedding. After all, we marry only once in our lives, and I do want him to have a splendid wedding."

"Very well. If that's your desire, we will have the wedding of the century. But we can't do it alone."

Alissa frowned lightly. "No, I don't suppose we can. Not in three days." Then she looked toward the windows where, in the garden outside, the shadows were beginning to lengthen, and said in a whisper, "Or two."

Ellen's brow was furrowed as well. "Let's think. Who can we get to help?"

"Would Lady Anne? With her soirée behind her, perhaps she would have time. So would Rosalynda. And there's Emily Townsend and her aunt, and then . . ."

The rest of the day passed in a flurry of notes and plans and answers to notes. By bedtime both of them were exhausted, but plans were well under way.

And tomorrow was the beginning of the fifth day of Alissa's fateful week.

At Kantwell House, plans were being made as well. They weren't as appealing as those being made by the ladies, but they were even more important.

Michael said, "We have to deploy in the best positions to watch Collington House to keep Lady Alissa safe from whatever her uncle might plan to delay her wedding. I don't want to use the footmen, as we don't want the gossip they'd start."

"We can use Bow Street Runners to fill in," MacLain suggested.

"Huh!" Stone scoffed. "After the way they refused to see to her concerns over the disappearance of her friend, Sir Thomas Lane, I fail to have much confidence in their attitude should we ask them to help guard her."

MacLain thought briefly, then seconded him. "Best do it ourselves, then. Shame we haven't some of the other chaps here from the regiment."

"I'd settle for what's left of 'The Lucky Seven.'" Stone counted. "Us three, Harry and Bly. May be only five now, but we could get the job done."

"We will get the job done. We haven't a choice." Michael threw himself back in his chair, "Damnation! Even if we use the cook's spit boy, we're going to have a hell of a time covering all the possibilities."

Rubbing the cleft in his chin, Stone said quietly, "True, but look." He used the tines of his dinner fork to draw a rectangle on the damask tablecloth. "If one of us is positioned at each of diagonally opposite corners of the house, we can cover the sides of the building that connect to that corner. That way, one man can see two sides of the mansion, necessitating only two men to cover the whole."

Michael clapped him on the shoulder. "Excellent. And I can take the alley behind Collington House as my post. Whatever might be going to happen will be likely to start from there."

Stone started to speak but held his tongue.

Michael went on. "Palmer can act as messenger between us, to keep us all in touch."

"Well"—MacLain's voice held an odd note—"not really."

Both other men turned their gazes on him.

He squirmed down lower in his chair. "You see, I, uh,

wrote a letter to Bly telling him all that was going on, and I, er, I sent Palmer to Cliffside with it just after you got back from your ride." He finished in a rush, then added, "I hope you don't mind."

Michael took a deep breath and was very still for a minute. Then he said, "We can still manage. We'll just use the system of whistles we used on the Peninsula."

MacLain said, "I'm sorry, Michael, I didn't think."

Stone bit back a comment.

"It's all right, Mac. We'll manage."

"Oh, that's good." MacLain was visibly relieved.

Stone walked over to the window, pulled aside the drapery and looked out. "Dawn's breaking. Too late to worry about mounting guard tonight."

Michael grunted agreement. "Tomorrow night the three of us cover Collington House as agreed then, right?" His expression was grim.

"Very well. It's a workable plan, and I don't see that we have any other options," Stone admitted.

"Yes, the plan will work, I'm sure." MacLain was frowning a little. "But there is just one thing that puzzles me. What does that leave for the cook's spit boy to do?"

Chapter Twenty-three

Lights were blazing from every window of Collington House as they approached to mount guard. Michael said to Stone, "What the devil? They should all have been asleep hours ago! Something's happened!" He started for the door, but Stone pulled him back into the shadows.

Just then the door opened and a liveried footman came out of it as if shot from a cannon. Behind him in the lighted doorway, Lady Ellen shook a finger at the youth and said in no uncertain terms, "You tell that man I want a church full of flowers Saturday morning or he will *never, ever* get another single order from anyone in the *ton* if I have anything to do with it. *Then* we'll see if he gets out of bed to listen to you! The idea! Turning a Collington footman away! Go! And don't stop pounding on his door until he has my message, do you hear me?"

"Y-yes, Countess!" The footman, probably the youngest on Alissa's staff, took off at a dead run, his powdered wig clutched in his hand.

Stone chuckled. "Nothing wrong, Mathers. You're just seeing the logistics for your wedding."

"Good Lord! It's chaos in there. Just look in the window. There must be ten women in that room, and they all appear to be shouting orders and scattering papers around." Michael laughed. "Heaven help you, Stone. You may get trampled out here in front."

They watched another footman fling himself down the steps and rush off into the night. "I leave you to it. I'll have a quieter time in my alley, I'll wager."

"Shouldn't be hard to do unless that little fire-breathing general needs her carriage, or decides to mount one of her messengers. Then you'd sure as hell better get out of the way, too."

Michael punched his friend on the shoulder and left to take up his position in the alley behind the stately mansion. Stone went to his own prearranged post. Both men moved quietly through the shadows.

They'd taken the precaution of putting MacLain in place first. They'd agreed that was wise, just to be on the safe side.

With the stealth of a cat, Michael slipped along the tall granite wall that marked the end of the Collington House garden and arrived at the deep stand of ancient evergreens he'd chosen as his station. The evergreens offered the best cover in the broad alley. And he was right about the alley being quiet. It was quiet as the grave compared to the minor uproar that continued in the front of the house. He was smiling and distracted as he slipped into the shelter of the trees.

"Good evening, your lordship." It was the leader of the men who had attempted to abduct Alissa. Even in the dark shadows here among the evergreen boughs, Michael could make out that he held a large pistol pointed straight at Michael's heart. So did the three men behind him.

Michael knew the odds of ducking four pistol balls all

too well. He was careful to stand very still and keep his hand in plain view. Pretending to relax, he said, "Good evening. Lord Withers's lackeys, I presume?"

The man refused to be baited. "Correct. Lord Withers told us you'd choose the alley as your post, as he was certain you'd decide it was the most obvious place from which we might attack. He said, too, that you'd be the one to man this particular spot, as you'd never sent men into more danger than you faced yourself. Clever of him to deduce all that, don't you think?"

"And your plans are?" Michael was unable to detect a knife anywhere. The fact that he couldn't made him uneasy. That would have been the most sensible weapon. Dispatching him with a knife would be silent and efficient, and would call no attention to his murderers. As seconds passed, he wondered just what was going to happen.

There was one thing to be pleased about. At least it seemed to be going to happen to him instead of to Alissa. He was grateful for that even as he worried about what would happen to Alissa without him.

Strange how ironic life could be. He'd come to London to have his life ended for him in some city street. Somehow, though, he'd imagined it would be in the Rookery or Seven Dials, not behind one of the finest mansions in Mayfair.

Oddly, too, he hadn't thought about dying in quite a while. It was almost as if he'd changed his plans. It certainly looked as if he were going to be forced to think of dying now, though.

The important thing, however, was saving Alissa. His mind was working quickly, coolly. Stone or, God forbid, MacLain would have to take his place as her bridegroom day after tomorrow. Stone would work it out when they found his body.

Getting the special license would be the trick. Unless they found him soon, time was going to be tight.

Michael heard a soft sound behind him, but he didn't bother to turn his head. Since there was no hint of surprise on his captor's face, he could be certain it was another of the gang.

The man holding the gun on him chuckled. "I'm glad to see you're going to behave. Shooting you here would cause you to miss what my employer has in mind for you. Believe me, the experience will be interesting. Quite unique. And related, by the way, to the events of your somewhat daring rescue of Lady Alissa the other day."

"Really?" Michael sounded bored. "I simply can't imagine wha . . ."

His sentence ended as a blunt instrument smashed into the back of his head. He dropped where he stood.

When Michael regained consciousness he had a foul taste in his mouth and the dim memory of a rough carriage ride and some obnoxious liquid being forced down his throat. When he opened his eyes, he found himself in a nightmare!

Dizzy and nauseated, he closed them again. He didn't want to consider the scene before him until he had his wits back.

"Are you awake at last, Kantwell?"

Michael spun his head toward the voice, was immediately disoriented, and fell back on what he now saw was a filthy straw pallet. "Withers," he rasped, his voice barely a whisper, his throat raw from whatever drug this bastard's henchmen had forced down it.

"Yes, it is indeed, I, Lord Kantwell. I wanted to come see for myself how you liked your accommodations."

"Where am I?" Michael's head was pounding, his vision blurred. He tried to raise his hand to his brow. His good hand was chained to his useless one by a foot or so of heavy iron links. The heavy belt that had held his bad arm to his side was on the floor beside him.

He was in manacles! Again!

With an inhuman roar, he lunged for Withers.

Withers laughed and easily shoved him back down with the tip of the cane he was carrying. "I hardly think you are up to that sort of thing yet, Kantwell."

Michael called him every filthy name he could think of.

"Oh, my. You're really not being very nice, are you, my boy?"

Michael found more names.

"Very inventive. Your years in the army certainly taught you a lot more than just fighting, didn't they?"

Michael gritted his teeth and glared.

"You should be grateful."

Michael remained silent.

"Aren't you even curious as to why I think you should be grateful?"

Michael stared at him.

"Well, I'll tell you anyway." He pointed across the huge room. "See that?"

Michael couldn't help it, he looked.

What he saw made his gorge rise.

Three men in shapeless, dirty, white robes surrounded a similarly attired woman. One man was slobbering kisses over her face, and another was pawing her breasts. A third man danced around the group like a child, chanting "Can I do it, too?" over and over.

The woman stared sightlessly into nowhere, seemingly unaware of the men. Her madness was her armor against the world.

Michael turned his face away and tried not to vomit in front of his tormentor.

Withers's cool voice penetrated Michael's horror. "One wonders if the woman were quite that mad when she came here. You'll observe she doesn't even seem to notice what is happening to her. I should think that sort of treatment might aggravate her condition at the very least, wouldn't you?"

"For God's sake. Call an attendant!"

"Do you think they care, Kantwell? You are not in the finest asylum, you know. This one is, alas, one of the worst. While the guards do not seem interested in a hag like that woman, I've heard that the more attractive female inmates are . . . shall we say given the same special attention by the keepers?"

"You bastard!"

"Why, Michael, you seem to be repeating yourself. You have said that before." Withers rose, and a man in a loose gray uniform of some sort took the chair he'd been sitting in and went to stand by the metal door of the cell. "I grow bored with you, Kantwell. You fail to realize that your being here has spared my niece coming. I'd expected you to be grateful."

Michael cursed himself, now, for he actually *felt* a flood of gratitude toward this monster. He did. God knew he'd be driven to madness himself if he'd ever had to think that Alissa might be here, in the hands of madmen. In his heart he was, curse him, truly thankful that Withers had imprisoned him instead. He must be mad enough to belong here!

"When I get out of here, Withers, I'll tear your black heart out with my bare hands."

"What a gruesome thought. I actually believe you mean it, too."

"Count on it!"

"I have some difficulty picturing the event, however. You only have one hand, you see." He smiled sweetly. "Evidently you forgot in the heat of anger."

Michael kept silent.

"I'm afraid you are doomed to disappointment, in any case, my lord. I've told the keepers that you are my younger brother and have lost your mind and tried to kill me, your loving sibling. A nice touch, don't you think? As head of our poor, distressed family, I have—sadly, of course—had to commit you."

Michael gave him a look full of promise.

"Rot in peace, Viscount Kantwell. No one else knows where you are. There's no way out of here for you."

Michael lunged for him.

Withers slashed his cane across Michael's jaw, and he fell back on the vermin-ridden straw, unconscious again.

Chapter Twenty-four

Alissa was running toward the study to tell her grandmother that the fourteen seamstresses London's most sought-after modiste had working on her wedding gown had nearly finished it when a thunderous knocking sounded throughout the house. Since she was the closest person to it, she answered the door. "Before the person pounding on it knocks it down," she muttered. Scowling, she threw open the door.

Suddenly, it was as if the very sunshine had been sucked out of the day. A subtle feeling of dread came over her and the hairs at the back of her neck rose. In the doorway a tall, still figure clad entirely in funereal black stood, unsmiling, his hawklike gaze bent on her. Held captive by the power that blazed from his narrowed eyes, Alissa could almost smell brimstone.

Involuntarily, she dropped back a step. When she did, the man swept, unbidden, into the house. He ripped his hat from his dark head and thrust it at Quillen with a force that knocked the butler back a step. Blue eyes as cold as an arctic sky pierced Alissa through. "Is Kantwell here?"

"No he is not." Alissa was having trouble adjusting to the man's abrupt manner. "He has not been here for . . ."

The apparition cut her off by demanding, "What the hell does *this* mean!" and thrust a letter at her.

Alissa was rapidly regaining her scattered wits and had opened her mouth to tell him what she thought of his manners, when her grandmother came out of the study and cried, "Chalfont Blysdale! I haven't seen you in years! What brings you to Collington House?" And she whispered to Alissa, "Close your mouth, darling."

Bly fumed, "The frequent appearance of the words 'Collington House' in this idiotic missive has brought me here." He paced two steps away and whirled back to her grandmother as if he were a panther pouncing. "I was coming to Town on business when I met Kantwell's groom bringing this to me. Attempting to decipher the ravings it contains has brought me here to you."

"And just in time for breakfast, too." Lady Ellen slipped her arm through his and headed for the breakfast room, saying mildly, "My granddaughter is getting married tomorrow, and we are all at sixes and sevens just now."

She introduced Alissa, who was following hard on their heels, uncertain whether her grandmother was safe with this overpowering man. "This is another of the legendary 'Lucky Seven,' Alissa, Michael's commanding officer, Colonel Blysdale."

Blysdale acknowledged the introduction as if Alissa ranked right up there with the scullery maid.

While Alissa fought down her outrage, Lady Ellen said sweetly, "But tell me about your letter. It looks like a very long one."

"And the blasted thing's incoherent."

She patted his arm. "There, there. It'll make more sense after coffee."

Quillen, rubbing his midsection and wishing he had the courage to glare at the man he now knew was the legendary Colonel "Beelzebub" Blysdale, entered the breakfast room immediately behind them. Almost frantically, he gestured to one of the footmen to set a place for their guest.

Colonel Blysdale seated her grandmother, then turned his hawk's gaze Alissa's way. To keep from having him come near enough to help her with her chair, Alissa slithered into it with an audible plop, thankful the table was between them.

"Won't you have breakfast, Chalfont?" Lady Ellen asked him. "Cook has a wonderful way with shirred eggs."

Alissa would have offered him a dish of horseshoe nails if it had been up to her. He certainly had the air of a man who habitually chewed them.

"No. Nothing. Just coffee and help me decipher this"— he gestured disgustedly at the pages lying on the table— "this chicken scratch." Turning his intense gaze on her grandmother, he said, "I'm having one of my forebodings, Ellen. You know I always get them about my men."

"Yes, dear," Lady Ellen said in a troubled voice, "I do."

"This one's tearing my guts out."

Alissa was surprised her grandmother allowed such an expression at her table, but she saw no censure, only a grave concern on Lady Ellen's face. That dear face went as pale as the cream for their coffee. Then she asked, as if fearing his answer, "And for whom are you so worried this time?"

"Mathers is missing. I must find him before it's too late."

"Michael!" It was a breath, a sigh, a prayer. Alissa slumped in her chair as the world whirled and crumpled around her.

Lady Ellen gasped, "Alissa!"

Quillen rushed forward to catch her before she could slip to the floor. One of the footmen was close behind him.

Alissa rallied even as they reached her. "Thank you." She looked up at the butler without seeing him and spoke the formula of the well-bred. "I'm quite all right."

She put her hands on the table to help her sit up straight. They were trembling uncontrollably.

"Bring her some brandy," Blysdale ordered. He strode around the table and clasped her hands in his own. His grip was firm, almost bruising. "Forgive me. I had no idea you loved him."

Alissa could only look in surprise at him. Many a young woman of the aristocracy would have the vapors if faced with the redoubtable Beelzebub, yet he knew instinctively that her near-swoon had nothing to do with him. How could this stranger know that she loved Michael?

And how could a man who positively radiated violence gaze at her with such compassion?

"I'll find him," he told her. "I'll bring him back to you," he promised. "Never fear."

Alissa gazed up into his eyes and knew that he meant what he said. Knew that he *could do* what he said. Strength flooded back into her. "I'll help." She stood and went around the table to the letter they had all momentarily forgotten.

"This was written by Lieutenant MacLain, wasn't it?" she asked after a moment.

"You recognize his hand?"

"No." She smiled in spite of herself. "I recognize his thought processes."

With a snort of laughter, Blysdale muttered, "Or the lack of them."

Together they bent over the papers. Bly said half under his breath, "It seems he's outlining a plan they'd decided on to guard you. He and Stone were to take the house, with Mathers taking the alley as his post."

He looked across the room at nothing. "Hmmm. Of course. The alley would be the most dangerous spot. And anyone who knew Mathers at all would know that he would assign himself to the place where there was the most danger. Does his enemy know him well?"

"Everyone knows him from the dispatches, of course." Alissa sighed. "But the enemy is mine, I fear." And she told him the whole story from the day she had received word from her uncle of his base intentions.

When she had finished the story, Bly sat drumming his fingers on the tablecloth, his chin on his chest and his eyes narrowed to slits. When Alissa started to ask him something, he held up a hand. She waited.

Finally, he lifted his head and looked at her. "If you have told me all of it, I know what to do." He rose and started for the door.

"Aren't you going to let me help?"

"Help?" he asked sardonically. "How can you possibly help? You have a wedding to get ready for."

Alissa bit her tongue until the front door had closed behind his tall form, then burst out, "That seems horribly pointless when there isn't any groom!" Then she threw herself back down into her chair. With all her might she fought back the sobs that threatened. She felt as if her heart would break.

Her grandmother came to her and smoothed her dark curls for several minutes. At last she said, "My dear, if anything can be done, you may be sure that the man who just left here can do it."

"But suppose my uncle has . . ."

"I refuse to believe Michael is dead. Blysdale has always had an uncanny sense about these things. He would not go searching if it was already too late."

Alissa began to dry her eyes.

"Search your own heart, dearest. You love Michael, and I know that he loves you." She ignored the small start those words gave her granddaughter. "If he were dead, wouldn't *you* know it?"

Alissa looked as if she were discovering some marvelous truth. Her eyes brightened and a smile touched the corners of her mouth. "Yes. Yes! I *would* know. I'd know because there'd be something missing. I'd feel as if a large part of me had been swept away. And I don't. I still feel complete!" She put her arms around her grandmother. "Oh, dearest, he is alive. Somewhere out there he's still alive."

Lady Ellen hugged her fiercely.

They were both laughing a little in relief, crying a little in gratitude.

Quillen was looking from one to the other and experiencing a great and extremely unfamiliar indecision. He looked at the brandy decanter he'd been ordered to bring and wondered if it might be time to offer it again. He went to the sideboard, picked up two wineglasses, and approached his ladies.

Alissa smiled through her tears. "No, thank you, Quillen."

Lady Ellen smiled and motioned him away.

Quillen, retreating as ordered, shook his head and looked from the decanter to the glasses. After a moment, he poured himself a generous amount and downed it.

Chapter Twenty-five

Bly took a heavy purse of coins into Seven Dials, the roughest part of London, where he expected to find word of Mathers. Though he'd refused the support of Stone and MacLain, actually laughing in MacLain's face when he'd said to Stone that Colonel Blysdale needed their protection, Bly wasn't surprised to see both his old comrades trailing after him from shady tavern to sleezy pub as he made his inquiries and ostentatiously clinked his bag of coins.

In the tavern just before the one in which Bly made his last stop, he picked up a group of murderous-looking men who were more than slightly interested in the heavy bag he carried. Ignoring them as he strode into the dim cavern of a public house next door, he held the bag aloft, then spilled a few of the shining coins it contained on the greasy counter in front of the barman.

"I seek assistance, gentlemen. A recommendation, if you will." The men sitting around the common room looked at him as if he'd dropped off the moon. Bly went on smoothly, "Can any of you recommend a private asylum for the insane to me? One that might hold a fellow aristocrat who can comfort my poor uncle during his bouts of insanity?"

"Wot's 'e think?" One of the drinkers punched his companion. "Do the likes of us look like we can sport the blunt ta put somebody in an asylum, private like?"

A man across the drink-slopped table answered, "Tha's a'course should we have any crazies in the fambly." He nudged the man next to him—"Like ye do, Kenny!"—and went into gales of laughter.

More ribald laughter and coarse advice about what Bly could do with his uncle followed Bly's question. Two men, however, did not laugh. Instead, they exchanged meaningful glances.

Bly added incentive. "I'm willing to pay good coin for the name of such a place."

The two men began to exchange comments.

Seeing them do so, Bly was confident that he'd found the source of the information he was seeking. Like a spider settling into the center of his web, he told himself to be patient and wait for the men who possessed that information to come and claim the bag of coins.

Watching without seeming to, he saw them argue for a moment, then confer briefly. He had no doubt that their greed would win out over their common sense. Smiling inwardly, he sauntered over and leaned casually on the bar, waiting. He didn't have to wait long.

"Yer say yer wantin' a place where your loony uncle can fin' another swell to talk ta?"

The speaker's companion tugged at his arm. "Don' give away how we know!"

Bly was now certain he had the right informers. Elation filled him. He was careful to let nothing but faint boredom show in his face. With a smile that would have done a crocodile proud, he offered, "Gentlemen, let me buy you some gin."

Ten minutes later he walked out of the Sleeping Bull without his sack of coins and went swaggering up the filthy lane toward his two waiting guardians. As he passed the ragged group that had followed him from the previous den, he said, "Bad luck, boys. Two of your friends inside have already relieved me of my purse."

The thugs jostled each other as they ran for the tavern's door. There they momentarily jammed in the doorway, each trying to be first to discover who had the sack of coins they'd been lying in wait for. They'd lost interest in the dangerous-looking Blysdale with a strong feeling of relief.

"Done, lads." Bly smiled his tight, crooked smile at Stone and MacLain. "Mount up, we're off."

Miles away in Padnum Asylum, Michael was working at the mortar that held the ring through which the chains that bound him to the wall passed. With the buckle of his carelessly discarded belt, he had scraped it half away, working only when no one was looking his way. He also had to be greatly cautious that no one noticed the sound of his labors. It made the work painfully slow, and Michael was not a patient man. Another half hour, he estimated, and he would be free.

Gritting his teeth against the terrible frustration that rode him as he worked, he cast frequent glances at the grimy, barred window high in the wall across the large common room in which he and fifteen other male inmates were being kept. Beyond its dirty glass panes, the sky was darkening. Ribbons of salmon and gold threaded it, and caught among them, drifting clouds gone dark with approaching night glowed deep gray, their edges luminous with the sunset.

Damn and blast! The day was almost over, and tomorrow was his wedding day! How the devil could he marry

Alissa and save her inheritance for her if he was chained to yet another wall? He fell to cursing, long and well. Unfortunately it was also long and loud, and he drew the attention of one of the warders.

"'ere, now. We don' need none o' that." He came over to Michael, slapping a slender cane against his palm.

Michael could see the man would love an excuse to use the cane, and felt like telling him to strike and be damned. That would accomplish nothing but a little release of his own foul temper, however, and he had to hide his handiwork. Leaning against the wall to shelter the scraped place and the telltale pile of mortar dust, he told the man, "Sorry. I didn't mean to disturb you." He manufactured a doleful sigh. "I'm just angry that I don't know why I'm here."

The warder, placated by Michael's apology, said, "Ye're not the only one 'ere that feels that way."

Michael chuckled as if sharing a joke with the man. "Yes, but I'm not crazy."

The warder just stared at him for a while.

Michael had to grit his teeth to maintain his casual pose. He wanted information if he could get it, not a confrontation. Finally he tried another tack. "Of course, you have no idea why I'm here, either. There's no way they'd tell you."

The stratagem worked! His pride punctured, the warder told Michael, "Now *there* ye're off. I 'appen ta know that ye're in here 'cause you got in a sartin lord's way. But if yer behaves yerself, ye might be out 'o 'ere as early as next week."

Next week! So! Withers fancied he was a master at mental torture, it seemed. He'd deliberately let Michael believe he'd never be free, enjoying his captive's despair. All the while he planned to let Michael go so that he could observe the drastic consequences of his failure to marry Alissa.

Damn the man! What good was freedom in a week? It might as well be next year for all the good he'd be to

Alissa. All that he'd be able to do by then would be to put a period to the man who tormented her and had had him brought to this hellhole.

He looked down at the manacles that held him, and for an instant all the horrors of the caves rushed into his mind. He was helpless again! But the former nightmare was nothing, compared to the present reality. For where did this leave Alissa and her family?

At the mercy of a man who could do *this*? He rattled his chains.

Rage at his helplessness sent a surge of strength flooding through him. "God!" he cried in his despair, yanking at his chains.

"'ere, now. Yer settle down!" The warder moved in with a well-aimed kick.

Stunned by the discovery, Michael felt the ring through which they'd bound him to the wall give a little. With a lunge, he threw all his weight into snatching the ring free of the ancient mortar that remained around it. Amazingly, it came free!

The warder went down like a poleaxed ox as Michael smashed the manacles into his jaw. Minutes later the man was bound with his own belt and gagged with the rag he carried for a handkerchief.

Standing over him clad in the man's loose-fitting uniform that he'd donned, with considerable difficulty, over his own clothes, Michael held aloft the keys he'd taken from his victim's heavy leather belt and laughed triumphantly.

"A chance, by God! *Now* we have a chance, Alissa," he whispered.

Then he turned his attention to the ticklish business of getting out of the asylum. By the time he'd managed to escape undetected, night had fallen.

• • •

They came thundering down the highway toward the drive
to the asylum. Bly was in the lead, Stone and MacLain
close on either flank. Night was falling fast and the moon
cast strange shadows on the snow-laden moor as it moved
in and out of the wind-driven clouds. The light gave the
land an aspect as foreign as that of a frozen moonscape.

At last the asylum came into view. Bly raised his hand
and the three of them drew rein. "We'll proceed at a more
decorous pace now, lads."

"What excuse are we going to give for showing up here
at all?" MacLain wanted to know.

"We are, ostensibly, coming to make suitable arrangements for my dear lunatic uncle," Bly answered him. "I
shall deplore the lateness of the hour in my usual supercil-
ious manner, and demand a tour of the place."

"I'm certain you'll get it, too. You always get what you
want, whether or not you're acting high-handed."

Stone swallowed a laugh.

"Yes, *Captain* Stone?" Bly's left eyebrow was near his
hairline.

Stone decided he'd just as soon not tell his former
colonel that he was always high-handed. "Nothing, sir!"

MacLain was still trying to figure out their plan of attack. Finally he asked, "What good'll that do?" MacLain
cocked his head, thought a minute, then said, "Besides, I
never heard you had a lunatic uncle."

"Dear God!" Stone burst out. Exchanging looks with
Bly he stated, "We could easily convince them that we
wanted a place for *him*!"

MacLain laughed aloud, saw that Bly hadn't found anything to amuse him in Stone's pronouncement, and went
quiet immediately.

Bly worked to control the upward quirk of amusement
that threatened his lip. "We shall keep him awhile longer,
I think. He's always proved useful in a fight."

Stone relented. "Aye, Colonel. That's true enough."

"What *are* we talking about?" MacLain asked plaintively.

"You don't want to know." his companions said in unison.

MacLain subsided, frowning in puzzlement, as they reached the forbidding gates of the Padnum Asylum for the Insane.

Michael saw them charge up the drive, slow down, converse, and go on again. He didn't dare shout to draw their attention for fear of sounding the alarm for his escape, and he was too far away to head them off. "Damn and blast!" he muttered. "Rescue is at hand, and the most they'll be able to do is point out to the warders that I'm missing!"

Having realized that that was exactly what would occur, Michael set himself to putting as much distance as possible between himself and the great gray pile in which he'd been imprisoned. That it also put him farther from his would-be rescuers didn't trouble him. After all, there was only one road out of here, and it was undoubtedly the way they would return. He just had to make certain that he hailed and stopped them this time. It was colder than the hinges of hell, and the lack of his heavy greatcoat was in no way compensated for by the light uniform of his warder. Freezing to death God only knew where wasn't in his plans.

He'd walked almost a mile before he heard the sound of galloping hooves coming up fast behind him. Stepping into the center of the road, he hoped the fickle moon wouldn't dive behind the clouds before it gave his comrades-in-arms light enough to avoid riding him down.

The moon did better than that. Having hidden itself behind a thick cloud that offered utter darkness to the land a moment before, it suddenly reappeared and displayed Michael's upright and gesticulating figure in the brightest moonlight of the evening just as the three horsemen arrived. The flapping of the warder's uniform accomplished more than Michael had hoped for. The apparition he presented sent the horses into terrified sliding stops that caused Stone and Bly to fight to keep their seats and MacLain to fly over his mount's head into Michael.

While Stone pulled Michael and MacLain to their feet, Bly caught MacLain's horse and asked conversationally, "Just how the devil did you get loose, my boy?"

Chapter Twenty-six

In the perfectly appointed blue drawing room at Collington House, Alissa paced the floor, wringing her hands. Lady Ellen watched her with increasing anxiety. It was almost ten o'clock, and they still had no word of Michael.

"Try to sit down and relax, dear." Lady Ellen offered the advice automatically. Even as she did, she felt certain it would do no good.

It didn't.

"Sit?" Alissa exploded. "Look at me!" Her voice was plaintive as she lifted her hands toward Ellen. "I never wring my hands, you know I don't. I can hardly remain inside my skin, even by pacing. This inactivity is driving me crazy. If only I knew that he was safe. That no one had hurt him. If only there was something I could *do.*"

"I'm confident that Bly is doing all that can be done."

Alissa hesitated a moment, then, glad of a new subject for her thoughts, said, "He's a strange, hard man, Grandmother. Your obvious liking for him puzzles me."

"I've known him since he was born." Lady Ellen's face closed. "I knew his mother, you see."

"And?"

"And I understand why Chalfont is the man he has become."

Alissa didn't ask what her grandmother had thought of Colonel Blysdale's mother. She knew, without asking, by the shuttered look on her grandmother's face. Pensively she said, "There's no softness in him. He rather gives me the shivers."

"Kate, his wife, I'm sure would disagree. But I see what you mean. Colonel Blysdale is . . ." She paused, seeking the right word, ". . . a fierce man."

Alissa made another turn around the large Oriental rug. "I'd have said ruthless."

Lady Ellen pursed her lips in disapproval. "You'd have been wrong." Then she relented, struggling to be fair. "At least he is ruthless only to those who deserve it."

Alissa took another agitated turn around the room. Going to the window for the hundredth time, she pulled back the draperies Quillen had closed at dusk and searched the vacant street.

"If only they'd come! If only they'd send word!" She let the blue brocade fall back into place over the windowpanes and came to perch for a moment beside her grandmother. "Do you really think they will find him?"

Lady Ellen heard the agony in her voice, and took her hand. "Dearest, if anyone can find him and bring him back, Colonel Blysdale will."

"Is he so able, then?" Alissa didn't even know what she'd asked. Her mind was all on Michael, all on trying to reach out to him, trying again for that tenuous link that had assured her he was alive before.

Her grandmother saw her distraction and sympathized with it. Even though she knew her words wouldn't penetrate through to Alissa's mind, she answered anyway.

"Colonel Blysdale is a legend. He does what he says he will do no matter what the cost."

Alissa turned to look at her. "Oh, Grandmother. I love Michael so. It's not just to foil Uncle Gerald's plans that I want to marry him, you know."

Lady Ellen smiled. "Of course I know that, dearest. And it makes me so very happy. I only hope you can convince Michael."

"I only hope that I'll get the opportunity to try to convince him. I really wan . . ."

The sound of a sharp pounding on the door sent her heart into her throat. Alissa leapt to her feet and flew toward the front door. "Bly has found him!" Relief flooding her and her eyes full of glory, she wrenched at the handle. "Thank God!" she cried as she flung the heavy door open.

Michael and his friends made as good time as they could, coping well with the problem of four good-sized men and only three horses. Captain Adam Stone was so large there was no chance of his horse sharing the burden of a second rider, so MacLain's and Bly's alone were put to service.

The manacles and their chains that bound Michael's good arm to his useless one made it impossible for him to handle reins, so he was forced to ride behind MacLain for the first half of their journey, then, as Mac's horse showed signs of fatigue, behind Blysdale to Collington House.

"We must stop there first," Michael insisted. "I must put her . . . *their* minds at ease."

Blysdale allowed it because Alissa's home was on the way to Kantwell House, and the horses were sorely in need of a breather. Walking them the last few hundred yards gave them all a chance to catch their breaths, and the men to notice a large traveling coach drawn up in the street in front of Collington House.

"What the devil!" Michael began to curse under his

breath. "If that's Withers tormenting her, I'll have his blasted heart out."

"Peace, Major," Bly commanded calmly. "No self-respecting nobleman would have so cumbersome a vehicle. Whoever it is, it's not your enemy."

They halted their exhausted horses behind the coach, dismounted, and started for the front door. The scene that met their eyes, however, stopped them in their tracks. As still as amateur players in a living tableau, they gaped at the doorway.

A tiny lady with a hat full of ostrich plumes was assaulting the door with the silver handle of her parasol while her footman stood just behind her, holding a beribboned pug in his arms. With every stroke of the lady's battered silver parasol handle, the squirming pug let out a yap.

Almost immediately, the door flew open and they heard Alissa cry, "Thank God!" Immediately, the radiant glow that had been in her face as she opened the door faded, and they heard her gasp, "Aunt Izzy! What are *you* doing here?"

The tiny lady thus addressed informed her, "I've come for your wedding, of course, you foolish gel. Did you think I would not?"

At that moment, Alissa looked beyond her and saw, standing at the edge of the lamplight, her beloved Michael. Her heart almost stopped.

He stood tall and straight, his broad shoulders and handsome head held proudly in spite of the cruel manacles and heavy chains she saw on him. She knew that they must be causing him great discomfort. As she moved toward him, she could see in his face the deep lines of pain that having his injured arm dragged down by the weight of the irons had put there. She could see, too, that the firm line of his jaw was blurred by a day's growth of dark beard, and a livid bruise showed through the stubble.

She rushed the last steps to his side. "Michael. Oh, Michael, you're safe."

They stood staring into each other's eyes.

"Ellen!" Isabelle's strident call echoed throughout the staid neighborhood. "Come here this instant!"

"Here I am, Isabelle." Ellen's voice was calm, but it held a distinct note of resignation.

"I demand that you tell me the meaning of this! Who is this—this disreputable creature that my grandniece is—is *touching*?"

And Alissa *was* touching him. She ran her hands across his chest and shoulders and down his arms to the manacles, satisfying herself that he was here. That he was whole and safe. Safe, thank God!

Completely unaware of anyone but Michael, Alissa took the first full breath she'd taken since she'd learned he was missing. Her heart in her eyes, she traced her fingers over Michael's bruised jaw and on to his upper lip. Smiling tremulously, she whispered, "Are you beginning the mustache you promised Robin you would grow for him?"

Michael quivered under her touch.

"Take your hands off that dirty man, Alissa Collington!" her great-aunt shrieked. "Take your hands off him this minute!"

Lady Ellen passed her fuming sister at the edge of the broad porch and came down to where the men stood. "Welcome back, Michael." She tiptoed to kiss his cheek. "I am so very glad you are safe." She slipped an arm around Alissa, and put a hand on Michael's arm. "We've been so worried."

"Now *you* are doing it, Ellen!" Isabelle cried, stomping down the steps to where they stood. "Have none of you any sense of propriety? You, gel! You're to be married tomorrow. Behave! Go into the house this instant!" She came storming at Michael flailing her parasol. "Get away! Go away! Scat!"

Bly stepped forward to keep her from striking Michael. "Madame." His tone would have stopped a cavalry charge. It even stopped Isabelle. "This is Lady Alissa's bridegroom."

"Ah, no! Never!" Isabelle whirled around and confronted her kin. "Explain yourselves! What have you done! Are you so desperate that you've had some scurvy debtor dragged out of prison for my grandniece to wed? Why, just look at him. He's still dripping chains!" She whipped back around to the men. Addressing Bly she ordered, "Take him back. You take him right back!" Turning to her sister, she said, "No matter what is going on, things can't be *this* bad."

Lady Ellen said, "You have no idea what is going on with us, Isabelle. If you will just come inside, I will explain it all to you."

"Nonsense! I won't stay a single minute in this madhouse! I want nothing to do with these havey-cavey goings on. I have my reputation to think of!" She snatched to her bosom the dog her footman proffered, turned her back on her twin sister, and ordered one of her footmen, "Peters! Take my trunks upstairs. Quillen will tell you where." Stalking back up the steps with every ostrich plume shaking, she announced, "I should have come days ago. I knew I should have come. Then things wouldn't be at such a sorry pass!" In a shout she ordered, "Quillen, attend me!"

Quiet fell around them like a heavy velvet cloak as the reverberations from Isabelle's slamming of the great front door of Collington House died. In the blessed silence, Blysdale took charge. "I should take Michael home and try to make him presentable for tomorrow, Lady Alissa," the man she had called ruthless told her gently.

Gratitude welled up in her. "Colonel Blysdale, I shall be forever in your debt. How can I ever thank you?"

Instead of offering her some polite convention in answer, Blysdale looked down at her thoughtfully. After studying her face a long moment, he said, "I shall hold the debt until I decide what can best be done with it. Then we will discuss what you can do to repay me. Right now, I must find a blacksmith to strike these chains from Michael, and I suggest we all seek our beds. Tomorrow is your wedding day, and you will want to be your most beautiful."

He turned to her aunt Isabelle's driver. "You there, John Coachman. Move over. I've need of you and your mistress's carriage for a quarter-hour."

Bundling an exhausted Michael into the ancient but ridiculously comfortable vehicle while the coachman stared, Blysdale then leapt to the box and gave him directions to Kantwell House. Instinctively, the coachmen knew better than to protest.

Alissa and Lady Ellen stood on the steps and watched until they were out of sight. Stone and MacLain rode behind them leading Blysdale's horse.

"They are very—able, aren't they?"

"Yes, my dear. He is safe now." She gave her granddaughter a kiss on the cheek. "You can rest."

"Yes." Alissa smiled down at her, and they started up the steps into the house. She chuckled. "I can rest, but with Aunt Izzy in the house, will anybody else?"

Ellen sighed. "From past long experience, I can absolutely guarantee that they will not."

As they opened the front door for themselves, Quillen came running, full of apologies for having failed to be there to get it for them.

"Don't apologize prematurely, Quillen." Lady Ellen told him. "I fear this is only the beginning."

Chapter Twenty-seven

Alissa kissed her grandmother good night and went to her own rooms. She was so excited and nervous about tomorrow that she knew she'd never get to sleep.

Her heart was singing. Michael was safe. He'd been dirty and disheveled, not to mention being in chains, but he had never looked better to her because he was *safe*. She recalled how handsome and proud and—and exhausted—he'd been as he'd stood there and looked into her eyes in a way that told her he cared for her. She knew that she had only the fact that he was worn to a thread to thank for letting her see that expression in his eyes. She sincerely doubted that he was aware of it.

She had vowed then and there that somehow, no matter what she had to do, she would see that expression of loving care again. And she would see it frequently, no matter how determined he was to hide it from her. One day, she promised herself, she would see real love for her in his eyes.

She had but one assurance that she would be able to accomplish her vow. Easily she called to mind that assurance, for it was one she'd never forget. Not if she lived to
be a hundred. When she had touched his face there on the
front steps, Michael had trembled at her touch.

Surely there was hope for them. Surely they would
make a wonderful marriage. Even if he never realized that
he cared for her, she loved him enough for both of them.

Lying there letting herself imagine what it would be
like to be held in his arms at night, to talk, to make love,
warmed her cheeks. Alissa could almost feel the lean, hard
length of his body next to her own. Could imagine the
warmth and strength of it there. Blushing faintly, she imagined herself carrying his child. She touched her abdomen
as if his child already grew there, and was overwhelmed by
love for him.

Tears of sheer joy trickled from the corners of her eyes.
She was to be his *wife*—Michael's *wife*! And their lives,
from tomorrow onward, would be forever entwined.

But most important of all right now was that, whatever
had happened to him, he was safe. Safe. Her heart swelled
with gratitude to Bly for finding him, to Stone and
MacLain for helping bring him to her, and to her Maker for
bringing it all about.

Somehow, in His benevolent wisdom, He had given her
the desires of her heart. She was going to marry for love
after all. She was going to marry Michael. Dreams *could*
come true. Her heart felt as if it would burst with the emotions that ran through her.

Somewhere between her prayers of thanksgiving and
her prayers for a happy future with Michael, exhausted by
worry and waiting and overwhelming joy, Alissa fell
asleep.

A few minutes later, as was her habit, Lady Ellen looked
in on her granddaughter. Standing at the foot of the bed, she

saw her precious Lissa relaxed at last. "Thank Heaven," she whispered.

The girl had been as taut as a bowstring ever since the awful letter from her uncle Gerald had arrived. Now, Lissa lay on her back for the first time all week. A peaceful smile was on her lips, and her hands rested beside her head on the pillow. Both were open now, with her fingers curled slightly. Before, every night during this dreadful week, Ellen had found Alissa curled in a tight, defensive ball with her hands fisted so hard that the nails bit into her palms.

Ellen sighed. They were almost through this. Tomorrow Alissa and Michael would wed, and Gerald, her own son Gerald, would no longer be able to do anything to hurt them, praise God.

While she was praising, she thanked God for Michael's safe return and for the fact that, in coming, he had brought into their lives friends like the "Lucky Seven." On all points, these four men of that legendary group had lived up to their sterling reputation.

She smiled as she recalled to mind how she had seen them just an hour ago. No wonder she'd thought of them as the Horatii of Roman legend defending the bridge when she'd seen them standing shoulder to shoulder on the steps while Isabelle pitched one of her silly fits. With the bond they so obviously shared, it was clearly "We fight as one!"

Until Alissa stirred, Ellen didn't realize she'd spoken the oath of the Horatii aloud. Quickly she tiptoed to the door. She must leave Lissa to sleep in peace.

Besides, she had one more duty to perform before she could seek her own bed, weary as she was. Closing Alissa's door softly, she went down the hall and around the corner to the best guest room and knocked on her twin sister's door.

"Enter!"

Ellen did, and announced without preamble, "Sister, if you do anything to diminish my granddaughter's joy on her wedding day tomorrow, be careful never to eat in one of my houses again."

"Why ever not?" Isabelle was astonished.

Ellen's voice was as firm as her tread as she went back out into the hall. Her words were clear. Very clear. So was their promise.

"Because I shall *poison* you!"

And she slammed the door for emphasis.

At Kantwell House, a bone-weary Michael stood beside his cook's chopping block and waited. The blacksmith Bly had dispatched Stone and MacLain to find was not yet in evidence.

Michael let out a sigh and Bly turned toward him, his eyes assessing. "You love her, don't you, boy?"

Michael turned on him as if he were an enemy. "Of course I love her! Who wouldn't?"

Bly hitched a hip onto the edge of the large center table on which vegetables were prepared and meals were put together. In the dim light from the banked kitchen fires that were the room's only illumination, his saturnine features took on an almost satanic aspect. "You love her." The simple statement was a challenge.

"Yes, damn you. I love her. I love her with all my heart. I would give my life for her." His eyes were full of anguish. And determination. "I *will* give my life for her!"

Bly barked, "And just what is that supposed to mean, damn you right back!"

"That means"—Michael drew his lips back in a snarl, hating what he must say, hating what it meant he must do—"that when Alissa meets the man she really wants for her husband, I shall see to it that I am no longer alive to keep her from marrying him!"

"Suicide?" Bly's scathing tone showed what he thought of that.

"Suicide is for fools and cowards." Michael's own tone gave away his feelings on the subject.

"And forbidden by Almighty God." Bly was standing now, looking as if he were ready to leap down Michael's throat.

"Hell, Bly, there are a dozen causes—worthwhile causes—that a man can die for."

"True. But you'd be wasting your time." He clapped a hand on his friend's shoulder. "She loves you, you know."

"Impossible."

"Why should it be impossible?"

"Look at me!" Michael shook his manacled hands at Bly, letting him see how his useless arm and hand dragged down his good arm, letting his friend see, as he had never permitted another to see, the pain the weight of it caused him. "How can she love me? Look at me! I'm half a man. I can't even make love to her without letting my weight crush the breath out of her!"

Bly did look at him. "Strange. I seem to see a great deal of man left when I look at you. Your fighting spirit, however, seems to have deserted you. Pity. In the regiment, you were one of the best."

"This isn't war, Colonel," Michael grated out harshly.

"Oh, yes, it is, Michael. Yes, it is. It's the war for your happiness."

"My happiness? What the devil does my happiness have to do with anything? I'm merely a chess piece. A pawn. A block, if you will, to stop Alissa's uncle from . . ."

Michael was cut off by the precipitous entrance of Stone and MacLain as they frog-marched into the kitchen a muscular man with sleep in his eyes and blacksmithing tools in his hands.

"Here we are!" MacLain announced the obvious. "Had the devil's own time finding one, but we've brought him."

Stone stopped and leaned against the jamb of the door

leading out of the kitchen. If the scowling blacksmith decided to take to his heels, he wouldn't get far.

Michael slammed his hands down on the chopping block he stood beside and ordered, "Strike off these manacles."

The smith scowled. "I've no liking for freeing felons."

"I'm no felon. An enemy has done this. Free me."

Still the smith hesitated.

Bly made a quick movement with his arm, and a throwing knife appeared in his hand. The other hand produced a golden sovereign. He tossed both to the chopping block beside Michael's hands. The knife quivered upright in the block, light from the kitchen fire glittering on its polished edge.

Michael grinned at Bly, then fixed a severe gaze on the blacksmith and spoke a single word. "Choose."

The blacksmith wasn't a stupid man. He caught the inference immediately. With a gulp, he scooped up the gold coin and began work on the manacles.

Michael flinched once when the blows of the smith caused a pain to shoot up his useless arm. Blysdale stepped forward immediately. "You flinched. You didn't flinch when he worked on your good hand."

"I wasn't expecting pain. I haven't felt anything in that hand for so long, I was taken by surprise."

"Are you continuing the exercises Griswold taught you?"

"Gris isn't here."

"Blast it, Michael, don't insist on being difficult with me. I've no patience for it!"

"I lack a valet currently."

"Hmmmm. When I get home, I'll send Gris to you."

"No. He's your man, through and through. Have him train someone and send them, if you are so set on the continuation of his torture."

"I should think that that torture would be preferable to

a withered claw in the eyes of a man who is as overfastidious as you are proving to be."

Michael could feel himself pale at the mention of a withered claw. "I'd have it cut off rather than wear it!"

Bly murmured, "Yes, I can easily imagine that you would. There will be no need of such drastic action, however. I shall send you a well-trained valet."

With one final ringing blow the irons fell from Michael's wrists. He wished he could rub them, but of course that was not possible. He contented himself with pressing the wrist of his good hand lightly against his waist and thanking the blacksmith. "I apologize that my need for you has disturbed your rest, Smith, and I thank you for coming."

The blacksmith looked surprised at the courtesy, bobbed his head, gathered his tools and made good his escape. From his place at the exit, Stone closed the door and locked it.

Michael smiled around at them all. His heart swelled with pride to have these men as his friends. That pride shone from his eyes. So did his gratitude. But all he said was "Well, since there is no way I can ever thank you, I'm going to bed. I suggest you do the same."

Laughing, they marched up out of the kitchen, more than content to follow their host's example.

The next day, the fateful day, Alissa's twenty-fifth birthday, dawned bright and clear. Every trace of snow had melted except in the deepest shadows. There was not a cloud in the sky, and the wind was still. By early afternoon, the day was even lovelier, the harsh chill of the morning having been chased away by the sun.

Alissa stood looking out the window. The exquisite gown the modiste and her fourteen tireless seamstresses had fashioned almost overnight flowed about her in shining folds of pristine white satin.

Lady Ellen stopped in the doorway and drew a quick breath. "Oh, my dear, your gown is beautiful." Tears came into her eyes. "You're beautiful."

Alissa said softly, "Look, dearest, the sun is shining."

"Ah. You're thinking of that old saying, aren't you?"

"Yes, I am." She quoted it, " 'Happy the bride the sun shines on.' " She smiled radiantly at her grandmother. "But I truly think I should be happy married to Michael if I were to marry him in the middle of a horrible thunderstorm."

Lady Ellen laughed. "I don't have to tell you how happy I am for you, do I, Lissa?"

"No." Alissa laughed, too. "I think you fell in love with Michael even before I did."

Ellen straightened a fold of Alissa's train, and said, "Of course I did. With more years come more experience and wisdom. I've seen many, many men, so it was not at all difficult to judge the exceptional quality of your Michael."

There was a flurry of silk at the door and Alissa's aunt Isabelle bustled across the room to her. "Let me see you," she commanded, making a circle in the air with an index finger. "Turn around."

Alissa obeyed, turning slowly so that her aunt could view her from all sides.

"Well. You will certainly do. You look quite lovely. I only hope the young man you . . ." She stopped herself and cast a hasty look at her twin.

Fully intending to keep Isabelle from forgetting the threat she had made last night, Lady Ellen spoke in her severest tone. "It is high time that you learned the name and rank of the gentleman Alissa is going to wed, Isabelle. He is Guy Michael Mathers, Fifth Viscount Kantwell, and one of England's heroes." Her expression dared her twin.

Isabelle said weakly, "Well, I suppose one can't be expected to find a duke in a week."

Ellen cleared her throat.

Isabelle sought to save herself, assuring Alissa, "I'm

certain that the Viscount will be quite presentable when he is clean and, er, not wearing chains." She turned to Ellen. "Why, in Heaven's name was he wearing chains in the first place, Ellen? I simply don't understand why he would come to visit Alissa looking like that!"

Ellen, her face determined, took Isabelle's arm in a firm grip and walked her to the door, Isabelle's shoulder on that side jammed into her ear. "As to that, sister, you will have to ask your favorite nephew!"

"Gerald?"

"Yes, Gerald." Ellen propelled her twin into the hall. "And you will have to do it after the wedding." She looked at her sister meaningfully. "I *strongly* suggest that you set your mind to quiet enjoyment of the ceremony for the present. *Strongly.*"

"Really, Ellen. There is no need to threaten me." Ellen gave her a final push, and Isabelle squawked, "And please don't shove!"

Alissa chuckled at the scene she could imagine was taking place in the hall, but she refused to let even Aunt Izzy's foolishness ruin her enjoyment of this day. She went back to looking out the window at the clear blue sky and let happiness wash over her.

A moment later, she was enchanted to see the carriage that was to take her to the church pull up outside. It and the horses were garlanded with white roses.

Quillen summoned Lady Ellen, and Lady Ellen came for her. Alissa and she descended the stairs, with the maids Ellen had brought back to the room with her holding Alissa's train. At the front door, Quillen wrapped her in an ermine cloak to keep her from the chill of the bright, brisk day, and she was on her way to her wedding in a haze of perfect happiness.

Lady Ellen and Aunt Isabelle and Button followed in another carriage. Robin had gone ahead that morning so that he could be familiarized with the layout of the part of the church in which the wedding would take place. John Coachman drove to the church by a circuitous route to give Quillen and Cook and several of the other old servants time to reach the church to attend the wedding.

Behind Alissa's carriage, Stone and MacLain rode at a discreet distance, armed to the teeth. Blysdale would accompany Michael. They were taking no chances.

The church was filled to overflowing with friends. The ladies who had thrown themselves wholeheartedly into arranging Alissa Collington's wedding in a single frantic day had done their job well, and everyone she could wish for was in attendance.

Alissa stepped down from the carriage onto a carpet of white rose petals. Their fragrance filled the air. The dim interior of the ancient church was filled with the same fragrance. Roses were everywhere. Robin, bursting with pride, was waiting just inside to escort her up the aisle.

The thought that there must not be a single hothouse in all of England that had a rose left in it crossed Alissa's mind. A deep gratitude for the kindness of friends welled up in her. Everyone had done all they could to make this hurried wedding memorable.

Tears of joy misted her eyes for only an instant. She blinked them quickly away. There was no way she was going to miss any part of this day even if she was overcome with the thoughtfulness of friends. She kissed Robin's cheek, then slipped her arm through his, and they began the long walk up the church aisle.

Robin, having studied the church floor carefully with the sexton earlier, took her forward confidently. Alissa started to whisper encouragement and appreciation to him, but then she saw Michael, and everything else ceased to exist for her.

He was there at the end of the long aisle. Michael, who was soon to be *her* Michael, her husband. He was standing in the jeweled sunshine that streamed down from the great rose window high in the wall behind him, and the sight of him took her breath away. She wasn't even certain how she got up the aisle to him, wasn't aware of the reassuring pressure of Robin's arm holding her own close to his side. She was only aware of Michael.

He stood between the vicar and Blysdale, his best man, watching Alissa come to him. An awesome sense of tenderness, responsibility, and a piercing sadness flooded him. She was so beautiful, her face aglow with the happiness that belonged to every bride. And she was his to protect, and to cherish, and defend against all harm.

But, a cold inner voice told him, *not yours to bed.* He closed his eyes for an instant against the pain of that particular torture, and concentrated instead on the fact that he could serve her all his days. Right up to the one on which he learned she had at last discovered the man she could truly love and would really want for her husband.

Michael would absent himself from her life then, of course, and from his own, so that she would be free to wed.

Ironic, he thought, *how one changes one's mind only to be brought back to one's resolutions.* He hadn't thought seriously about seeking death since he'd met Alissa. She had wiped from his mind all desire to "shuffle off this mortal coil." Being her protector and the friend of her family had temporarily negated that, had given him a purpose for which to live. And now he wanted to live. He wanted to be with her for as many days, even moments, as he had left.

Right now, he seized the immediate present. Watching the vision she made coming to him here at the altar rail, he let go of all the grim thoughts of duty and his own electedly uncertain future to bask in the presence of his beloved and share with all sincerity in the bonds by which they soon would be joined.

The ceremony passed quickly. Too quickly for Michael, who spent it gazing down at his bride.

When it was over, MacLain called from the back of the

church, "Kiss the bride!" Good-natured laughter and repetitions of the cry rose all around them as they turned from the altar, and Alissa lifted her arms toward him, certain that this might be her last chance for a kiss from Michael for a long while, for who knew how long it would take her to make him love her?

Michael bent his head toward her, his intention a chaste brush of his mouth over hers.

Alissa had a different idea. If Michael intended merely to play at being a husband—acting as her spouse in name only—then she was going to take from him, and thoroughly enjoy, at least this one kiss. To that end, when Michael's lips touched her own, she threw her arms around his neck, twisted her fingers in his crisp, dark hair, and kissed him with all the fervor of her longing to truly be wife to him.

When her slender body molded itself against him, Michael's steel will deserted him. Head spinning, he let his own desperate desire to take from the woman he loved just one memorable kiss overcome him. Now, while she was being encouraged to play the part of a happy bride by the laughing comments of her surrounding friends, he'd seize the advantage that gave him to take, to cherish for the rest of his life, a single kiss.

Chapter Twenty-eight

"You really can't just stand here like that, you know, Major."

Bly's dry comment roused Michael enough to realize he still had his arm around Alissa, still had her clasped tightly to him as if he would never let her go. Alissa was staring up into his eyes with stars in her own, and he counted the world well lost.

Duty called, however. "Of course," Michael murmured, and released her with great reluctance.

They turned to accept the congratulations and wishes for happiness from their friends. Their long training as social beings stood them in good stead, for the kiss had left them both so shaken that the crowd of well-wishers had to propel them out of the church.

Then, laughing, the group left Alissa and Michael waiting in the shadowy vestibule of the ancient stone edifice while they scattered for their carriages. Hastily, they set off for Collington House to be there when the newlyweds arrived for the wedding dinner.

Michael looked down at his bride. "Alissa, I . . ." He didn't get to finish his sentence.

Suddenly, the archway was blocked by a dark form. "This is not the end of it, Niece," Lord Withers snarled. "I shall see to it that you never have a moment of peace. I shall . . ." His sentence ended, incomplete, in a choking gasp.

Michael's steely grip on Gerald's throat stopped him from uttering another word. "If you so much as look at my wife harshly, Withers, you're a dead man!"

Alissa's uncle clawed at Michael's hand with both his own, but to no avail. Michael held him until his eyes rolled up in his head, shook him like a dog shaking a rat and dropped him. Withers fell, half-senseless and whooping for breath, to the flagstones.

"Well done, Major." Blysdale walked sedately past them and out into the bright sunlight to hold open the door of their carriage.

Alissa was transfixed, staring down at her semiconscious uncle.

"Come, children," Bly called.

Michael laughed exultantly. "Yes! We wouldn't want to keep our guests waiting." He threw his arm around Alissa and swept her out of the dark vestibule into the glorious day and down the flagstone steps to Bly and the waiting rose-bedecked carriage.

Still smiling, Michael settled her with her train and her veil around her and thanked Bly as he closed the door for them. Then they were alone in the carriage, and with the sudden cessation of congratulations and kind comments from the crowd of friends at the wedding, a pall of silence seemed to envelop them. He'd been careful to arrange her satins and laces on the seat so that there was really no room

for him beside her without deliberately crushing some bit
of expensive fabric.

Michael felt safer sitting opposite her, safer from his
own desire to sweep her onto his lap and convince her that
he could be more—much more—than just a safeguard
against the piratical intent of her uncle. He had never
wanted anything as desperately as he wanted Alissa
Collington Mathers as his wife in more than name only. He
wanted her to be his helpmate, his dear friend, his lover.
He wanted to lead her through the enchantments of the
magic that two people in love could explore. He wanted to
pleasure her beyond anything she could ever have imagined, to lead her to the heights of human passion and
plunge with her off the dark precipice of desire. He
wanted . . .

But that was not the bargain they had struck. Or, rather,
the bargain he and Lady Ellen had struck. He wasn't husband and lover, he was her guard and, if he were truly fortunate, her fond companion.

Abruptly he turned away from staring at the beautiful
woman who was now his wife and looked out the window.
In quiet anguish, he recalled the bitter cold of the winter
snows in which he'd often fought. Pictured the desperate
struggles to keep the men and horses from starving. The
hopeless task of keeping them warm. The snows, the ice,
the frozen waters. And finally, with aching inertia, the fires
raging in his body subsided.

"I asked if you minded." From across the carriage,
Alissa was looking at him with concern.

"Minded?" he repeated more sharply than he'd intended. "I'm sorry, I was recalling something and didn't
hear your question. I apologize. Would you mind repeating
it?"

Alissa frowned a little as she said again, "I hope you
don't mind Grandmother having arranged for us to stay at

Collington House. It was a decision she came to with Colonel Blysdale, I understand."

Michael regarded her steadily. "I have no objection to the arrangement. The Colonel thought"—his hesitation was scarcely noticeable—"that since Kantwell House will be full of bachelors, you might not be comfortable there." On purpose he neglected to tell her they had decided that one house would be easier to keep guard over than two, given that there were only Bly, Stone, and MacLain to mount guard. Considering the vindictive nature displayed by Alissa's uncle in the vestibule of the church, Bly and he had deemed it necessary to protect Lady Ellen and Robin as well as Alissa for a while.

Alissa looked at him speculatively. She wondered why he'd hesitated. Obviously there must be something more to it, but the idea of denying MacLain the opportunity to set off fireworks outside their bedchamber or some other nonsense was reason enough for her.

Like Michael, she found something she wanted to watch in the passing scene, and their conversation died. Later she would find out what he was keeping secret from her.

Coachman Green drove them close to the front steps of Collington House, and they were rushed by gleeful friends to stand just inside the front door, beside Lady Ellen and Aunt Isabelle, to formally receive their guests. By the time the happy crowd had passed, each one of the number delighting in calling Alissa by her married name, into the ballroom where tables, gleaming with silverware and four-branched candelabras, were set up to accommodate them, it was dark outside.

After the sumptuous dinner and enough toasts to the new couple to put a regiment under the table, Michael and Alissa were escorted to the master suite with much good-humored laughter. There the guests left them and returned to the ballroom to dance.

Michael looked down at Alissa. "Do you mind awfully?"

Alissa frowned, puzzled. "Mind what, Michael?"

"I think it is usual for the bridal couple to waltz once before they retire."

"And?"

"And we did not. Certainly your friends decided that I should be unable to hold you for a waltz." He was stiff with wounded pride, but forced himself to add, "It was very kind of them."

Alissa saw that her next comment might very well set the tone of the rest of their lives together. Her thoughts were as quick as runaway horses. She had no intention of treating this magnificent man as if he were somehow deficient because he had the use of one less arm than the rest of his kind. Hadn't he proven time and again that he did as well with one as the others did with two?

Taking a deep breath, she lifted her chin and began as she intended to go on for the rest of her life. "Then we shall just have to work out suitable adjustments, for I do dearly love to waltz."

Michael took a sharp breath of his own. Whatever he'd expected, it wasn't this. "If you are so fond of waltzing, I have friends who can waltz very well with you."

"And I have a strong desire to waltz with my own husband, thank you." She was staring at him sternly.

"Good God, Alissa, are we having our first disagreement after only two hours of marriage?"

"I don't feel we are having a disagreement at all. I'm just making a preference known to you."

Even with its stubborn expression her face was beautiful. Michael tried not to smile as he told her, "It would seem you are not shy about making us a public spectacle."

"Why, as to that, we can waltz alone in the music room here at Collington House, if you prefer." She thrust her chin at him, daring him. "I do not, however, mind if people stare at us waltzing. They have always stared, and will no doubt continue to do so, because I am beautiful and you are handsome."

Michael was disarmed, and a little taken aback. "Alissa," he said, laughing, "you are shockingly lacking in modesty. . . ."

Button appeared around the corner of the hall and stopped in confusion to see them standing outside the double doors to the master suite. "Are you not yet ready for me, your ladyship?"

With difficulty, Alissa put down the temptation to tell Button that she wanted her to go away. To Michael she said, "We will have to continue this later, Husband. You can apologize then."

"Apologize!" Michael was astounded. "Whatever for?"

But Alissa had swept through the doors into the sitting room of the master suite, crossed it, and disappeared into the bedchamber on the right.

Button said, "Please excuse me, your lordship," brushed past him and went on to close the door to Alissa's bedchamber softly behind them both.

Michael stood, deep in thought. Alissa had called him "Husband."

Black, the butler from Kantwell House, appeared just then and cut off his speculations. "I have come to act as your valet, your lordship."

Michael smiled at him. It would certainly be more comfortable to be helped by his old retainer than to have to call on some Collington servant he didn't know. "Thank you, Black. This is most thoughtful of you."

As they finished and Black slipped Michael's useless hand into the special deep pocket constructed at the side of his dressing gown to hold his arm steady, Michael ordered, "I shall wish to dress at dawn. Can you be here then?"

"Of course, your lordship. Will there be anything else?"

"No, thank you, Black." He waited until his butler had

reached the outer doors to the suite, then added, "And thank you, Black."

Black smiled, dipped his head jerkily, and closed the door noiselessly behind himself.

Alone, Michael took a deep breath. He walked to the window fronting on the square. In the dark park across the street from Collington House, he saw the figure of MacLain leaning against a tree at a vantage point from which he could survey the front of the mansion and see the approach of anyone coming to this side of the square.

To check to see if Bly and Stone were in place guarding the rear, it would be necessary to look out the windows on Alissa's side of the suite. There were things he must tell her, and, he thought with a small smile, he had an apology to make to her. Having thought about that while Black undressed him, he knew it was because he had taken the Lord's name in vain in front of her. Cursing in front of one's wife was not done, and it looked like Alissa had no intention of letting him get away with it. She was going to be a very interesting wife.

It was time to face Alissa. He squared his shoulders and raised his hand to knock on her door.

In the bedchamber designated for the mistress of the house, Alissa lay in the huge four-poster and waited for Michael to come. Her heart pounded so hard and so rapidly she was amazed it didn't shake the bed. Her thoughts ran through her head like ill-behaved children.

What would Michael do? Was he going to be a husband in name only? Her grandmother had, after all, coerced him into marrying her with her plea that he foil her uncle's plan to steal her inheritance. What if Michael truly felt that was all they wanted of him? Wouldn't he be hurt to think that? In his place, she would feel used and rejected.

Of course, he wasn't her. He was a man, and they were a strange breed. It could go either way. He could decide that he had served his purpose and was needed for nothing more—or he could decide that they were married in the eyes of God and man, and that he had every right to claim her body and live with her as his wife.

With all her heart, Alissa hoped he would do the latter. It would be so much easier to convince him she loved him and to make him love her if their bodies were joined as God intended. Surely there must be a way to turn simple physical desire into a loftier passion, and that into true love. Surely, there was someone from whom she could learn how to . . .

There was a soft knock at the door that joined their quarters. Michael! He had finally come. At least that was a first step. What should she say? Enter? Come? Oh, dear Heaven. Who would have thought that she'd be ignorant of the proper call to one's husband to enter one's bedroom? Why hadn't she found that out from her grandmother?

She was saved from saying anything. The door opened slowly, as if she were being given the opportunity to refuse him entrance. She sat up in bed and stared at it. Then it opened at normal speed, and Michael stepped into her bed-chamber.

He seemed taller than before, and his shoulders were wider. His dressing gown was a dark silk that clung to his frame and outlined it to her distraction. Without his cravat, there was a strange intimacy about his appearance that made her a little uncomfortable.

Great heavens! she scolded herself mentally, *it's not as if he came bounding into your room stark naked, Alissa. Stop acting like a ninny!* She fought down a hysterical giggle, not at the thought of Michael coming in unclad but at her own unladylike hope that someday he might. It was clear from the way the silken robe he wore caressed his shoulders that there was no nightshirt under it, and that knowledge filled her with an eager heat that she was certain she should be ashamed of.

She was assailed with a terrible desire to rise from her bed and go to meet him. To stand before him as an equal, not sit like a quaking maiden awaiting her conquering lord. Unfortunately there were two problems with that. First, she didn't know whether Michael had conquering on his mind, and second, she wasn't clad for standing up in front of a man, even a husband—at least not a brand-new one—in the nightrail she had chosen.

Diaphanous in the extreme, it was sheer enough to see through, as if she wore nothing at all. Only the very expensive fullness of lace at the low-cut neckline—which did, admittedly, just barely hide the tips of her breasts—offered any protection from Michael's eyes. Exactly as she had intended.

Unhappily for her urge to stand, though, there was nothing to guard her modesty anywhere else, and she was therefore reluctant to get out of the bed and relinquish her sheet. She wasn't averse to letting the sheet fall into her lap, however, and was fiercely elated to see Michael suck in his breath when she did.

"Yes, Michael?" She felt a small surge of power in being a woman, as he fought to drag his eyes from her. Deliberately taking a deep breath, she held it so that the lace at her neckline lifted ever so slightly. She saw Michael's lips part and a fire begin to burn at the back of his eyes.

Then she saw him make a monumental effort to drag his gaze from her almost bare bosom and could have cursed, if only she had known how! Winning him was going to be difficult, she could see. She had just used all her ammunition, and her target had managed to escape. Obviously she knew no more about seduction than she did about cursing!

Michael walked to the window, his pulse racing and his body almost beyond his control. Breathing deeply, he forced his attention to the garden below him. Yes. There was Stone, and he was certain that Bly, whom he could not discover, was on guard as well.

Excellent. His plan to keep Alissa, Lady Ellen, and Robin safe was in operation, and he was filled with gratitude that he had friends like these who could implement it. He couldn't continue to depend on them, however. Tireless as they seemed, they weren't indefatigable. Soon he would have to get reinforcements, and a defensible position.

The city was so busy that an army of enemies could approach undetected. He intended to move his new family to the country, where every stranger stood out like a sore thumb. That would greatly simplify matters. Which of his estates he would use, he hadn't decided. And, right now, he faced the problem of telling Alissa. Would she object to being married one day and carried off to the country the next? There was only one way to find out.

"Alissa."

"Yes?"

He turned away from his vigil at her window to face her, and the battle for self-control almost began again. Forcing his mind away from such thoughts and fixing his gaze on the top of the bed's headboard, he told her, "Tomorrow I plan to leave for the country. Possibly Kantwell Hall in Kent."

Alissa was astonished, "Why?"

"I feel we will be more private there. That it will be easier to protect all of you if your uncle should try to make good on his threat to ruin your peace. He might seek to injure Robin or Lady Ellen, you know."

"Yes, I see." She sat with the bedclothes clasped under her chin and frowned. "Could we not go to Collington Park, then?"

"I don't know it. I know every inch of my own estate in Kent."

"But Robin knows every inch of Collington Park. The house, at least, and though he has been very good about it, using his cane to get around while we've been here has been difficult for him."

"Of course. Collington Park it will be then. I'll be inviting Stone and MacLain. I hope you don't mind." *How stilted this blasted conversation is!* Michael fumed inwardly. *You'd think we'd been married years and years and were bored silly with each other!*

"No, of course not."

"Very well. We'll leave day after tomorrow, then." With that he turned and left her room.

Alissa flung herself back on her pillows so hard she bounced. "Wonderful!" she muttered. "Not only is my husband totally uninterested in me as a wife, but he has to invite friends to visit to ease the boredom of being in my company!" She knew she wasn't being fair. Nor even truthful. Michael was taking his comrades to help him guard her family. But it was her wedding night. And she did love him. Terribly. And she was certain now that the great idiot was completely unaware of that fact. And worst of all, she knew that she had no idea of how to go about making him see.

Most of all, she was feeling very frustrated. That wonderful sense of womanly power that had so lifted her spirits had gone, and her dreams had collapsed like a house of cards! She felt curiously flat.

She heaved a tremendous sigh. Not only had she failed as a seductress, but she felt neglected. Very neglected. Now she just wanted to feel sorry for herself, for she knew she richly deserved to.

So, holding that thought firmly in her mind, Alissa turned over, buried her face in her pillow, and, concentrating very hard on doing it, finally managed to cry.

Chapter Twenty-nine

Alissa went down to breakfast late the next morning and found Colonel Blysdale in the front hall with her grandmother.

"Alissa! Come and say good-bye to the Colonel. He is about to leave London for Cliffside and his Katherine."

Alissa hurried across the parquet of the foyer and grasped Blysdale's hand. "I shall always be indebted to you for bringing Michael home safe." She laughed. "And in time to save us."

Blysdale looked straight into her eyes, and Alissa felt as if he were penetrating to her very soul. She lowered her lids to safeguard her innermost thoughts. It was too late. In an agony of embarrassment, she heard him ask Lady Ellen, "May I be permitted a word alone with your lovely granddaughter, Ellen?"

"Of course, Chalfont."

Alissa wondered if sleigh-driving Russians fleeing

across the snow threw their children to the wolves as casually!

"Shall we?" Bly offered her his arm, leaving the choice of a place to talk up to Alissa.

She chose the yellow drawing room. It was the cheeriest. It was also farthest from the front hall, so there was less chance they would be disturbed—or overheard.

In silence, Blysdale escorted her across the pale Oriental carpet to a settee covered in yellow damask. He waited for her to seat herself comfortably, then took his place beside her and turned so that his piercing regard was full on her face.

The effect this had on Alissa astonished her. She burst into tears.

"So," he said handing her his handkerchief. "Mathers did not consummate your marriage."

Alissa's tear-drenched eyes flew wide with shock.

"You are shocked?" he murmured. "That is a very great pity, for there is nothing I can do for you if you cannot bear plain speaking."

Alissa gulped back a sob and wiped away her tears. She could bear anything if it would help her marriage. Straightening her shoulders, she looked Bly straight in the eye and demanded, "What must I do?"

"Good girl!" He clapped a hand on her knee in approval and rose. Standing in front of her, he began. "We have established the fact that you owe me a debt for having brought Michael safely back to you. It is my desire that you cancel that debt."

If Alissa hadn't known that Colonel Blysdale was wildly in love with his wife, she might have quailed at his intent stare. "Yes?" she managed.

"I shall consider that your doing of what I am about to suggest will discharge your debt to me. Is that agreeable to you?"

"Yes, of course," she said with a caution born of a sudden instinct for self-preservation, "if you wish."

"Very good." He clasped his hands behind him in the position of a soldier at ease and rocked from heel to toe for a moment before he went on. "It is my intention that you shall make Major Mathers the happiest of men."

Alissa couldn't help it, laughter bubbled out of her. When Blysdale looked at her in astonishment, she told him, "There is nothing I'd rather do more!"

"Excellent. We are in accord.

"First, you must know your husband's history insofar as it applies to your problem."

Alissa nodded.

"Michael was the most social and charming of all us Lucky Seven. He could charm the blasted birds out of the trees. Quickest to laugh, he was the most sought after at social gatherings, received the most invitations, and was the most welcome at parties. Beyond even that, Michael was the delight of more ladies than all the rest of us put together were privileged to pleasure. His prowess as a lover was a well-known fact."

Bly stopped and scowled at Alissa. "Please stop gaping and attempt to control your blushes. You've agreed to plain speaking, and I've no time for anything else."

Alissa balled her hands into fists and told him in a tight little voice, "Go on please. I shall do my best."

"Very well. This man, my friend and your husband, came across a band of men last year who were abducting women to be sold as slaves in the Eastern bazaars."

Alissa gasped.

Bly ignored her and continued. "Interfering as any true Englishmen would, he killed two of the slavers, and put others out of the fight, you can be sure. Fighting alone, however, he really didn't have a chance. They overcame him, took him prisoner. They took Smythe, another friend, as well. He was Michael's traveling companion but he had absolutely no skills as a warrior. David's excellent mind had been employed in planning battle strategies rather than in fighting them. He was, therefore, of precious little help."

Alissa's fists crushed into the bosom of her dress to still the wild beating of her heart. Michael in danger, even in danger past, filled her with anguish.

Her reaction seemed to please the saturnine Bly, so he went on in a tone that suggested the slavers reacted in exactly the manner one would have expected. "The blackguards hung Michael in chains against a damp cave wall, and proceeded to beat him senseless for the deaths of their comrades."

Alissa couldn't help it. She began to cry again, big silent tears that simply spilled over and ran down her cheeks as she saw in her mind's eye her beloved Michael hanging in a dark cave in chains. She could see manacles on his wrists as she had seen them the other night, could see his lithe body stretched against the wall, and could see brutish men, bent on vengeance, approaching him.

She refused to permit herself to "see" more than that. Anything else would be beyond her ability to endure.

Bly was not so considerate. He went on matter-of-factly, "In subsequent beatings Michael was struck on the shoulder by a club with enough force to destroy his use of that arm."

He peered at Alissa and found her pale as chalk, but still upright. He nodded his satisfaction.

"Shortly thereafter he contracted the fever that killed many of the captives held with him. He told us that Smythe died in that minor epidemic. For some reason, he thinks he's responsible for his friend's death." Bly considered that for a moment then announced, "Asinine of him, of course. He was out of his head and has no idea *what* happened to Smythe, and he certainly had no way of preventing it."

Alissa regarded him unblinkingly.

"Good," Bly approved. "You've managed to get through the worst of it."

Alissa wiped the tears from her cheeks and kept her gaze riveted on Blysdale's face.

"And there you have it. By the time we rescued him, Michael was a shadow of himself, fever-ridden and half-starved. A man full of unreasonable guilt for the death of a friend, rendered a partial cripple by a wound not the result of battle—which I'm certain he could accept with better grace—and no longer possessing his ability to . . ." He stopped abruptly.

Alissa regarded him steadily. Her eyes told him she would hear the rest if it killed her.

"Plain speaking," Bly reminded himself as well as Alissa. "Michael had enjoyed his reputation as a ladies' man. After all, he had the little darlings falling over themselves to get him into their beds."

Alissa felt as if she would burst with jealousy. It was a new emotion for her, and it took her completely by surprise.

Recognizing her expression, Blysdale cleared his throat and started on another tack. "Now we find this man who has always been, shall we say, more than able to please the ladies, maimed."

Alissa felt her temper flare. "Don't use that word about him! That creature at the ball used that word, and I wanted to tear her hair out."

"Oh? That was merely one of his, er"—he searched for a word that wouldn't be too shocking for a gently bred female—"*chères amies*, paramours." Bly's shrug was as Gallic as his words had been. "No one to take seriously. He had dozens."

"Dozens!" Alissa was scandalized.

Bly considered her reaction and decided that more needed to be said. "I told you he had an eye for the ladies, and a highly competitive attitude when it came to them and his fellow officers. But you will notice I have used the past tense. That man was not the Michael you have met. He is a very different man from the charming rogue he was before his experiences in that prison cave under Cliffside."

Alissa was regarding him with eyes that seemed to fill her face.

"It has taken the better part of a year to nurse him back to health, and we have all been deeply concerned at the changes in him. There is no frivolity left, you see. I fear that he had every intention of . . . But that is beside the point. Now that he has met and fallen in love with you, I have great hopes for his future. We have only to get him over this little hump, and all will be well."

"What 'little hump'?"

"The hump of being reluctant to be a true husband to the woman he loves, and who loves him, of course."

"Of course." Sarcasm dripped from Alissa's words. "Little" looked like a mountain to her.

Bly decided to ignore her and get on with it. "Any man with his lover would like to have the use of both hands to, ah, bring the object of his affection to the place at which she is eager to join him in the act of love."

Alissa held the breath she had just drawn, fearful that she might show the depth of the embarrassment she was suddenly feeling. Her eyes went wider and rounder in spite of her best efforts.

"Even more to the point in Michael's case, a man making love to a woman holds his weight off her as he does. This takes two hands. Michael no longer has the use of both his hands."

He stopped and watched Alissa until she finally took her next breath. "That's better."

Alissa willed him to continue.

"You, Alissa, will have to, er, take charge, so to speak." His cheeks colored.

Emboldened by Bly's having come at last to a subject

he wasn't altogether comfortable with, Alissa demanded, "And just how do I do this?"

"No," Bly said firmly, "Your first problem is how to get to the point that you are given the opportunity to do it."

"Granted!" Alissa felt the faint stirring of exasperation. "And how do I do *that*?"

Blysdale cocked his head and considered. "For that you need a tutor."

"A *tutor*?" Alissa was scandalized again. Surely Colonel Blysdale didn't think she would engage in such a conversation with *another* man. It was only Blysdale's legend as having the ability to totally detach his mind that had gotten her this far!

"I suppose I mean a 'tutoress,' if there is such a word."

Thank Heaven! At least she wouldn't have to face another man with her questions about marital intimacy. Alissa was conscious of a great flood of relief. It was doomed to an early death, however.

"Yes, Lady Alissa. It will be necessary for you to hire a consultant from the ranks of the city's, er, courtesans. And you must do it quickly, as you are to leave tomorrow."

"I beg your pardon!"

"What about? I've made myself perfectly plain. Send your butler out to hire a prostitute to teach you what you must do." He frowned at her. "Where else do you think you'll learn how to seduce a man? Do you think any of the frozen wives of your overpolite friends can help you? Ha!"

He walked across the room and scooped up his hat from the chair on which he'd flung it as they'd entered. "No. Only a woman who must rely for her very living on her ability to please a man can teach you what you must know."

Alissa stared at him.

"It has been a pleasure meeting you, Lady Alissa." He bowed and opened the door. "I trust I have been of some small assistance, but now I must go. My wife awaits."

"But . . ."

He smiled, and she would swear she could smell brimstone as he ordered quietly, "Go hire a yourself a whore, Alissa."

Chapter Thirty

She came swathed from head to toe in heavy veils, led in from the back of the house by a thoroughly disapproving Quillen.

Waiting in the study, Alissa, her grandmother, and her aunt Isabelle were showing diverse signs of nervousness. They were seated in a semicircle facing the vacant chair that awaited their guest.

Quillen brought the courtesan into the study with his nose so high in the air that Alissa wondered how he avoided tripping over something.

"The *person* you asked me to bring to you, madame," he announced.

Oh dear, demoted from ladyship to madame, Alissa thought. *I must have really blotted my copybook this time. It's going to take a long time to work my way back into Quillen's good graces, and we leave tomorrow.*

"Thank you," Lady Ellen told the butler in a frigid tone. "That will be all."

Quillen spun around to face her, his expression incredulous. In his turn, he'd been reduced from butler to a servant not deserving the use of his name. When Lady Ellen met his shocked gaze and held it with a steely one of her own, he got the point. Walking stiffly to the door, he turned and offered, "Would your *ladyship* like tea, Lady Alissa?"

Alissa took pity on him and accepted his apology. "Thank you, Quillen. That would be very nice."

His composure restored with the tacit acknowledgment of his proper station, Quillen bowed himself out of the study.

As the door closed behind him, Alissa spoke to the figure in the chair she faced. "Wouldn't you like to take off your veils? The room is warm."

"Thank you." Her voice was low and breathy. As she removed her veils, letting them fall to the floor around her chair, she displayed the skillfully painted face of a woman past her prime but still attractive.

Alissa sighed a sigh of relief. This was no green girl. From this woman, she should be able to learn what she wanted to know.

"Did my butler explain to you why I asked him to bring you here?"

"No, he did not, but I think I can guess."

"Oh?"

"Yes. I imagine you want to know either how to give your husband or lover greater pleasure in bed, or how to avoid conceiving a child."

Isabelle gasped. "Well, I never!"

Ellen said, "Hush, Izzy."

Alissa recognized the defensiveness behind the woman's provocative comment and understood it. With a kindness she hadn't know she was going to feel, she said, "This must be as difficult for you as it is for me."

The woman colored, raised her chin, and began as if she were delivering a lecture. "There are a thousand little gestures that move a man. If you touch your mouth frequently, for instance, he is intrigued. If you suck at a finger, he is undone."

"Why is that?" Isabelle wanted to know.

The courtesan looked as if she would like to answer, but decided not to. "Running a finger from your lips down your chin and, if you have the courage for it, close to—or best yet, into—your cleavage will drive him wild."

"Like this?" Isabelle traced the route in less than a second.

"No, madame. Definitely not like that. Like this." And she put her head back, lowered her eyelids till her eyes were slits, assumed a dreamy expression, and, as if she were unaware of what she did, traced the path ever so slowly with her index finger, lingering on her lower lip before starting. "Like that."

Alissa drew a breath. It made her realize she had been holding hers.

"Yes," Ellen whispered from beside her. "She does have that effect."

Satisfied that she had their undivided attention, the woman went on. "Touching is very important to a man. Touch him as often as you can find an excuse. Run your fingers through his hair if he will permit it, and end by resting your hand on the nape of his neck."

Isabelle informed her with some heat, "My grandniece would never do such things! Why, a lady doesn't behave in that fashion."

Alissa said quietly, "This lady shall, if it will help her marriage."

"Ellen, are you going to let this shameful proceeding go on?" Isabelle demanded.

"Izzy, either be quiet or be gone." Ellen looked hard at her sister, and finally Isabelle sat back with her lips firmly closed.

Alissa looked at the courtesan. "I pray you will continue."

"Whisper when you wish to tell him something. Don't lean forward like a schoolroom miss with a ruler up her back. Lead with your breasts, try to touch them to his shoulder first, then bend your head in toward him to whisper." She rose and demonstrated the movement. "Like this."

There was something so seductive in the courtesan's almost sinuous movement that Alissa felt her pulse quicken. She *was* going to learn how to seduce Michael!

"When you whisper, make certain you blow just a breath behind his ear. This is done as you approach the ear, saying 'Oooh, John,' as if you are trying to get his attention. That 'oooh' is the breath that will touch his neck and or behind his ear."

"I see." Alissa wanted to say something that would encourage her instructress.

"Be certain, too, that your breast touches some part of him. Arm, shoulder, back, or chest. It will depend on his position and your approach."

"Of course."

"Whispers are very useful unless you are flat-chested, which I can see that you are not." She smiled a tight little smile, as if waiting to be reprimanded for her familiarity.

Lady Ellen stated firmly, "No, my granddaughter is not flat-chested. I perceive that it is necessary for you to evaluate her weapons, as it were, and do not take it as an impropriety."

Isabelle gasped.

The courtesan smiled. "You are a very perceptive woman, milady."

Lady Ellen acknowledged the compliment with a nod. "Pray continue."

"Touch your gentleman as often as you can with your

breast. For some reason a woman's bosom seems to fascinate men more than any other part of her body."

Isabelle burst out, "I can't see how a lady can go around pushing her chest at every gentleman she meets."

The woman laughed, a rich, low, pleasant sound. "No, I suppose not." Turning back to Alissa, she said, "When he offers you his arm, touch the side of your breast to his upper arm as you take it. If that is too intimate a position for the situation, you can always pull back. The damage will have been done. If you are able to leave it in contact with his arm, you may rest assured his blood will rush more quickly through his veins the longer it is there."

Alissa's eyes were a little wider than she wished them to be.

The woman's eyes took on a kindly expression. "I'm aware this must be embarrassing to you, milady. If you wish, please stop me at any time."

Alissa nodded, not trusting her voice.

"We shall," Lady Ellen told her.

"Certainly you realize that sitting on a gentleman's lap is forbidden in society for good reason, but if you can manage to sit on your husband's lap and squirm to get better settled . . ."

"Squirm! Like a fish? This is absurd!" Isabelle had opened a fan and was applying it vigorously.

"When you kiss him on the cheek, again lead with your bosom. Don't collide with him and spring away. Press yourself against him, rise on tiptoe for the chaste kiss on the cheek, and slide your breasts down his chest when you return to your flat-footed stance. As I say, a woman's best weapon is her bosom."

Isabelle demanded, "What if I have wiped my bosom all over him and nothing happens?"

"Why, then we go on to other tricks. At table, slip your foot from your slipper and run your foot up and down his leg. Very, very slowly."

Isabelle kicked off the satin slipper that matched her gown and wiggled her stockinged foot around in front of her. "And if that doesn't work?"

Lady Ellen was frowning at her twin.

"Then you must do something even . . . no, *much* more daring."

Alissa's eyes widened again. What could be more daring than the things the woman had already told them?

"You must trace his inner thigh with the toe of your foot."

"No!" Isabelle nearly fell off her chair.

"Ah, yes. It is quite effective, I assure you."

"What next?" Isabelle was breathless.

Alissa and Ellen were both staring at Isabelle.

"Next"—the courtesan leaned toward her and whispered dramatically—"you put your foot . . . so very gently . . . in his lap."

Ellen shot to her feet. "But that is where his . . ."

"Exactly!"

Isabelle cried, "His what? What is in his lap?"

Quillen, entering at that moment, nearly dropped the tea tray. Recovering quickly, he took his revenge for all the trouble Isabelle delighted in causing him and the rest of his staff. In his most formal manner he intoned, "His genitals, madame, his genitals." Then he turned to Alissa and inquired serenely, "Will that be all, milady?"

Ellen flapped him out of the room with her free hand while she and Alissa hung onto each another to keep from falling out of their chairs with suppressed laughter.

Chapter Thirty-one

Michael arrived a few minutes later from Kantwell House, where he'd gone to make last-minute arrangements for their removal to Collington Park on the morrow, and had ordered the knocker taken off the front door to signify his absence. Black had grumbled that he had just barely gotten the knocker *up*, and Cook had wailed that she had purchased all manner of good food to prepare for him and his guests and had started to throw her apron over her head to shelter herself for a good cry.

Seeking to avert the threatening flood of tears, Michael had suggested that Cook really ought to be busy preparing a great many of the treats she'd bought for him, so that he and his guests could have a picnic to sustain them on the trip to Collington Park. That turned the trick, and Cook had gone back to her kitchen eagerly, her step light.

Now, as he handed his hat to Quillen, who was obviously striving to conceal laughter, he had to step aside to avoid being run down by Alissa's aunt Isabelle and her grandmother. Isabelle had Ellen by the hand and was pulling her along, saying, "That was surely the most interesting and eye-opening lecture it has ever been my good fortune to attend."

Ellen murmured, "Great heavens."

"But it has left me feeling a trifle warm. Surely we can get ices at Gunther's even if it *is* winter. I really would like one, wouldn't you?"

"I . . ."

The end of Lady Ellen's reply was lost as the door closed behind them.

Bemused, Michael asked Quillen, "What was that all about?"

"I couldn't say, your lordship." His twitching lips betrayed his duplicity.

"Oh?"

"Miss Isabelle is given to strange fits and starts, you see. Quite unpredictable."

"Ah, well. Yes." Michael gave up trying for information. Through one of the front door's sidelights, he stared at the two elderly ladies being helped into their waiting carriage. "So long as nobody lets her get hold of a parasol."

"Quite so, sir!" Quillen barely made it out of Michael's presence before he was doubled over with laughter.

Michael shook his head, convinced that his own remark had not been that amusing, and went to find Alissa. He finally located her at the end of the back hall. She was bidding good-bye to a tall, slender woman wrapped in veils who seemed determined to leave the house by the back door.

"Don't forget," the woman was saying to his wife, "if the dining table is too wide, you can always play cards." With that enigmatic comment she slipped out the door, and was gone before Michael reached them. When Alissa turned, she gave a start that Michael could only interpret as guilty. "Oh! Michael! It's you."

He frowned slightly, "Is everything all right, Alissa?"

She took a deep breath and hid her hands behind her in case it became necessary to cross her fingers at any time in their conversation. "Aside from the rush to get everybody packed for the move to Collington Park, all goes . . . as planned." She could hardly say "as usual" because it was certainly not usual to visit with a woman of ill repute, but she definitely did not want her new husband to become curious about what had been going on here this morning.

Michael smiled down at her, and she was struck again by how handsome he was. She was indeed a fortunate woman. She had married the man of her dreams in spite of the greatest odds against that happening. Doing so had saved her family by saving her inheritance, and she had just been given a plan by which to seduce the tall, serious man in front of her. And more.

She rose on her tiptoes and fought down her inbred tendency to keep from making physical contact. It really was quite difficult to overcome years of training, but she managed it. She pressed her chest against Michael's broad one.

She felt the quick intake of his breath, and was ridiculously pleased. Planting the kiss a little closer to the corner of his mouth than she had intended when she began, she could feel the second quickly drawn breath.

Michael's eyes looked a little wild for a moment, and Alissa knew he was fighting not to take her in his arms. He loved her, Bly had told her so. He wanted her, she knew it with a wonderful certainty. From the heightened color in his cheeks and the careful way her new husband was controlling his breathing now, she felt certain that she'd had a little bit of an effect on him. The knowledge gave her such a heady sense of power that it almost made up for her feelings of inadequacy on her wedding night.

Last night. That was only last night! He'd walked out of

her bedchamber without making her truly his wife only last night. He had left her crying and incomplete. Surely the man deserved no mercy.

She decided she had let him off too easily with that one chaste kiss on the cheek. Especially when she had the most pressing urge to grab him by the ears if she had to, in order to kiss him full on the mouth! Slipping her arm through his, she purred, "Shall we go see all that I have done?" She shoved her ladylike training aside and made very sure the side of her breast was firmly in contact with Michael's upper arm as they moved.

After all, Blysdale had assured her that Michael loved her, so she felt no shame that she was engaged in a campaign to push him past his rigid self-control. She was totally and firmly committed to forcing him to admit his love for her.

Alissa had made up her mind.

All unwittingly, Michael foiled Alissa's best plans. He spent that night at Kantwell House organizing the caravan that would be going to Collington Park. Early the next morning they picked up Alissa and her family and the baggage wagon they needed now that Great-aunt Isabelle had decided to join them for a brief visit. It took the better part of the day to get everyone under way, and thanks to all the delays, they got only as far as the inn at which they had stayed before.

There was still snow on the landscape to remind them of that subtle magic of moonlight on snow during their last stay. Today, however, the magic was held at bay. Alissa wanted to kick Michael for riding Gladiator instead of keeping her company. But she had her grandmother and her aunt as well as Robin with her in the comfortable Kantwell coach, and knew he was right not to crowd them. Even with Button riding in the servants' carriage, there was still not room enough for a man as large as Michael without crowding someone.

When he bespoke separate bedrooms for them, Alissa wanted to scream. All her newly learned expertise was useless if she couldn't get near him! *No matter*, she told herself firmly. Collington Park was only half a day away now. She would be able to seduce her husband once they were safely there, she knew. And, as Michael had said, "All of us will be better for a good night's sleep."

Other than being frustrating, the trip was uneventful. Evidently, Alissa reasoned, her uncle had decided to give up his foolish threat. She was greatly relieved. One could live on one's guard only so long.

They swept through the gates at Collington Park and the gatekeeper sounded the horn that would alert the house to their arrival, while his family stood proudly behind him and waved. They stared so hard at Michael that Alissa knew they'd had word of her marriage. She marveled at how news traveled among servants. She had let Kemp know they were coming just yesterday.

She settled back to watch her new husband as he rode easily beside the carriage. Gladiator seemed tireless, but that was because Michael had enforced periods of walking that had refreshed all the horses. Alissa smiled. There was certainly an advantage in being married to a cavalryman. Under her uncle's control, they had worn teams out and had to replace them with inferior post horses frequently.

Michael looked tireless, as well. He seemed part of the horse, and as relaxed as if he sat in a chair in his study. But then, he'd spent long hours in the saddle during the war with Napoleon, so she supposed it was to be expected. Hours in the saddle might cause him to be slender, but none of that guaranteed he would be as handsome as he was. She smiled as she studied him.

"Good Heavens, Alissa," Isabelle said, "you really

mustn't look as if you're the cat who ate the canary, you know."

Alissa looked at her, startled and not understanding.

"It's not fashionable to be so in love with one's husband in high society."

"Leave the child alone, Izzy. She's extremely fortunate to love the man she's married to. Few women in our class have that blessing."

"Oh, tush, Ellen. You loved your husband."

"Finally, yes."

"Well, I suppose it *is* nice that Alissa is starting out in love." She sighed heavily. "From all I've learned, it doesn't last long."

"Oh, for Heaven's sake, Izzy. Don't be such a wet blanket."

"Wet blanket? Me?" Isabelle drew herself up haughtily. "I am merely giving her the benefit of my experience."

Ellen leaned toward her sister. "Izzy, you don't *have* any experience." She drew the words out carefully. "You're a spinster."

"Well, I've heard a lot from my friends." Izzy flounced around in the seat to turn a shoulder to the others and sulk.

Robin asked in a small voice, "Are we there yet?"

Alissa took his hand. "I can see the towers over the tops of the trees. Only a few more miles left, dear."

Stone and MacLain had seen the towers, too. MacLain said something to Stone that Alissa couldn't hear and they tore off. She assumed that they were bored with outrider duty and had decided to race. As she watched, Gladiator threw up his head and whinnied, yearning to race after them. Instead of holding him back, Michael galloped him in a large circle on the deep green turf of the park, letting him work some of his enthusiasm off without leaving the carriage.

Alissa caught her breath at the ease with which her *husband* managed it, then leaned back and basked in the enjoyment of his mastery. A spine-tingling thrill went through her to see him once again prove that he was able to do with one hand what most men could not have accomplished with two. The big thoroughbred's blood was up, and racing ran strongly in it, but Michael turned him effortlessly with rein and leg, casually preventing the great horse from tearing off after his friends.

A few minutes later, they had arrived at the terraces on which the sprawling manor of Collington Park stood. The rose brick of the manor was warmed by the setting sun, and every window glinted with the light of the sunset. Alissa wondered if she had ever seen her home look so beautiful, or whether the boundless happiness she felt at being Michael's wife colored everything around her.

Stone and MacLain's race had had the desired effect, and the entire staff of Collington Park stood in a long double line that formed a corridor from the bottom terrace at the spot where they would arrive to the front door, all waiting to greet the new master and to welcome Lady Ellen, Alissa, and Robin home.

When the coach pulled up and stopped, the Collington Park butler, Kemp, hurried forward. Grooms came to take the horses from their riders, and two took charge of the coach. Footmen broke out of the line and swarmed down to unload the baggage wagon as it pulled up. Amid the hubbub Alissa, smiling radiantly, introduced her old friend Kemp to her new husband.

Then the newlyweds passed through the double line of servants. As they went, Alissa nodded and smiled and presented the older ones to Michael. When they were at last inside and the crowd had gone back to its duties, Michael grinned. "For a moment there, I was afraid I'd married the queen."

"Oh, Michael, I know there are a great many of them, but Collington Park is so vast, it really does need an army to run it. And they are all your responsibility now, you know."

Michael saw that she was holding her breath and looking at him earnestly, anxiously, as if she feared any decision he might be about to make.

He put his hand under her chin to lift her face and looked deep into her eyes. "Remember me?" he asked softly. "I'm the man who's come to guard your life, not to change it. These people have long been in your service, and I think I'm right in surmising that they have been your friends."

He smiled gently, letting her see that he understood her anxiety. Now that she was his wife, everything she had owned, all she had been responsible for, was his to do with as he would. He bent his head and kissed her forehead. Then he said, teasing, "I'm sure they won't be any more difficult to look after than a full regiment."

Tears sparkled on her lashes, and she reached up and touched his cheek. "Oh, thank you, Michael. I was so afraid . . ."

"That I would take over and make drastic changes in your life?"

"Yes. No. No, just the servants. I trust you. It's just that there are so many of them, and some of them are rather old. But they . . ."

Michael just stood looking down at her, until she ran out of breath suddenly and dropped the subject. She trusted him with her life, now she trusted him with those of her servants. Now, all her only worries were past—except one.

Michael handed her his handkerchief and she wiped away her tears. "Thank you. I must see to our guests, and to dinner . . . and to Aunt Izzy before she attacks Kemp." She gestured to a waiting footman. "John will show you to the master suite."

Michael just smiled at her, white teeth flashing in his tanned face. "It's rather nice to see you a little flustered."

Alissa's heart tripped, stopped, and took up its rhythm again a little wildly. Taking a steadying breath, she stood looking at him for a long moment, admiring his broad shoulders and military bearing, and the way his windblown hair curled around the nape of his neck. How fortunate she felt. How cherished and blessed and protected.

Michael looked back at her and wondered how he would feel if this brave, delectable woman were really his wife. Even though that wish was denied him, it was still balm to his spirit to see her able to relax the iron control under which she'd held herself. He'd done that. He had, by marrying her, granted her the safety she had lacked. He'd served his God-given purpose, and his heart swelled to realize it.

As he watched, Alissa pulled herself together. With another radiant smile, she met his gaze with one that told him she was glad he was here. That she was happy to have his protection over her life. She turned to go about her duties as hostess, then quickly turned back.

Michael halted the footman who had started to lead him to the master suite. "One moment, John."

When he'd given her his undivided attention, Alissa took a deep breath, gave Michael a mysterious little smile, and told him, "By the way, after dinner we'll play cards."

Chapter Thirty-two

Dinner had been served at seven, in keeping with country house hours, and everything had been perfect. Alissa had changed to the special gown she'd had made for just this night, and everyone else had bathed and changed, promptly gathered in the drawing room.

Michael had been the last to come down because he'd had to have John, the young footman who'd been assigned to take him to his rooms, aid him in dressing. When he'd entered the room and seen his wife in the clinging silk gown she'd selected, he'd stopped dead in his tracks.

"'Bout time you got here, old boy." MacLain, oblivious as ever, had broken the spell. "Picnics are all very well. In fact, your cook's was splendid, but I like my wineglass to sit before me on a firm surface, don't you know."

Now they were all in the library, even the two older ladies. In spite of the fact that Lady Ellen had complained of being a little tired, and had tried to get Isabelle to go to bed as well; they were both sitting near the card table Kemp had had set up for the four who were to play.

Isabelle looked so alert and attentive, one would have thought that she was learning the rules of the game by observing the players. Lady Ellen, looking grim, jabbed at, instead of stitched, the piece of embroidery she had picked up.

"She is going to . . ." The whisper came from the corner where Lady Ellen and Isabelle sat.

"Shush!" was Lady Ellen's rejoinder.

Michael was curious, but somehow he couldn't get his eyes to move from Alissa, much less turn enough of his attention their way to determine what the two were talking about. She stood calmly waiting for him, her slender body sheathed in a column of white silk that gave him the feeling she was wearing nothing under it, for it seemed to cling lovingly to her every curve. Her dark curls were brushed back from her face and threaded through with a white silk ribbon embroidered with tiny red roses. Her cheeks and lips seemed rosier than usual, but he put it down to the fact that it was considerably warmer in the room than he'd expected it to be—and the temperature was climbing.

There didn't seem to be as much air here in the spacious library, either. Or, if there was, he wasn't getting his full share of it. To remedy that, he consciously took a deep breath and then had to try not to let it go in too much of a rush. Alissa was so beautiful. She was so hard to resist. Especially for a fool who wanted her more than he'd ever wanted anything in his life.

Standing there, smiling gently, she represented everything he had been looking for. She was intelligent and brave and kind, and the fact that she was beautiful as well was simply a gift. It was taking all his strength to remember that she had married him for safety, not love.

Blast it! Why did she have to look at him as if his presence added something wonderful to her evening?

Alissa moved close and touched his arm. Softly she said to him, "I hope we'll be partners, don't you, Michael?"

If he had to be honest, Michael would rather have MacLain as his partner. That arrangement would have demanded that he put all his concentration on the game, at least. Focusing all his attention on the cards might spare him some of this gut-wrenching yearning after Alissa.

Stone stepped forward and picked up the pack of cards. In one long, smooth gesture, he fanned them out on the tabletop, and the four of them each withdrew a card from the deck. Partners thus chosen, they took their places. Both Stone and MacLain helped seat Alissa, for she'd gotten *her* wish and was Michael's partner. Thus, she sat across the table from him.

Michael regretted the arrangement. He'd really counted on partnering MacLain. Then the game would have distracted him.

It didn't. Shock, however, did. When he felt Alissa's foot touch his leg, he threw his cards down and shot to his feet. Stone and MacLain looked at him in surprise as he said, "Gentlemen. Ladies. I know you will excuse us."

"Oh, dear!" Ellen was taken by surprise as well.

"Oh, good!" her twin crowed.

Michael took Alissa by the hand and pulled her from the room.

"Oh, I say," MacLain murmured. "I had rather a good hand."

Stone, smiling after the newlyweds, invited, "Ladies, won't you join us for a game or two of cards?"

Michael didn't slow until he reached the master suite. Alissa ran to keep up with him, her skirt clutched in her free hand to keep her from stumbling over it in their haste.

When they reached their private sitting room, the draperies had not yet been pulled across the tall windows. Through them, stars glittered in the cobalt vault of the sky and added their faint light to the glow of the few candles Kemp had lit.

The soft light showed Alissa that Michael's face was as set as if carved of granite. She hadn't said a word the whole way up the stairs and down the long hall. Strangely, she wasn't nervous, just wondering what Michael was going to say or do. After all, she had begun this. There was nothing to do but await the outcome. With a monumental calm she had never felt before, she knew exactly what *she* was going to do to precipitate that outcome, and she waited for Michael to make the first move before she did it.

"I suppose Colonel Blysdale put you up to that." It was a grim-faced accusation.

A thousand answers seemed to crowd her mind, but she spoke without consciously choosing any of them. "He helped me to find a way to be your wife."

"What does that mean, Alissa?"

It was time to take charge of this situation. She had no answers she was willing to give him—indeed, she wasn't certain she had any answers at all—but she had no intention of losing the battle in which she feared they were engaged. She moved closer. Reaching up, she began loosening his cravat.

Michael's eyes widened. "Alissa . . ."

"*That* means that I have every intention of being a wife to you, Michael." She freed the knot, and saw his nostrils flare. "I do not want a marriage of convenience." She began to pull the untied cravat from around his neck. "It is true that you have saved my family and fortune by marrying me," she began. She had been looking at his cravat. Now she raised her great gray eyes and looked straight into his startled blue ones. "But that is really beside the point now. Now you are my husband in the eyes of God and man, and my husband you shall be." She slid the rest of his cravat from around his neck and dropped it. Working slowly, one at a time, she undid the buttons on his vest.

Michael was looking at her with something akin to horror as she reached for the buckle of the belt that held his maimed arm to his side. "No," he cried hoarsely. "Don't."

"Yes, I shall." She unbuckled the belt and caught his arm as it was freed of its support, then lowered it gently to his side. He started to speak again, his face pale, his breath coming a little more quickly. Alissa didn't let herself think. She eased his coat from his shoulders and let it fall after his cravat. "I'd call your valet, but you don't have one yet."

White to the lips, Michael didn't answer.

Alissa reminded herself that he loved her. The Colonel had told her so, and supposedly he knew Michael better than anyone did. She knew that she would have to force her new husband to admit that he loved her, now, tonight, or she would lose him forever to whatever warped gallantry held him aloof from her.

She slid her hands inside his vest, and caught her breath as she felt the warmth of his flesh under his fine linen shirt. She couldn't help it. Her gaze flew to meet his, as a tremor went through her. She had never touched a man so intimately in her life, and the effect was electrifying.

Michael, high color in his cheeks now, a half-smile on his face, caught one of her hands in his hand and carried it to his lips. His blue eyes burning at her, he kissed her fingers and whispered over them, "Are you very sure this is what you want, Alissa? Because shortly it will be too late for you to change your mind."

Tears swam in her eyes as she strove for an answer. Tears of relief that he was saving her from going further down a path with which she was totally unfamiliar, tears of joy that she had won him. "Yes, my darling Michael. This is what I want. I want truly to be your wife."

He swept her to him and kissed her then, and the room

spun around them. Alissa thought that no woman on earth had ever received such a kiss. It took her breath away and removed her from the here and now to a paradise in which there were only the two of them.

She wasn't even aware of how they got into the bed-chamber, but they were there, beside the big four-poster that had been the bed of her parents and her grandparents and ancestors before them. The draperies had not been pulled across the windows in this room either, and the re-flection of moonlight on the snow outside bathed the room in a dim radiance as they stood there, locked in an em-brace. Their shadows, silvered by the light from the moon, fell across the counterpane as if they were cast by a single form, so closely did she cling to him.

Soon, Alissa had been kissed and caressed and was dizzy with wanting more. With wanting her husband, her Michael.

Somehow, Michael had removed her gown and his own remaining clothing, and lay beside her in the great bed. He slowly kissed and caressed her until she was half out of her mind.

Languorous desire filled her, heightening her senses. She quivered as fire trailed the touch of Michael's hand on her body. Everything the courtesan had told her had gone right out of her head, lost in a delirium of passion that shook her to the very roots of her being.

Michael lay on his useless arm and held her close. His mouth plundered hers, stealing her breath, stealing her soul. His lips were slow, sweet torture on her flesh. The de-manding words he whispered against the rapid pulse in her throat served as bonds that would unite them forever.

Alissa twined her arms around his neck and held herself as close as he would let her, and when he made her his own, the very stars seemed to enter the bedchamber to ex-plode and sing.

Hours later, when they lay exhausted with love, Alissa chuckled.

The sound was so at odds with the occasion that Michael was instantly alert again. Frowning, he asked, "Is something amusing you?"

Alissa laughed aloud, then, clinging to him, kissing his scarred shoulder. "It was just a silly, unexpected thought, and it caught me unaware."

"Please tell me. I'd be interested in anything that caught *you* unaware, wife."

She snuggled closer, burying her face in his throat and whispered to him.

Michael's own laughter, exalted, triumphant, echoed through the bedchamber. He kissed her again and told her, "Go to sleep, darling. Go to sleep."

Closing drowsy eyes, Alissa gave a sigh of deep content and did so.

Michael lay awake longer, listening to her even breathing, marveling at what she'd said. He both took comfort from and reveled in her words. His precious Alissa had told him what had made her laugh. She'd said, "I was just trying to imagine what more you thought you could do if you *had* the use of both your arms."

Chapter Thirty-three

The next few days passed with a delicious feeling of leisure after the hectic pace of the preceding week. More snow had fallen, both shutting them all safely away from the outside world in an unbroken blanket of white, and heralding the approach of Christmas.

In addition, the obvious happiness of the newlyweds had transferred some of itself to the guests and staff at Collington Park. Alissa and Michael were never apart, and spent a great deal of time gazing into each other's eyes as if they could never get their fill, and sharing whispered secrets that made them smile.

Lady Ellen was so content that even the presence of her twin couldn't chase the smile from her face. She and Robin played the games he liked best and laughed together a great deal.

Stone and MacLain, glad to see Michael happy and settled at last, were content to stay casually watchful over the couple's safety in spite of the fact that there was no sign of any threat to it.

Even the staff was affected by the air of contentment that pervaded the estate, and service, always good, became excellent in every way. Several of the downstairs maids, and even the scullery girl, had had to be reprimanded by Kemp for singing while performing their duties.

Lady Alissa, the new Viscountess Kantwell, allowed that it was quite in keeping with the season, and told Kemp that she could see no harm in the maids *humming* quietly, as long as it was some of the carols of the season. This dispensation pleased everyone but Isabelle. "I really think you are making a mistake to let the servants make that noise, Alissa. Anyone can plainly hear they hum off-key!"

As Christmas drew nearer, the pace picked up again. Stone and MacLain, suffering a little from inaction, announced to their host and hostess that it was time they took their leave to spend the days of Christmas with their respective families. Alissa and Michael were sorry to see them go. Stone smiled to see them so wrapped up in each other and said, "I doubt if you will even know we're gone."

Alissa blushed becomingly and told him, "Well, tonight we must have a gala dinner to celebrate the time we've had together." Alissa turned to MacLain. "You must tell me your favorite foods."

"Ah, I'm not the famous gourmet trencherman of the 'Lucky Seven.' That's Smythe."

Michael turned to stone. All the guilt he felt about the death of his good friend David rushed to the surface.

Alissa saw, and slipped an arm around his rigid waist, saying softly, "Oh, my dear. My very dear."

Stone glared at MacLain, and MacLain looked from one to the other of them, bewildered. "What happened? What did I say?"

Finally Michael managed, "Smythe is dead, Justin."

MacLain flinched. "I'm in the soup for sure. You called me by my Christian name, Michael." He hung his head. "And it's only gonna get worse."

"Why worse?" Stone demanded, suddenly suspicious.

"Well, because." MacLain looked as if he wanted the earth to swallow him. "It looks like I forgot to tell you something important."

Stone was the first to guess. "Oh, dear God!"

Michael took a step forward as if he would shake MacLain's important news from his friend, his face a strange mixture of blazing hope and savage anger.

MacLain hastily retreated behind Stone. Alissa pulled Michael beside her and kept a firm grip on his good arm to hold him there.

"Tell me," Michael grated out.

"It's just that Smythe ain't dead, is all. Bingley—remember Bingley? He was in the artillery with—"

Stone erupted. "Get on with it or I'll murder you myself!"

MacLain looked at his best friend reproachfully. "Well, you don't need to get nasty." Turning back to his host, he said, "Bingley escaped from the heathens over in Araby last month and brought news that Smythe is working for some sultan as a slave in his mines."

Michael sagged with relief. "Thank God!"

Alissa felt tears spring to her eyes.

MacLain looked a little puzzled. "Well, he *was* a slave in the mines, anyway. Bingley said he heard a rumor just before he scampered that some Englishman had led a revolt in that particular mine and had got clean away when it was over. Scattered with the other slaves, don't you know?" He cocked his head. "Think Smythe swam out to one of our frigates, if I remember rightly."

Michael looked as if he were ready to do murder. Stone appeared ready to help. Alissa looked from one man to the other and said, "Gentlemen, I think perhaps drinks are in order."

When no one moved, she said, "I must insist," and led the way to the study. The men had no choice but to follow their hostess, but there was considerable milling around before she could get them all to sit down.

Kemp filled their glasses and Alissa set about saving her dinner party. "Friends," she began firmly, ignoring the glares directed at MacLain, "we have just gotten the most wonderful news imaginable, and I strongly suggest that we concentrate on the joyous nature of that news instead of its tardiness."

There was dead silence as they each absorbed the good sense of her comment. Finally, Michael raised his glass and offered a toast. "To His Grace Michael David Lawrence, Ninth Duke of Smythington. Long may he live!"

"Hear, hear!" Stone's rejoinder was hearty, MacLain's a timid echo.

Again silence reigned for a moment, but this time it was a tribute to their absent comrade. Then Michael signaled to Kemp.

"Yes, my lord?"

"Find my secretary, please, and ask him to join us."

"Very good, your lordship." Kemp bowed and left.

MacLain, relieved that he was going to be permitted to remain a friend, asked, "What are you planning, Michael?"

"How better to locate and assist David than to have my secretary devote all his time to inquiries about Smythe?"

"Splendid," Stone agreed.

Alissa herself took the brandy around and replenished their glasses, grateful that peace had been restored among the friends. Having done that, she left them to go to the chapel to give thanks that the awful burden of guilt her husband had carried had been lifted from him, and to ask that his friend Smythe—or David, as Michael preferred to call him—find his way back to England's shores soon and without undue difficulty.

When she finally felt the peace of the chapel settle around her, she was certain that her prayers were heard. Slipping out, she hurried to the kitchen to order the serving of the gala meal she had promised the men.

The next morning, as planned, Stone and MacLain took their departure. Michael and Alissa, wrapped together in his old campaign cloak, stood on the terrace saying goodbye.

"Thank you for everything, Lady Alissa," MacLain said cheerfully. "Especially the feast last night. I won't have to eat all the way home."

"Thank you for everything," Stone echoed. But his tone was serious, and his gaze flicked to Michael before it returned to Alissa's face. "Everything," he repeated solemnly, and Alissa knew that he was thanking her for all the happiness that belonged to her and Michael.

Alissa gave him a quick hug. "Thank *you* for all you have done. I shall be forever in your debt," she told him earnestly. "Please come again, often and soon."

"Thank you, Lady Alissa. I'll look forward to seeing you again." Clapping his hand on Michael's shoulder, he told him solemnly, "Send for me if you need me. Keep me abreast of news of David."

"Of course."

MacLain promised to return when Stone came, and Alissa gave him a hug as well. MacLain blushed like a boy. "Well! I say now! A fellow would come back anytime for one of those."

They all laughed, then Stone and MacLain mounted, saluted, and were gone. Alissa and Michael stood looking after them until they could see them no longer, then Michael kissed her and Alissa melted against him under his old cloak. Her body against his, she could feel that the tenseness that had always been in her beloved husband's frame had left him, and knew it had been caused by the guilt he'd carried so long.

Gratitude that he was free of it filled her. Tears came and spilled over.

"What?" Michael teased. "What is this? Will you miss those two so much?"

Smiling through her tears, she told him, "Of course."

Michael laughed down at her. "Poor darling." And he kissed her tears away.

Preparations for the season filled everyone's minds, and a heightened spirit of gaiety permeated the huge house.

"Garlands," Alissa cried, "we must have evergreens from which to make the garlands to decorate the house."

Michael laughed. "To decorate *this* house, you'd have to denude the entire forest of evergreens."

Alissa ran to him and flung her arms around his neck. "We don't do the entire house. We would, indeed, need more than our fair share of evergreen boughs."

Michael kissed the tip of her nose. "I'm relieved to hear it. I was afraid there'd be no place left for the birds to nest in the spring." His tone was light, but the way he held her tightly to him before letting her move away gladdened Alissa's heart.

Robin came up behind them. "I just hope you'll warn me where you're going to pile the boughs. Last year I went neck over teakettle when I tripped over the pile of them you left in the front hall!"

"Indeed you did." Alissa put out her arm and scooped him into the embrace she was sharing with Michael. "And you frightened us half to death doing it, too."

Robin squirmed free. "I'm not a baby anymore, Cousin Lissa."

"And what is that supposed to mean?"

"You can't go hugging me like that in front of the Major."

"Oh, I see." She made her voice very serious, a difficult task when her every hour seemed to glow with happiness and every remark to hold hidden laughter. "Is it all right if I hug you when I come to hear your prayers?"

Robin gave the question serious consideration. "I suppose so. But not for very much longer. I am growing up, you know."

Alissa's face held a sweet sadness as she answered him. "Yes, dear, I know."

When he had gone, she turned back to Michael. "What will the future hold for him? Oh, if only he could *see*."

"This spring we will take him to London to consult a physician I know who has been able to help several comrades of mine who were blinded in the war." He put his finger on her lips to stop her joyous cry. "But we must remember that those men were not blind from birth, darling. You must not get your hopes up. Nor his."

She nodded, not trusting her voice.

Michael bent his head and lightly kissed her.

Alissa smiled. "It's a very good thing that our servants are so good at pretending they don't see us. I fear we are behaving quite scandalously."

"I think they can bear it. After all, even scullery maids fall in love."

"Oh, Michael, I feel so fortunate. Grandmother said just last week that love came more surely for scullery maids than for ladies of the *ton*. How truly blessed we are to love each other."

He swept her into his embrace and kissed her with a rough hunger that told her what her statement had meant to him.

"Oh, Michael," she sighed as she melted against him, "do you think we could go to bed early?"

• • •

Later, after they had lost themselves for hours in tender lovemaking, in the deep part of the night when the stars ruled the sky alone, Alissa stirred and cried out, "Thomas! Oh, dear Thomas, beware! Beware!"

Michael awakened at her first cry. His heart stopped and his blood ran like ice water in his veins. Great God! Was he deceived? Could everything he'd believed be untrue after all? Could this marriage be a farce?

The poignancy with which his beloved Alissa had just spoken shook his confidence in his own senses. Was this Thomas to whom she'd cried out in her dreams the man she'd really wanted to marry? Was the anguish in her voice because she was no longer free to be the man's wife?

Even as he kissed and soothed Alissa back to pleasant dreams, icy bitterness and flaming jealousy vied for mastery over him. Alissa! Ah, God, Lissa. Nothing in his life had prepared him for the strength of the emotions he was experiencing. He fought them with a fierceness that shook him to the core.

The stars had lost their dominion over the night sky to the pale first rays of sunrise before Michael forced his staring eyes closed. Finally, he had won his battle.

Lying there with his whole reason for being sleeping beside him and the darkest of despair in his soul, he vowed to find this Thomas for his beloved wife.

In the morning, Alissa woke to find her husband gone from her side. Quickly she padded into her own room and rang the bell that would summon Button.

"Button, dear, hurry and dress me. Michael has gotten up, and I must find him. I can't imagine why I have slept so late."

Button looked at her, fighting to repress a smile. "Yes, milady."

"What are you grinning about, Button?"

"Was I grinning?" Button broke out into soft laughter.

"You know very well you were!"

"Well, Lady Lissa, I suppose it was a little bit of joy sneaking past my guard, so to speak. We are all so glad to see your happiness with the master."

"Yes." Alissa blinked. "He is master here now, isn't he."

"Aye, and your master, as well." Button watched for Alissa's reaction to her statement.

For a moment, Alissa looked as rebellious as she felt, then she remembered how cherished and loved and . . . Well, she wasn't going to admit, even to herself, that she was pleasured beyond reason by this man her servants called master, but maybe, just maybe, she would let Button call him *her* master too. At any rate, recalling for an instant his wondrous and very satisfying mastery over her last night, she was willing to let it pass for now.

Button hid her smile and brought the dress she had selected for Alissa to approve. "Your bath is on its way. With such a lusty man in your bed, you'll no doubt be glad of it."

"Button!" Alissa was shocked. "I . . . !"

While Alissa sputtered to a stop, Button was quick to turn the conversation to a safer subject. "The master's new valet arrived at dawn. Kemp was more than a little put out at the hour, I can tell you. One-legged he is. From the war. The new valet, not Kemp, of course."

"Of course not Kemp." Alissa could feel herself frowning mightily. Lusty, indeed! Was her husband's prowess as a lover a subject of discussion among the servants? Obviously it was. She would have to get Michael to agree not to kiss her in front of them anymore.

The decision left her feeling curiously depressed.

Her bathwater arrived just then, and she couldn't scold Button as she wanted to. Not with the two maids who remained after the procession of footmen had departed with the empty copper canisters.

She heaved a deep sigh. The first fly had just been

dropped into the ointment of her happiness, drat it, but such was life. Hating the necessity, she made up her mind to find Michael the minute she was dressed and to tell him that they would have to be more discreet.

Chapter Thirty-four

Alissa found Michael closeted in the study with the new valet. "Mi . . ." She stopped dead and stared, his name unfinished on her lips. Her husband sat on the edge of the desk, bared to the waist, and he was magnificent.

In the night, Alissa had caressed his chest, but it had been dark, and she had never seen it. Now, she was seeing for the first time the wide bands of muscle across his chest and shoulders and the definition of the long, strong sinews in his arms. The sight of them made her palms tingle in remembrance and took her breath away.

She saw, too, the ugly scar caused by the crushing blow from the club that had maimed him. Suddenly, she could feel again the rough texture of the skin there from the time she had kissed it, and she grew warm all over. She felt as if her knees were going to give way and drop her with a thump on the parquet floor of the study. Desire for this husband of hers was reaching ridiculous proportions! If she stood there gaping another instant, she was going to blush.

Michael's low voice was saying, "My shirt, Webster."

The valet stopped massaging his employer's lame arm and reached for the article in question.

"No," Alissa managed, lifting her fascinated gaze from her husband's broad chest with a difficulty that surprised her. "That won't be necessary. The matter can wait until you are through with your—" She didn't have a word. How annoying.

"Treatment, milady," the tall, peg-legged man said helpfully.

"Thank you, Webster," Alissa answered. "Please continue. What I wanted to say will wait." She turned and fled.

Michael sat and watched her go, a slender vision in a wonder of the couturier's art—a long-sleeved crimson wool dress frogged across the bodice with gold braid. The braid and the color of the dress were intended to put one in mind of the dress uniform of an army officer, he had no doubt. He wondered if she had worn it to honor him.

Was she aware that she had cried out another man's name in her sleep? Was she wearing that gown as some sort of apology? That thought cut through him like a knife. Ah, God! Surely their life together—the life that had so briefly been sheer bliss—wasn't going to become a lifetime of Alissa's trying to make up to him for the fact that, while she had given him her gratitude, her heart really belonged to another! *No! Oh, dear God, no.* There was no way he would permit that. It was past bearing.

"I can't do this if you tense up like that, sir."

"Then don't," Michael snapped. Instantly contrite, he said, "You've had a long night of travel, Webster. You could do with some rest and some time to settle in. That's enough for today."

"Very well, sir." He helped Michael get his shirt back

on. "But you don't want to let that arm stiffen, and it's begun to."

Michael's thoughts went savage. *What the blazing hell difference does it make? Without Alissa, what the devil difference does anything make? I can drag the damned arm around withered as a twig while I look for this Thomas for her! Who would care?*

His inner voice was snarling, but he strove hard for a calm tone as he addressed his new valet. "You'll set it to rights, Webster, I've no doubt of it."

"Thank you, sir. Until tomorrow, then." He saluted as if they were both still in the army and marched from the room.

Michael went to the window and stared out. The whole outside world glowed in the light reflected off the snow. In Michael's heart the candle of hope had gone out, and the only thing he could relate to in the landscape was the silent, bitter cold.

He took a deep breath, straightened his shoulders, and began to plan his next move. He let the breath go in a despondent sigh. There was nothing else he could do but to start . . .

"Michael! Michael! Come!"

Alissa's glad cry galvanized him into action. He dashed out of the study to find her. She was at the front of the house, standing in the huge double doorway, staring out over the snow.

As he ran up to her, she cried, "Look! Look there. Riding that old farm horse. It's Thomas! He's safe! Oh, Michael, thank God!"

Michael murmured, "Not bloody likely!" as Alissa ran out of the house. He snatched the cloak Kemp had magically appeared with and threw himself out the door in pursuit of his wife. By the time he caught her at the foot of the terraces and wrapped her in the sable-lined cloak, the approaching rider had seen her and kicked the huge nag he rode into a shambling gallop.

As the ludicrous pair neared them, Michael saw that the man had a bandage around his head and one arm in a sling. *So*, he thought acidly, *it would seem we have two things in common. Alissa and a useless arm.*

The bandaged blond adonis wrenched the great ugly beast to a halt and threw his leg over the animal's neck in a graceful dismount while Michael wished he'd fall on his face. "Alissa!" the intruder cried, spreading his arms wide, sling and all.

So they hadn't two things in common. This man could still use *his* arm, sling or no.

"Thomas!" she sobbed as she threw herself into his arms. She touched the bandage that circled his head. "Are you all right?"

"Right as rain." He gave her a cheerful smile.

He has good teeth was Michael's next sour observation, then he stood like stone and watched as they babbled reassurances of Thomas's health and of Alissa's continued ownership of Collington House. Jealousy consumed him. It was the second time in his life he had felt it, and he decided he hated the sensation.

"Come, you must meet my husband." Alissa swiped at her eyes with the back of her hand and tugged the other man toward Michael. "Michael, this is Thomas. Sir Thomas Lane. I thought my uncle had murdered him, but look, he's all right!"

"So this gentleman is the reason for your trip to Bow Street," Michael managed. It wasn't the most welcoming thing he could have said, but at least he hadn't challenged the man to a duel. Yet.

And, surprisingly, he wanted to. Far from slinking off to find a way to get himself killed, he fully intended to stay and fight for what he wanted. After all, Alissa was his wife. His! He was the first man to possess her, the first to pleasure her into delirium with his lovemaking, and by God, he was going to be the last. Alissa was *his*, and he was going to keep her.

These thoughts, brought on by the sight of the man he'd proposed to give Alissa up to, were so at variance with all his previously held intentions that he laughed.

"Well, now." Thomas seized Michael's hand and shook it heartily. "That's infinitely better. I thought for a moment you were going to eat me! I'm no threat," he said with a winsome smile and a gleam in his eyes. That glint told Michael more plainly than words would have that Sir Thomas Lane sensed his jealousy. "I'm a family friend, husband to Alissa's best friend, my late wife."

Michael's smile was genuine as he returned Lane's handshake. "We're glad to see you safe. Alissa has been worried about your welfare and feeling guilty over your disappearance."

Lane turned to Alissa. "Thank you, silly goose, but as you can see, I'm fine."

This less than loverly speech completed the reassurance Michael needed more than he needed the very blood in his veins. They were friends, not lovers, this handsome man and his own cherished wife. His sense of relief was enormous. "Come in," he invited. "I think we are close in size, and you look as if you could do with a bath and a change of clothes."

At that moment, the sleigh arrived that he and Alissa had ordered earlier. Their intent was to use it to spy out where best to gather evergreens for garlands on the morrow and to spot which oaks had mistletoe for use in the great house. Robin, his face already red from the cold and excitement, was beside the coachman, Green, who was driving.

"Oh, dear," Alissa told the two men, "we can't disappoint Robin. I'll have to go." She put her hand on Michael's arm. "You take Thomas in and get acquainted.

I'll take Robin for the ride we promised him." She kissed
Thomas on the cheek quickly, then rose up on her toes and
kissed Michael.

Michael clasped her to him strongly, overcome with relief at knowing she was truly his that was still surging
through him. Looking down into her face, he sought and
found needed reassurance.

Alissa's eyes softened, and she answered him again
with a much longer and more lingering kiss—not a pas-
sionate one, but the kiss of a woman who loves tenderly
and deeply, from her very soul. Then she pulled away, her
gaze holding his for a long moment. Her eyes expressed
the depth of her love, and Michael's last doubts fled before
that glory.

Alissa laughed a little shakily from the strength of that
silent exchange, and said with an attempt at gaiety, "Be
kind to Thomas and find out all that happened to him for
me." She ran toward the sleigh. The cloak Michael had
draped around her swirled as she turned back again. "And
be especially sympathetic. After all, if he hadn't fallen off
the bridge, he'd have married me before you got the
chance."

"Minx!" Sir Thomas scooped up a handful of snow and
using his injured hand to help, clumsily formed it into a
loose ball and threw it at her. "You could at least stay long
enough to offer me tea!"

Alissa laughed at him and told Green to drive on.
"We'll be back in an hour! Please have your sad story suf-
ficiently condensed so that there is time for me to tell you
all *my* news!"

Even Michael was laughing as he clapped his hand on
his new acquaintance's shoulder and offered, "What do
you say to something stronger than tea while you tell me
what the devil happened to you?"

"An excellent suggestion. We'll save the tea for the

ladies!" Thomas's long-legged stride matched Michael's as they headed for the brandy.

When they entered the study, it still smelled faintly of the liniment that Webster had used on Michael's arm. "Sorry about the odor, Lane."

"Don't apologize, it goes well with my fragrance of farm horse."

They threw themselves down in chairs, dispensing with courtesies and graceful posturings since there were only the two of them. Kemp, alerted as the men had come in from outside, brought a pair of goblets with an inch or so of brandy in the bottom of each. "Will that be all, my lord?"

Michael grinned at him. "Just leave the brandy here where we can reach it."

"Very good, my lord." Kemp bowed himself out.

They sipped their brandy for a moment, then Michael said, "Tell me what happened. I came in at the middle of the story. All I know is that Alissa was determined to get to Bow Street to avenge you."

"It's a simple tale. Alissa wrote to me, asking me to marry her to save her inheritance. Not for the money, you know, but for her independence. Her uncle is a nasty piece of work, and she was afraid of being in his power. Afraid of what he might do—or, for that matter, not do—to, or for, her family. Her servants, too, I expect."

Michael offered him more brandy by lifting the decanter toward him.

"Thanks." Thomas held out his crystal goblet. "I had just lost my wife and son in childbirth the year before, so Alissa knew there could be no one else in my life."

"And she was desperate."

"Yes. I was willing to start out for Collington Park immediately, but she'd asked me to find an old army friend to accompany me. She was worried that I might not be safe coming alone." He swirled his brandy and frowned.

"And?"

"I went to the club to find the friend I wanted to take with me. He wasn't there, but her uncle, Lord Withers, was." Thomas looked up with a crooked grin. "You can guess what stupidity I performed next."

Michael grinned back. "You did just what any Englishman, and I, myself, would have done. You taunted him with the fact that you were going to marry my wife. Er, Alissa."

Thomas laughed. "Precisely!"

Michael's grin widened and he shook his head. Then he raised his glass. "To English manhood!"

"Hear, hear!" They tossed down their brandy.

"And then?" Michael's smile faded. "What did the bastard do?"

"Withers played all the right tunes. He first intimated I was a fortune hunter to rattle me, then remarked that the weather was turning chancy. Said a bit about the roads to Collington Park being difficult in snow. Then he implied I was afraid to make the trip alone, and of course—" He gestured as if tipping his hat to his own gullibility.

Michael understood, and chuckled.

"To make a long story short, he and three of his thugs were waiting for me at the bridge that is just before the drive into Collington Park."

"And they tossed you into the river." Michael wasn't laughing now.

"Right. Luckily for me, a farmer was downstream gathering his cows to herd into the barn. He pulled me out of the water and kept me warm until I woke up two days ago."

"With the water freezing this time of year, I'd say you had the devil's own luck."

"And I'd agree. Pass the brandy."

"Alissa will be back soon." Michael glanced at the tall

clock. "She won't want to risk Robin taking a chill. I'll pass on this round."

"Ah, my new friend, henpecked already."

Michael just smiled. He could afford to, now. He sat back and basked in the knowledge that he could smile for the rest of his life, now that he knew that his lovely Alissa, his wife, was truly his own.

Chapter Thirty-five

Robin cried, "Faster!" and Green cracked the whip above the horses' backs. Snorting plumes of warm breath into the freezing air, the matched bays lunged ahead, enjoying the snow and the bright day as much as their human cargo.

Alissa held tight to her cousin and laughed her own delight as he enjoyed the sensation of speed and the feel of the wind against his face. *If only he could see!* She kept up a running description of the beauties of the day and the brightness of the sun glittering on the snow, the tall evergreens with their branches bowed under the weight of the snow. She had long grown accustomed to telling Robin about the sights around them by relating colors to temperatures he could feel, but the day was so glorious, she was having to strive for new comparisons.

"The trees are covered with heavy burdens of snow. They are dark in color. Green like the smell of new-mown grass, but darker. They are bent down under the weight of—"

There was the crack of a shot, and Green fell sideways. Alissa cried, "Hang on, Robin!" and lunged up out of her seat to keep the coachman from falling from the sleigh.

Without his hands on the ribbons, the team was faltering, slowing, unsure of what was wanted of them. Then a rider came blasting out of the trees and hurtling toward them, shouting, "By Heaven, you'll not thwart *me* and live to gloat about it!"

"Uncle Gerald!" Alissa shrieked, as he whipped the bays into a dead run. "Have a care! You'll hurt Robin!"

Laughter was the only response. It was the last thing she heard as the sleigh careened wildly and slammed into the trunk of a tree. Stretched as she was between the grip she had on Green and the attempt she was making to hold Robin, Alissa didn't have a chance. When the sleigh struck the giant oak, she was thrown into the snow.

As Alissa lost consciousness, she saw her uncle charging down on her.

Thomas Lane laughed. "That's the third time you've glanced at that clock, Kantwell. Not getting anxious for Alissa's return, are you?"

Lane was teasing, but Michael didn't give him the sheepish grin his guest was expecting. His eyes serious, he told him, "Yes, I rather think I am. Would you like to ride a better horse than the one you arrived on?"

Lane was instantly grave. "You're worried."

"Uneasy," Michael admitted. He strode to the door and bellowed, "Kemp! Two horses!"

Michael went to a case on the desk and withdrew a pair of pistols. "I keep them loaded, so have a care."

They were fastening their cloaks when the horses arrived from the stables. A moment later they were tearing off down the drive, watching for the tracks that would indicate the path the sleigh had taken into the woods. When they saw hoofprints in the snow that indicated a rider had intercepted its course and followed the sleigh, Michael cursed, signaled Lane, and sent Gladiator into a full gallop.

No more than a minute passed before they saw the destruction. The sleigh lay on its side, hopelessly wrecked. Green was sprawled in the snow with a patch of crimson widening under him. Robin's limp body was near his, blood staining the whiteness under his head. But Michael had eyes only for his beloved.

"Alissa!" he screamed.

She lay in the snow, unmoving, and her uncle was attempting to force his horse to trample her. Untrained in war, the animal was refusing to step on a helpless human.

His mind encased in icy hatred, Michael drew his pistol and fired at Withers. Gladiator hit a buried log at just that moment. The great horse stumbled badly. Michael's shot went wild.

Thomas reined in and steadied his good arm with his injured hand, his sling forgotten. He was farther away than Michael, but he winged the wild-eyed man threatening Alissa.

Withers yanked his horse around and fled, clutching his upper arm. As he galloped away, he shouted back, "Until the next time, Niece!"

Gladiator started after him, but Michael was intent only on Alissa. He halted the big gelding, jumped down, and fell on his knees beside his wife. It took all his strength not to gather her in his arms and pour out his love and his fears to her. Years of army discipline prevailed, however, and instead he felt her limbs for possible breaks. Then, steeling himself, he touched her head and neck gently. Nothing was broken. Thank God!

He bent to listen to her breathing, and was reassured. Experience on the battlefield told him she was not seriously injured. Nevertheless, it was with the greatest difficulty that he left her lying on his folded campaign cloak and went to Robin.

Lane had Green sitting up and was stanching the flow of blood from his shoulder. Green was striving to tell him what had happened, insofar as he knew it.

Michael held his breath as he approached Robin. His heart in his throat, he knelt beside the still child. Seeing the lad breathe, he drew a breath of his own, but the ugly head wound Robin had sustained caused him great concern.

Michael stood and called to Lane, "Ride back for the other sleigh."

Lane nodded, and placed his own cloak around the coachman before mounting. Then he immediately tore off for the mansion. "Take care Withers doesn't return," he called back as he rode away.

"Aye, my friend," Michael vowed quietly, "I'll take care he *never* returns."

Alissa was physically fine except for a slight headache, but she was worried half-wild about Robin. The boy lay absolutely still in his bed, his eyes closed and his breathing even, but he had not regained consciousness. He didn't move even when the retired doctor who lived in the village examined him.

Webster worked over him quietly, changing the pads soaked in half-melted snow that he had packed around Robin's poor head. On the other side of the bed Lady Ellen kept vigil silently, holding Robin's hand.

"Doctor, what can we do?" Alissa pleaded.

"There is nothing to do, Lady Alissa. The blow was a terrible one, but his skull is intact. Only God knows what will come of it. I wish I could do more, but there is nothing to be done. We must just wait. And pray."

Michael had seen the tenderness and care with which the man had worked over Robin. "Thank you, sir. Will you call again tomorrow?"

"Certainly, my lord."

The little old man took his leave, and Alissa leaned

against her husband, her body tense. "Oh, Michael, this is all my fault! I know what my uncle is capable of. I should have taken precautions. I should have . . ."

Michael stopped her words with a kiss. Then, kisses. When she finally relaxed against him, he kissed her once more and told her, "If this is anyone's fault, it is mine. I am the one who swore to protect you and yours, Alissa." His voice took on a bitter edge. "And I, too, had firsthand knowledge of what your uncle is capable of doing."

He tilted her face up and looked into her eyes. "Just take comfort in the fact that he will never bother you again."

Alissa startled back from him. "You . . . you won't do anything foolish, will you? Promise me!"

"I must ride for London now. I need to bring back another doctor for Robin."

"Promise me!" Alissa gave him a little shake.

He bent his head and kissed her. "Will I murder your uncle? No, my love, you have my word on that. I won't harm a hair on his head." He kissed her one more time and turned away, striding for the door. Softly he murmured, "But, I'll see to it that the blackguard will curse his Maker that I did not kill him."

Once down the stairs, he called, "Kemp, two riding horses and a closed carriage. It need not be a particularly comfortable one."

Thomas Lane stepped into the hall from the library. "How is the boy?"

"There's no change." He lowered his head like a bull about to charge, and Lane saw the cold determination burning in Michael's eyes. "I'm riding to London to fetch a doctor more conversant with head wounds. Would you care to join me?"

"Oh, yes." Lane had guessed what his host was about to do. And it wasn't ride to London for a physician. He understood and agreed with it heartily. "Shall we take pistols?"

Michael's face broke out in a grim smile. "Quite a few, I should think."

When they had spent several minutes in the study loading pistols, four for each of them, and writing a note of instruction for one of the grooms to take to London, they were ready.

"Kemp," Michael ordered, "Take care of the women. We will be back late tomorrow evening."

Kemp stood to attention. "Yes, sir!"

As he closed the door behind the gentlemen, he shook his head in a puzzled fashion and asked aloud, "Now why did his lordship not care that the carriage he was taking for the doctor be comfortable?"

Chapter Thirty-six

"You understand your orders?" Michael asked.

"Yes, your lordship," the eager groom answered, standing tall. "I'm to ride to London as quickly as possible, and to present this letter to . . ." He read out the doctor's name, holding the envelope up to the stable lantern nearest them. "Then I'm to bring him back here as quick as ever I can."

"Good man! Now be on your way."

"Yes, sir!" The groom leapt into the saddle and left them at the trot. As Lane and Michael listened, he picked up a canter, then was away at a gallop. Michael nodded his satisfaction at the man's treatment of his mount and turned to Thomas Lane.

Lane was watching him with a great deal of interest. "That done," he asked, "what's next?"

"Now I make certain that Lord Withers never troubles my wife again."

Lane saw him drop his hand to one of his pistols. They

each had two in their saddle holsters and two on their persons. "Are you going to shoot the blackguard?"

Michael sighed. "I promised Alissa I would not."

Lane raised an eyebrow. "If you're going to try to get me to do it, you'd better give me a moment to get used to the idea."

Michael gave a short bark of laughter. "Thank you, Lane, but no. I have another fate in store for the illustrious Lord Withers." He mounted Gladiator and sat looking down at his new friend, one eyebrow raised. "Well? Are you coming?"

"Wouldn't miss it for the world." Lane swung up onto his horse and the two of them rode down the long drive, the inferior carriage Michael had ordered rattling after them.

Behind them in Collington House, Alissa and her grandmother knelt beside Robin's bed and prayed.

"If only he would move. If only he would speak." Alissa turned anguished eyes to her grandmother.

"Michael has gone to London for the doctor, dear. It is obvious he knows someone he thinks will be able to help. We must have faith that he is right."

Alissa nodded. "I do have." She looked at the slight figure on the bed. "I do. But Robin is so still, and it has been hours since . . . since my uncle . . ." She stopped talking rather than relive the incident.

"I know, Lissa. But people with head wounds sometimes take days to wake up, and as you've said, it has only been hours. We must be brave and wait."

"You're right, of course." She smiled a tremulous smile. "But it's awfully hard when it's Robin, isn't it?"

Lady Ellen offered an encouraging smile in return. "It would be just as difficult no matter whom you loved lay there."

"Yes." Then, after a little pause, Alissa said quietly, "Grandmother, I'm frightened, too."

Lady Ellen started to rise, and Alissa was quick to assist her. "Of your uncle, you mean?"

"No, of Michael and what he may do. Though he promised he wouldn't kill Uncle Gerald, he also promised that he wouldn't let my uncle bother me again." She shivered involuntarily. "I'm really afraid for Michael." She shot a glance at her grandmother that made her look almost her old self, and said, "Mostly, I'm afraid he'll get caught."

"Don't fear for your husband, dearest. Clearly, Michael has a plan."

"Yes." Alissa pressed her hand to her midsection, where unaccustomed butterflies flew. "But what is it?"

The sky was still dark when Michael and Thomas reached Witherington, Gerald Withers's principal residence, but moonrise was not far away. Michael signaled the carriage that followed them to go on past the estate. The driver had been instructed to wait for them on the other side.

As he and Thomas rode through the tall gates, Michael led the way off the drive onto the turf so there was no chance that the sound of their horses' hooves would be heard. When they were still a hundred yards from the mansion, Michael drew rein and dismounted.

"Hold the horses and wait here while I reconnoiter," he ordered.

"Yes, sir," Lane mocked at being given an order.

Michael frowned at him. "I don't need to have you caught, too, if anything goes wrong."

"Yes, sir." Lane didn't mock this time, and his smile softened his sarcasm. "Be careful."

Michael nodded and moved quietly toward the great house, gliding from shadow to shadow like a shadow himself. He was in luck. As he reached his final hiding place, he saw a man come to the window just over the front door and begin drawing the draperies. A moment later, just before the draperies closed, Michael saw Withers, clad in a dressing gown, behind him.

Making his careful way back to Lane, he told him, "We're in luck. The window we want is the one over the doorway. The climb will be easy, even for me." He grinned. "As soon as he's had time to go to sleep, I'll *fetch* him."

"Like a dog with a bone, no doubt." Lane considered him for a moment before saying, "How the devil will you carry him down—and climb, too, Michael?"

Michael looked murderous. For an instant, he'd forgotten his infirmity. Then he laughed softly, mirthlessly. "Shall I throw him out the window and climb down after him?"

Lane chuckled. "Might be a bit hard on him. The terrace under the window is made of flagstones."

Michael became serious. "You're right, of course. I shall have to go inside and use the stairs. As soon as he's had time to go to sleep, I'll break in."

"*We'll* break in."

Michael didn't argue. They waited patiently while the light in the room they were watching dimmed and then disappeared as the candles were put out. Then they gave it twenty more minutes for their victim to fall asleep. The ten more it would take for them to break in and find their way through the house would make certain he slept. Lord Withers was not the sort of man to let saying prayers delay his night's rest.

Stealthily they made their way through the shrubbery to the French doors. The latch was old and yielded readily to the long knife Lane handed his friend. Once inside, they crossed the room to the hall doorway, opened that door carefully, and found themselves looking at the stairs to the first floor. Exchanging conspiratorial grins, they crossed to and went up them.

Moments later they were headed back down with a trussed-up, gagged, and, thanks to a sharp blow from the butt of one of Lane's pistols, unconscious Lord Withers. The bolts of the front door were well-oiled, and drew back without a sound. The two housebreakers closed it quietly behind themselves and their inert burden, and reached their horses without incident.

The rising moon lit the entire landscape brightly as they bundled Withers unceremoniously into the carriage waiting for them. Remounting, Michael led the way to their destination without the slightest further problem.

Late the next evening, Alissa was keeping vigil at a front window when Michael and Lane arrived back at Collington Park. The sight of her husband's tall figure on Gladiator sent her flying to the front door.

"Michael! Oh, Michael!" The men had hardly dismounted when Alissa threw herself at her husband and clung to him as if she'd never let go. "I was so worried. I was so afraid that something might have happened to you!"

"Thank you," Lane said in an extremely dry tone of voice.

Alissa laughed, a small, semi-hysterical bubble of a laugh. "Oh, Thomas. I'm glad *you're* all right, too."

"But you'll notice she's not hanging on *my* neck."

Michael looked up from kissing Alissa. "*You* didn't marry her."

Thomas smiled a crooked little smile. "Somehow I don't think I'd have elicited that kind of a response even if I had." He handed his hat, his cloak, and two pistols to the butler and demanded, "Kemp, where's the brandy?"

Kemp put Lane's pistols down carefully, deftly relieved his new master of two more, and, now that he could breathe easily again, answered, "In its customary place in the study, Sir Thomas."

Lane left Michael and Alissa staring into each other's eyes and went to find the brandy.

Later, when Alissa had proven to Michael how much she'd missed him, and how much he loved her, they bathed and changed and went down to join the other members of the household for a late supper.

Since Isabelle had asked for a tray in her room, they were free to talk. Lady Ellen broke the ice. "Well, gentlemen, just what have you done with my son Gerald?"

"Oh, Lord." Thomas was aghast. "I forgot Withers was you son!"

"No matter, my dear boy," Ellen reassured him. "He's a villain of the first water, if I may pervert a phrase, and he constituted a very real and continuing danger to my beloved granddaughter. I just hope you have removed him from our lives without any danger to yourselves."

Michael gazed at her a long moment, hating her hidden pain but knowing she was sincere. Gently he told her, "I have not harmed him, Ellen, though if I were in his place, I'd have preferred to die quickly."

Alissa's eyes widened. "Oh, Michael, that sounds dire."

Michael looked at her, and his face was grave. "Do you remember that he had me committed to an asylum to keep me from attending our wedding?"

"Of course I do. How could I ever forget?"

"And do you recall that Bly used the excuse that he was looking for a place to put his mad uncle in order to gain entrance to the asylum where I was a prisoner, so he could search for me?"

"Oh, Michael, I could never forget that. Your Colonel saved the day for us all. I'll never forget anything he did." She blushed suddenly, and shot a guilty glance at her grandmother, who blushed in her turn at being reminded of their hour spent with the courtesan. "So Bly pretended he was going to bring an uncle there someday . . . Oh!"

Alissa's lovely gray eyes were as round as saucers. "Oh, I see!"

"Exactly. I went to the administrator and told him I was Blysdale. To support my ruse, Thomas played the part of a devoted valet who was sorry to see that his master had finally gone mad. Your uncle ranted and raved and told everyone the simple, absolute truth. And no one believed him."

They sat silent for a while, each wondering if they should feel guilty about what had been done. Then Lady Ellen lifted her chin, signaled imperiously to Kemp, and announced, "Bring the port now, Kemp. Lady Alissa and I will join the gentlemen in drinking it tonight." Looking purposefully around the table at each of them, she added, "Gerald's awful malice has been . . . taken safely out of our lives, and Robin is improving thanks to the splendid doctor you sent for, Michael." Tears sprang to her eyes, and she blinked them away. "For the first time I have hope that he may see. All is well." She regarded each of them in turn. "We have much to celebrate."

Alissa and Michael's eyes met. They turned as one to look out the great dining room windows. Outside, the snow glittered like diamonds under the stars. And as they watched, the moon cast its magic across the shining landscape to remind them of that night at the inn—the first night they had known they were in love. Turning again of one accord, they each smiled radiant, loving smiles.

Celebrate? They had just begun!

Epilogue

It was spring again, and warm breezes ruffled the manes of their horses as Alissa and Michael sat them side by side on the ridge overlooking Collington Park.

Alissa was surveying the estate with a critical eye, carefully considering the fields spread out in front of them. It was all safely hers now, for her husband stood guard. Peace lay on the land and filled her heart. Never had she dreamed a woman could be so happy.

Michael sat watching his wife, enjoying the way the gentle winds lifted tendrils of her dark hair to drift tantalizingly around her pure profile. Moving his horse closer, he sought to catch the sweet feminine scent of her. His whole world revolved around this woman, and he never ceased to feel wonder when he allowed himself to dwell on the realization that she was truly and completely his.

His possessive perusal was interrupted when Alissa looked over her shoulder at him with a delighted laugh. "Look! Here comes Robin."

"You mean here comes Gladiator bringing Robin." He spoke in a dry tone of voice, but he smiled to see the big gray gelding coming up the hillside toward them bearing the young boy, so confidently erect.

"Oh, but darling, every day Robin sees a little bit more. Not just light and shadow, but real shapes. Soon he'll be able to give Gladiator back to you and ride any horse of his choosing."

"Indeed, Robin rides well enough to handle anything in the stable now." Michael encouraged his horse to sidestep even closer to hers so that his booted leg brushed against the side of her mare. He smiled down at his wife. "We have only to pray that he receives the rest of his sight quickly, so that he can safely guide the beasts. Few will take care of him as Glad does."

"Do I detect a note of excessive pride in your favorite charger, husband?"

"Always," he said firmly. Then he grinned down at her. "Can I help it if he is the cleverest animal in all of Great Britain?"

Alissa tried to suppress a smile. "I suppose I should be happy that your modesty constrains you to limit him to the Realm. At least you haven't claimed him to be the smartest horse in the whole world."

"Not yet. But soon, perhaps." He pointed down to where Gladiator was making a wide detour around a tree with low-hanging branches. "Just see the way Glad keeps Robin from being knocked out of the saddle by that bough."

They watched the two come on toward them for a moment, then Alissa's manner changed. She was no longer teasing. The expression in her eyes was serious as she said, "I suppose I can tell you now that I know myself to owe your Gladiator a terrible debt."

"A debt?" Michael was startled. "To Glad?"

"Yes, my dearest, to Gladiator."

Michael frowned lightly, caught between laughter and her grave manner. "How in the world?"

She regarded him steadily, her gray eyes solemn. "I well remember the day we met, Michael, and how you said you were looking for shelter for him. From the way you answered when Grandmother responded that you were surely looking for shelter for yourself as well, I knew in my heart that it was for his sake alone that you sought shelter. Possibly it was *only for his sake* that you had ridden long enough through the storm to come upon our stranded coach."

Color rose in Michael's face. Bowing to the truth of her statement, he dropped his gaze away from hers momentarily. Unable to deny her charge, he told her quietly, "Then I, too, must admit that I'm more indebted to Gladiator than I can express."

Silence spun a long moment between them. Then, softly, she asked him, "Do you know how very much I love you?"

The love in Michael's heart leapt into his eyes, and he leaned toward her. Bending his head down to her, his lips sought her soft mouth.

He was stopped from kissing her by Robin's cheerful cry. "Hallo! See me! I have made it all the way here from the house!"

"Good for you!" Alissa answered with a shout.

"Gladiator helped me come," the boy admitted as he approached. "But Grandmother sent me. She says you are to hurry home, it is time for tea."

"Very good. We shall go right down." Michael used the tone he'd use to praise one of his soldiers. "Well done."

Robin turned Gladiator and started back down the trail to the house. "Hurry, please. Cook has made her special cakes, and I can't wait to taste them."

Alissa sat still for another moment, her heart overflowing with happiness. Turning her face to Michael, she let him see it in her eyes.

Michael answered with his own, his eyes blazing his love at her. At his next move, tears of gratitude and joy blinded Alissa. Michael had simply reached out and taken her hand.

She felt as if her very heart would burst with the glory of that gesture, for he had reached out clumsily, and his grip was not firm, but the hand with which he lightly held her own as they rode back to Collington House was his *left* hand.